The
Juliette
Society

The
Juliette
Society

SASHA GREY

GRAND CENTRAL
PUBLISHING

NEW YORK   BOSTON

Grand Central Publishing
Hachette Book Group
237 Park Avenue
New York, NY 10017

www.HachetteBookGroup.com

Printed in the United States of America

RRD-C

First Edition: August 2013

10 9 8 7 6 5 4 3 2 1

Grand Central Publishing is a division of Hachette Book Group, Inc. The Grand Central Publishing name and logo is a trademark of Hachette Book Group, Inc.

The Hachette Speakers Bureau provides a wide range of authors for speaking events. To find out more, go to www.hachettespeakersbureau.com or call (866) 376-6591.

The publisher is not responsible for websites (or their content) that are not owned by the publisher.

ISBN: 978-1-4555-9945-5

LCCN: 2013941578

This is for all the women and men like me, who at one point only had literature and film as an outlet to feel comfortable with their sexuality.

Before we go any further, let's get this out of the way.

I want you to do three things for me.

One.

Do not be offended by anything you read beyond this point.

Two.

Leave your inhibitions at the door.

Three, and most important.

Everything you see and hear from now on must remain between us.

OK. Now let's get down to the nitty-gritty.

1

If I told you that a secret club exists whose members are drawn only from the most powerful people in society—the bankers, the super-rich, media moguls, CEOs, lawyers, law enforcement, arms dealers, decorated military personnel, politicians, government officials, and even distinguished clergy from the Catholic Church—would you believe me?

I'm not talking about the Illuminati. Or the Bilderberg Group, or Bohemian Grove, or any of those corny plot devices used to advance the commercial agendas of disingenuous conspiracy nut jobs.

No. On the face of it, this club is a lot more innocent.

On the face of it.

But not underneath.

This club, it meets up irregularly, at a secret location. Sometimes remote and sometimes hidden in plain sight. But never the same place twice. Usually not even in the same time zone.

*   *   *

And at these meetings, these people...let's not beat around the bush, let's call them what they are, the Masters of the Universe. Or the Executive Branch of the Known Solar System. So these people, the Executives, they use these private gatherings as much-needed downtime from the important and stressful business of fucking the world up even more than it is already and dreaming up ever more sadistic and devious ways to torture, enslave, and impoverish the population.

And what do they do on their off days, when they want to relax?

It should be obvious.

They fuck.

I can tell you're not convinced. Let me put it like this. Have you ever met a garage mechanic who doesn't have a thing for cars? A professional photographer who never takes a shot unless the studio lights are on? A baker who doesn't eat cakes?

So these people, the Executives, and let's not mince words again, are professional fuckers.

They will fuck you to get one over on you. They will fuck you over to get to the top. They will fuck you out of your money, your freedom, and your time. And they'll continue fucking you until you're six feet deep and in the grave. And then some.

So what do they do when they're not doing that? Naturally...

The other thing you need to know is this. Powerful people are like celebrities. They like to hang out together. All the time. They'll tell you till they're blue in the face that it's because no one else understands what it's like to be them other than people like them. The truth is they just don't want to mingle with the lower echelons, the hoi polloi, the uncouth and unwashed who take particular pleasure in witnessing the downfall of the rich and powerful by the one thing that always, without fail, stops them dead in their tracks: sex.

So these people, the Executives, the professional fuckers, they've worked out how to have all the sex they want, and indulge their most wild and debauched sexual fantasies, without the scandal. Which is a bit like someone claiming to have worked out how to fart without the smell, but anyway... they do it behind closed doors. And all together. In secret.

Henry Kissinger once said that power is the ultimate aphrodisiac. By that time, he'd been creeping around the corridors of power long enough that he probably knew exactly what he was talking about. This place is the proof.

You could call it the Fortune 500 Fuck Club.

The league of Immoral Mother Fuckers.

The World Bang.

Or the Group of Sex.

They call it the Juliette Society.

Go ahead. Google it. You won't find anything about it. Absolutely nothing. It's that secret. But just so you're not completely in the dark, a little background and a little history.

The Juliette this society is named for is one of two

characters—sisters, the other's called Justine—conceived (if that's the right word) by the Marquis de Sade, the 18th-century French nobleman, libertine, author, and revolutionary whose sexual adventures so outraged the noblesse oblige of the French aristocracy that he was locked up in the Bastille for obscenity. Which, in retrospect, was a really bad move because, sitting there in his cell, with nothing better to do than jerk off day and night, the Marquis was stimulated to create even more and greater obscenities. Just to prove a point.

During his incarceration he would write the greatest work of erotic literature the world has ever known. *The 120 Days of Sodom*. The only book ever written that outdoes the Bible for sexual perversion and violence. And almost as long. It was the Marquis, of course, who shouted out of the window of his cell in the Bastille to the crowds below that they should storm the place and so, inadvertently, started the French Revolution.

But back to Juliette. She's the lesser known of the two sisters. Not because she's the quiet one. Oh no, far from it. See, Justine is a bit of a drag and a prude, a compulsive attention-seeker who plays the victim till you're more than sick of her. She's like one of those celebrities who harp on about the disease of drug and sex addiction and hang on Dr. Drew's every word, tirelessly promoting their virtue to the public by appearing on every rehab reality series going.

And Juliette? Juliette is absolutely unrepentant in her lust for sex and murder, and any carnal delight that she hasn't yet tasted. She fucks and kills and kills and fucks, and sometimes does both at the same time. And always gets away with it and never has to pay a price for her indiscretions or her crimes.

Maybe now you start to get my drift. Maybe now you understand why this secret society, the Juliette Society, might not be as entirely innocent as it seems.

And if I told you that I'd managed to penetrate, pardon my French, the inner circle of this club, would you believe me?

It's not as if I belong there. I'm a full-time third-year college student. I major in film. I'm no one special. I'm a regular girl with all the same regular needs and desires in life as everybody else.

Love. Security. Happiness.

And fun, I love to have fun. I like to dress well and look good but I don't have an expensive taste in clothes. I drive a small hand-me-down Honda hatchback that my parents gave me for my eighteenth birthday and always seems to have random crap lying on the backseat that I never find time to fully clear out. It was the car I packed all my belongings into when I moved out of home to go to college. I left behind friends who I've known since childhood; some I've outgrown and find it hard to relate to anymore, others I feel will always be part of my life, and I've made a whole set of new ones who have opened my eyes and expanded my horizons.

And, at this point, I'm not going to come across like such a smart-ass anymore. Now I'm going to start sounding all homey and humble. Because, in truth, the closest I had ever come to the seat of power was in my head.

I have this recurring sexual fantasy. No, it's not about fucking Donald Trump in his private jet over Saint-Tropez at thirty-five thousand feet. I can't think of anything that would gross me out more. My fantasy, it's much more down to earth—more mundane and intimate than that.

A few times a week I'll go to pick up my boyfriend after work and sometimes, when he's there late and ends up being the last one to lock up, I fantasize about fooling around a bit with him in his boss's office—but we've never actually done it. Still, a girl can dream, can't she?

His boss is a senator. Or rather, a successful lawyer and would-be senator. And Jack, my boyfriend, is a staffer in his campaign office. As well as being an economics major. Which doesn't leave a whole lot of time for us to get together because, by the time his day is finished, he's usually so beat that he falls asleep on the couch almost the second he's kicked off his shoes. Mornings he's up early again for class and there usually isn't even time for a quickie. And you know what they say about Jack and work and no play.

So I fantasize about playing my part as the dutiful girl-friend and I have this all planned out. I'll dress for the occasion. Stockings and heels with my favorite double-breasted khaki trench coat, just like the one Anna Karina wears in Godard's *Made in U.S.A.* And underneath, some lingerie; maybe a sheer black bra and panties and a matching garter belt and suspenders. Or I'll go topless and wear knee-high white stockings and these cute little pink polka-dot panties I have that seem to drive him wild. Or else just heels and bare legs with nothing else but a slinky cream silk slip or a chiffon babydoll. But always a smear of ruby-red lipstick. Got to have the red lipstick. A girl's best friend.

The campaign office is in a storefront downtown. There are windows on all sides and the lights stay on all night to make sure that everybody who goes past sees the line of identical red, white, and black posters pasted along the windows with Jack's boss mugging for the camera under big bold type that reads VOTE ROBERT DEVILLE.

So the only place we could get a little privacy is the utility closet, the bathroom, or the office that Bob—he likes everyone to call him Bob—uses when he's there, which isn't very often. It's tucked right at the back, near the exit to the parking lot, so he can sneak in and out without having to waltz in through the front entrance, on the street, in full view of everybody.

I'm pretty sure there must be at least a few people in that office whose kink is to fuck in the bathroom or the closet during working hours and hope they don't get caught. But it's not mine, and certainly not when we have the run of the place to ourselves. And anyway, Jack usually lets me in the back door, which leads directly out into the lot where I park my car and the office is just…right there.

I should just say this again, because I really don't want you to get the wrong idea: We've never actually done this. We've never even discussed it, Jack and I. I'm not even sure he'd be into it. But in my fantasy, as soon as we get in that office, and the door's closed and the lights are off, all the kissing and cuddling is over, I'd take control.

I'd push him backward into the chair, Bob's plush leather

swivel chair, and we'd do it right there, in the "seat of power." I'd tell him not to get up, not to touch himself, not to move an inch, and do a little striptease, to show myself off for him. First undo the belt of my coat and slip it off my shoulder so he can see some skin. Then quickly throw one side open, keeping the other pressed close against my body, giving him just a glimpse of what's underneath. I'd turn my back, let the coat drop to the floor, bend over and touch my toes so he knows exactly what he's going to get if he's a good boy and does what he's told.

His cock is hard before I've even got his pants off. And when I do, I can see it bulging against the cotton fabric of his boxer briefs.

Then it's time for some close contact. But he's still not allowed to touch. I'd position myself in front of the chair, straddle his legs with my back to him, and grip the handles of the seat as I brush and bump and grind my butt, first soft and then hard, into his crotch. Then lower myself down onto it, hold him between the cheeks of my ass, and clench, feeling it flex and twitch and grow against the curve of my...

But I'm getting off the point. The point is, I had no business whatsoever being there, at the Juliette Society, among those people. And I didn't exactly answer an ad on Craigslist or go to a job interview to gain entry to it.

Let's just say I had a talent, a persuasion, a hunger.

And I was spotted.

We could argue back and forth forever about nature or nurture but this talent, it's not something I was born with. At least not that I'm aware of. No, this is something I realized. But it has been with me for a long time, hard-coded, buried like a switch in a sleeper agent, and only recently turned on.

And saying all that, how do I even begin to explain what happened that night? The first night I encountered the Juliette Society.

2

The first thing we ever learned in film class is this:

Plot is always subservient to character.

Always, always, always and without fail.

Any creative writing teacher worth his salt will tell you exactly the same thing and make you repeat it over and over and over until it's as recognizable to you as your own name.

As a general point of principle governing a fictional world, that's as immutable as Einstein's theory of relativity. Without it the entire fabric falls apart.

Take any classic movie (or any movie, really), strip it down to the basics, and you'll see what I mean.

OK, *Vertigo*, a movie that every film student like me is expected to know inside and out. Jimmy Stewart's character, Scottie, is a detective whose single-minded and dogged pursuit of the truth, coupled with a crippling fear of heights and an obsession for a dead blonde that borders on necrophilia, are the very things—his Achilles' heel, as it were—that blindside him to the elaborate con to which he falls prey.

Let's assume instead that Scottie was a cop with a sweet tooth. It would have been more realistic. But it just wouldn't have worked. He'd be a cop drawn inexorably to the donut stand instead of the femme fatale, and Hitchcock wouldn't have a movie.

There you have it. Plot subservient to character.

Let's take another example. *Citizen Kane*. Film critics love to call it the greatest movie ever made, and for good reason, because it's all in there. Subtext, art direction, mise en scène, all the things that make a great movie into a work of art and not an extended commercial for Microsoft, Chrysler, and Frito-Lay, the way movies seem to be these days.

So *Citizen Kane*, the story of a news mogul, Charles Foster Kane, felled by hubris and ambition—the self-same qualities that fueled his drive to the top, qualities derived from an overwhelming mommy complex that dwarfs his achievements, damns his marriage, and, ultimately, destroys his life.

Condemned by this vicious circle that reaches to the very core of his being, poor old Charlie dies alone and unloved, simply because he could never detach from his mommy's tit.

Or maybe not her tit...because the last word Kane utters with his dying breath, when his grip loosens and he drops that snow globe—or crystal ball, or whatever it was, in which he failed to see his immediate future, that his life was not just fucked but over—that word, Rosebud, was, so legend has it, a sly reference inserted by Orson Welles to the pet name used by William Randolph Hearst (the real Charles Foster Kane) to describe his mistress's vagina.

Rosebud. The first word heard in the movie and the last one seen, painted on a child's sled tossed into a furnace, as the flames lick at it and peel the word away to nothing.

Once you know that little tidbit of information, you'll never watch *Citizen Kane* again the same way. You hear Rosebud, you see Rosebud. You think "vagina."

You think Orson Welles might have been trying to tell us something? I think he was trying to tell us this: Charles Foster Kane was a real motherfucker. And that, not surprisingly, was the source of all his problems.

And again. Plot always subservient to character.

Don't forget it.

Just as an aside, there is one type of movie, and only one, that doesn't conform. One genre that flagrantly breaks the rule. Not only breaks it but also turns it on its head, just because it can, and it doesn't give a fuck: the porn movie.

But let's not go there.

Anyhow, this rule, I've realized it applies as much to reality as it does to fiction. That it's not only in the movies that what happens to us is subservient to who we are, how we act and why, but also the stories of our lives, the choices we make and the paths we take.

This path I'm on, you can't see it. It's not a yellow brick road, the lost highway, or a two-lane blacktop. And I don't even know that it's a road I've been traveling along until I reach my destination, look back at how far I've come, and realize that all this time the choices I made, the roads I took, were leading me to this place.

So here's the deal. In order to explain how I ended up at the Juliette Society, I have to start at the beginning.

Not right at the very beginning. We'll save all the embarrassing baby pictures for another day. And all those apocryphal childhood memories that locate the origins of traumas that have stayed with me ever since. Like the time I pissed my panties at Sunday school while Sister Rosetta was telling us about Noah and his ark.

So, no, not right at the beginning, but close to it.

And I need to tell you something about myself, my character, my Achilles' heel. I have to start with Marcus, my teacher, on whom I have a secret crush.

Doesn't every girl have a secret crush? An insignificant other who they can project their wildest sexual fantasies onto. Mine was Marcus who, unknown to him, became my fetish object the very first time I walked into his class.

Marcus: brilliant, rumpled, handsome, shy—shy to the point of seeming aloof—and intense. Marcus, who fascinated me the moment I first set eyes upon him. Nothing inspires the curiosity of a woman more than a man who's emotionally distant and hard to read, especially sexually. And I just couldn't get a peg on Marcus.

In film theory there's a term, "frenzy of the visible." It's something to do with pleasure. The intense pleasure we feel at looking, seeing, comprehending, evident truths of the existence of the physical body and its workings, writ large up on the screen.

That's how Marcus makes me feel. When I'm sitting in the front row of the lecture hall, where I can get the best view of him, projected against the whiteboard, illuminated by fluorescents that seem as bright as an arc light on a movie set. I sit in the same spot every class, in the front row of this huge hall that stretches back maybe forty rows, right in the middle of the row, directly in front of his desk, where he can't fail to notice me. Yet Marcus rarely ever catches my eye. Or even looks in my direction, but addresses the room—the entire room—except me, and makes me feel like I'm not there, that I don't even exist.

He's there, I'm not, and it's driving me nuts—a frenzy of the visible.

And I wonder if he's just playing hard to get because I'm making it pretty damn obvious.

On the days that I have class—Monday, Tuesday, Friday—I find myself dressing for him. Today is no different. Today, I picked out figure-hugging jeans that show off my ass, an underwired balconette bra to lift and separate, a blue and white striped tank top that accentuates my curves, and a navy blue cardigan that frames and directs attention toward them.

I want him to catch sight of my breasts and think Brigitte Bardot in *Contempt*, Kim Novak in *Vertigo*, Sharon Stone in *Basic Instinct*.

Is that obvious enough?

I hope so.

So today, as always, I'm sitting in class, pretending to take notes, and undressing Marcus with my eyes. Marcus is talking about Freud, Kinsey, and Foucault, about the spectacle of cinema and the feminine gaze, and I'm trying to trace the curve of his cock in brown suit pants that are just a little too tight around the groin not to be revealing.

He's half-standing, half-sitting against his desk with one leg splayed out along the edge, forming an almost perfect right angle with the other, which is firmly anchored on the ground. And I'm chewing on a pencil, counting a span of inches from the seam of his pants along his inside leg, taking guesstimates of girth and width and length.

I jot down the numbers neatly in the top right hand corner of my yellow legal pad, which, twenty minutes into class, contains nothing but scribbles, scrawls, and doodles. And when I tot them all up in my head, I'm impressed. Because Marcus clearly has a cock that's more than a match for the size of his brain.

I shouldn't be surprised. It's not as if I haven't done this close to a hundred times before. Every class, the same routine. And, miraculously, the same three numbers come up every time. Like I've hit the jackpot over and over and over. And I get that same little thrill shooting through my body every time.

Marcus, as I said, is oblivious. For all he knows, I'm absorbed in his lecture. It's not that I don't care about the subject or I'm not listening. I'm following his every single word and being distracted at the same time. I'm multitasking.

Marcus is talking about Kinsey and the conclusion reached in his landmark sex study that women don't respond to visual stimuli in the same way as men, and sometimes not at all. I beg to differ. And if Marcus only knew what he was doing to me, he would too.

He segues neatly from Kinsey into Freud—another old pervert with strange ideas about female sexuality—and now he's got all my gears churning.

He writes CASTRATION on the whiteboard. And PENIS ENVY. Then underlines each twice as he repeats them aloud for added effect. And you'd think that'd be one gigantic buzz-kill for my scholastic masturbation fantasy, right?

Wrong.

See, Marcus has a voice like brown sugar—soft, dark, rich. Just to hear him say anything makes me all gooey inside. But the words he says that really turn me on are the least sexy of all. Words that sound clipped and cold and technical, but when Marcus says them it sounds like he's talking dirty—in an intellectual way.

These words especially:

Abjection.
Catharsis.
Semiotics.
Sublimation.
Triangulation.
Rhetoric.
Urtext.

And last, but certainly not least, my absolute favorite, the one word to rule them all:

Hegemony.

When Marcus speaks, it's with such quiet authority that he has me in his grip and I feel like I would do just about anything he asked.

So when he says, "Penis envy," I hear him plead, order, and command, "Please fuck me."

And even though he's not looking at me, I know he's speaking to me, and only to me.

Only to me.

This has nothing to do with Jack, my infatuation with Marcus. I love Jack and only Jack. This is just an amusement, a little romantic episode I've dreamt up to amuse myself in class. A pedagogical daddy fantasy that's got me hot for teacher and flies from my mind the second the bell goes.

This time it doesn't even get that far.

I'm looking at Marcus's sinewy arms and long muscular legs and imagining what it would be like to have them wrapped around my body, my entire body, the way a spider holds a fly in place as it prepares to consume it. I want to be held by Marcus, consumed by Marcus, in that way. And I wonder if Marcus can fuck as expertly as he talks about psychoanalysis and semiotics and the auteur theory.

I let the question hang in the air.

The answer comes unexpectedly from behind, in a conspiratorial whisper.

"He's a freak."

I turn around and look directly into a pair of bright, clear, almost luminous green eyes and full, sensuous lips arched into a coquettish smile. And that's how I meet Anna. Leaning over me from the row behind, whispering into my ear, in full view of Marcus.

I know her, of course. She's in my class. Anna is blond, petite, and voluptuous, the super-hot girl at school who turns everybody's head. She's the girl everyone wants to be friends with, the girl all the guys want to fuck.

I was brought up Catholic and taught that sex was something you weren't supposed to seek or experience pleasure in. It wasn't until I started going out with Jack, long after I'd lost my virginity, that I stopped feeling so conflicted and started to enjoy it.

I look at Anna and see someone who's comfortable with her body, her sexuality, and the power it holds. She doesn't seem to have any of my hang-ups. She's flirtatious, free, and relaxed, always ready with an easy smile. And she intrigues me.

Have you ever met someone and thought, from the second you laid eyes on them, from the moment they first spoke to you, we're going to be friends.

That's how I feel about Anna, the instant she says, "He's a freak." It's like hearing my own voice, like she knows exactly what I'm thinking. And understands.

"How did you know?" I whisper back.

"How did I know what?" she says.

"That I have a crush on Marcus."

"It's pretty obvious," Anna says. "It's the way you look at him."

That's how it will be between us from now on. A secret bond.

What I didn't know is this:

She'd already fucked him, Marcus.

And on those rare occasions when Marcus caught my eye and I wanted to believe he was looking at me?

Well, he wasn't.

He was looking through me.

At her.

3

"Can you see my ass in the mirror?"

This is what I say to Jack in the hope of attracting his attention.

He's propped up on the bed one evening, shortly after the beginning of the Fall semester, reading some report or other.

I've just come out of the shower and I'm lying naked, face-down across the bed, with my arms folded in front of me and my head resting on them so I can look up at him. I'm displaying myself for him the way Brigitte Bardot shows herself off for her estranged husband, Michel Piccoli, in *Contempt*. I'm feeding Jack lines from the movie to see how he responds.

It's a game I like to play. Not to test his love but to interrogate his desire for me.

He glances up at the mirror, briefly, says, "Yes," and goes straight back to his reading material.

But he's not getting away with it that easily.

"Do you like what you see?"

"Why? Shouldn't I?" he says, without even averting his gaze from the page.

"Does my ass look fat?"

"You've got a beautiful ass," he says.

"But is it fat?"

"You've got a beautiful fat ass." He looks at me—at me, not at my ass—smiles, and returns to his papers again.

"How about my thighs?" I say.

I reach back and stroke my thigh just below the ass and, while I'm at it, I pull the cheek apart just a tad so he'll get a glimpse of my plump little pussy from behind.

"They're great," he says. This time he doesn't even look.

"That's all?" I say, "Just 'great'?"

"What do you want me to say?" he says.

I might be feeding him questions but I'm not about to give him the answers.

"Do they look thick, as thick as tree trunks?"

"They look just fine," he says.

Whatever he's reading, he's engrossed in it—the way I wish he would be engrossed in me.

I roll over onto my back, arch my shoulders, and cup my breasts, pushing them up into two rolling hills, and jiggle them a little.

"Which do you prefer," I say, "my breasts or my nipples?"

My body is still flushed with heat from the shower and the areolae are pink and round. I brush and circle my nipples with my thumbs until I start to feel them swell.

"Does one come without the other?" he says, showing not the least bit of interest.

"If you could choose," I say.

"If I could choose between nipples without breasts or breasts without nipples?" he laughs.

"Yeah," I say, "if you could have a girl who was totally flat-chested or one with tits so big the nipples were almost nonexistent."

"You, or someone else," he says. But, perhaps deciding this isn't a conversation he wants to have anyway, he doesn't wait for an answer. He says, "I like them just the way they are."

Damn you, Jack, I think, pay attention to me. Look what I have here for you! And you can have it on a plate. For free. No strings attached.

The less attention he gives me, the more childish and petulant I become.

"I'm thinking about shaving my pussy," I say, sliding my fingers into my bush and tugging at the tight brown curls of hair.

I say it because I know he won't like it, because he finds completely hairless girls a real turn-off.

"Don't," he says curtly.

"Why not?" I say.

Now I'm just trying to be provocative. Anything to get a reaction. And it works.

He stares at me over his knees, annoyed.

But he doesn't say anything and it doesn't make any difference because, now I know that I've got his attention, I decide to push him further.

"I might do it anyway," I say, as casually as I can.

"Don't," he says again, in a way that says, this is not up for discussion. In a way that says, leave me alone.

I stretch my arms up over my head, then roll onto my side, just to deny him the pleasure of seeing my breasts, my bush. I want him to kiss my ass instead. And I lie there, pretending to ignore him. As if he even cares.

That's the way it always seems to be with us right now.

No communication. No copulation.

At home, Jack's playful up to a point but, try as I might, I can't rouse his interest in taking it further. I can't make him fuck me. I rarely get it these days. He's too wrapped up in work.

Jack was working hard all through the summer vacation at the campaign office, and now the Fall semester's started, he's got even more work to do. Even less time for me. I don't even pick him up from the office anymore.

Before Jack, no man had ever come close to satisfying me in bed. Jack is everything that makes for a great lover—sensitive, caring, thoughtful, and kind. I'm crazy about him.

I look at Jack and think of Montgomery Clift in *A Place in the Sun*, intensely beautiful, square-jawed, the all-American boy. At least, that's how he looks to me. But it's not just about the way he looks. Whenever you see Montgomery Clift on-screen, he can be doing little else but staring into the middle distance, lost in contemplation, and you can see his mind churning. That's Jack. And it really turns me on.

When he's not around, I masturbate like crazy, fantasizing about Jack. About us. Fucking. At the office after hours.

Under the table in the college canteen. Between the book-shelves in the library. Not just sweet loving with nice cuddles and kisses, Jack pounding me hard. Sex that's dirty and raw.

He doesn't have any idea about these fantasies of mine, because I do it when he's not around and we never discuss them. But it's getting to the point where my fantasy sex life far outstrips the reality.

We live in a cozy one-bed apartment with rooms that all branch off the hallway. When things are good, it feels like we're living in a space capsule, locked together away from the world. Our intimacy seems to make the place seem much larger than it is. When things are bad—not really bad, just the little hiccups that happen between any long-term couple living in close quarters—it can feel stifling and claustrophobic.

On nights like tonight, when Jack comes home from class or working at the campaign office and goes straight in the bedroom to catch up on his reading, and stays there pretty much till he falls asleep, it feels like he's locking himself away from me on purpose, and I don't know why. I find myself coming up with reasons to walk around the apartment in my underwear or naked, flaunting myself in front of him, anything to attract his attention, arouse his desire and make him show he wants me.

I'll decide, on a whim, that I'm going to take a shower before dinner and start peeling my clothes off in front of him. But it doesn't make any difference because he doesn't even look up and I think he must be blind—blind to my love for him.

I take the shower as quickly as I can, because I didn't want or need one anyway, and it wasn't the purpose of this little exercise. I dry myself off and cream and oil my body so it glistens and shines. And I come out naked, smelling of jasmine. And then the games begin.

When we haven't had sex for a while, I smell sweet. Like a ripe apple or peach, dripping and ready to be eaten. Ready for someone to get to my core. I know that Jack smells me, but I always wonder if other people can smell me too. And if they can't, how is that possible? Maybe they just think it's lotion or perfume. Do they know that I'm ready and ripe and willing? And left wanting.

Tonight, Jack falls asleep on the bed fully clothed with his reading material fanned out on his chest. I gather up the papers and put a blanket over him so I don't have to wake him.

I'm left wanting again and I touch myself, imagining the way I want Jack to be, the way I want him to respond.

I'm lying naked on the bed, on my belly, and I say, "Can you see my ass in the mirror?"

He tosses the papers on the floor, leans over me, cups my cheeks in his hands, and kisses my butt.

"Who needs a mirror," he says, resting his head on my ass like a pillow and looking up at me with a grin on his face.

I say, "Do you like my thighs? Are they too thick?"

He walks his fingers down the back of my leg, then dips inside and nudges my legs apart. I don't resist.

"I love your thighs," he says. "I like them the best when they're locked round my head."

He slides his forefingers between my legs.

"Hey," I giggle, "that tickles."

I roll away from his touch, onto my back, pretending to play hard to get but really just giving him more of what he wants.

"How about my breasts?" I say, pushing them up for his inspection.

"Every time I see your titties, they fill me with joy," he laughs, launching himself upon me, sucking my breast all the way into his mouth, teasing my nipples with his tongue and letting me feel the sharpness of his teeth.

"And my bush," I say, "how does it feel?"

"Like the softest, silkiest fur," he purrs. "I wish I could hide myself in your hair."

He sinks his fingers into my bush, while his thumb explores my crotch, sliding down my crease and pressing against my pussy. I'm wet to his touch.

He buries his face between my thighs. I hook my legs over his shoulders, slide my calves across his back, pulling him down into me.

His fingers tug at the curls of my bush, his thumb presses against my pubic mound, his lips kiss and stroke me. I can feel hot breath on my groin and his tongue, lapping roughly at my crotch. I can feel myself open up for him. Willing him to dig deeper.

I run my fingers through his hair, clasping him to me as I arch my back and grind my hips up into him.

He enters me. I moan and grip him tighter.

He teases me. On the inside.

I howl with pleasure because I want him to know how good he's making me feel. That it's all about the motion. And hitting the right spot.

That spot.

Right there.

Don't stop.

With no letup until he takes me all the way.

And I let him take me.

Jack's fast asleep beside me but I imagine his tongue inside, taking me on the expressway to ecstasy. I imagine his tongue but my fingers are doing all the work. I'm shooting ahead in the fast lane, racing toward the curve, and I can feel it coming up.

I can feel it.

It's upon me.

I turn the curve.

My body is hit by jolt after jolt.

I call his name but he doesn't hear.

4

I'm sitting in class, waiting for Anna to show up. But she's late.

The one thing Marcus won't tolerate is tardy students. If ever someone arrives late to class, he goes through this whole elaborate routine just to intimidate them into never doing it again. He'll stop talking the second he hears the door to the lecture hall crack open. Not at the end of his sentence, in the middle of a syllable. He'll turn his head to stare at the door, just waiting for someone to step through it.

As they scurry inside and find a seat, Marcus's stony gaze follows their every step and he's so pissed you can almost see the steam coming out of his ears. But he still looks cute because he has these dimples—dark hair and dimples—and it always looks like he's smiling, even when he's really mad. But even once you've found your seat and settled in, with your legal pad in front of you and your pen at the ready, it doesn't end there. Oh, no.

Marcus will stand there in silence, bent over his desk, with his hands splayed out in front of him, staring down at his notes for a really uncomfortable amount of time. Almost as if he's willing someone to make a sound, willing someone to give him an excuse to explode. But everyone knows better than that.

We sit in respectful silence and when he feels he's tortured the class enough, and only then, however long that is, he'll continue the lecture, starting up again from exactly the same syllable he left off from.

Anna is always late to class. She's never absent or misses it entirely, but she always arrives at different times. It could be just as Marcus has started his lecture, or somewhere in the middle. Today is no different. Anna arrives fifty-two minutes late, less than ten from the end, right when I'd almost given up hope of seeing her at all. She waltzes in without a care in the world. Marcus looks up, see it's her, and continues his lecture as if nothing happened.

This is the way it always is when Anna walks in late, and I always wonder: why does she get special treatment?

So, one day, I ask her.

"Marcus and I have an arrangement," Anna says. "I do something for him. He does something for me."

"What kind of arrangement?" I say.

"Well," she says, "let me put it this way. Marcus has special needs…"

I'm wondering what those special needs could be.

Does Marcus ask Anna to lick his balls while he deconstructs *The 400 Blows*? Or fuck her from behind as he recites quotes from *What Is Cinema?* by André Bazin. Does he like Anna to stick her pinky in his stinky as he debates the ins and outs of abjection theory?

I can't wait for her to tell me. There are so many details I want to square with my fantasies of what turns Marcus on and how he fucks. And I can only think the reality is so much better than I could ever imagine. This is how we bond, Anna and I, over Marcus. Our mutual obsession. My secret. Her lover.

So, after class, we grab some coffee and go sit outside on a bench, as students rush back and forth around us trying to get to their next lesson. We sit under a tree, shielded from the mid-morning sun already high in the sky, because Anna's skin is pale and she prefers it to stay that way. "I burn easily," she says.

"OK," I say, "tell me. I have to know, because it's been driving me crazy, what is Marcus' special kink?"

"He likes to do it in the dark."

My heart sinks. Marcus sounds so depressingly normal.

"I thought you said he was a freak. That doesn't sound very freaky."

"Wait, let me finish," she says. "In a closet. He likes to do it in a closet."

I'm still not convinced and frown slightly.

"He's really shy, you know," Anna says, sensing my disappointment.

Marcus has this large closet in his apartment, and like everything in his apartment—which is huge and dimly lit and sparsely decorated—the closet is old, worn, antique, and wooden.

"There's nothing of any comfort in his apartment," she tells me. "No couches, no pillows, no throw cushions, no carpet, not even curtains on the windows."

"Not even a bed?" I ask.

"He sleeps on a mattress on the floor, but we've never fucked on it," says Anna. "And I opened his refrigerator once," she continues, "and it was almost empty. The only thing inside was tea. Not tea leaves, tea bags. A box of value-pack tea bags. No milk."

While Marcus' apartment is lacking furniture and sustenance, Anna tells me, there's one thing it's not short of: books and papers.

"There are books crammed into every inch of these floor-to-ceiling bookcases that line the walls," she says. "They're all meticulously arranged by subject: film and sex, art and religion, psychology and medicine. And when he ran out of space on the shelves, he started piling them up on the floor, on tables, chairs, the way a hoarder uses up every available bit of space at his disposal.

"Plus, where the bookcases aren't, the walls are covered in art. Erotic art. Nothing very pornographic," Anna says, "just strange dirty pictures."

Anna tells me about the blurry photographs of couples fucking that look like paintings by Francis Bacon. Street scenes of prostitutes. Salacious cartoons. Things that don't even look like erotic art at all—dense, sprawling collages of clippings from newspapers and magazines of faces, places, and objects—but that clearly serve some erotic purpose for Marcus. And things that can't be mistaken for anything else.

She says that there are two paintings in particular that have captured her interest more than any of the others. They're hung side by side in a little alcove off the entrance hallway, right when you come through the front door, and whenever she goes to visit Marcus, she'll just stand there and stare at them for a while.

One painting is of two women lying side by side, the curvature of their bodies forming a pair of lips. They both wear suspenders and stockings and have pert orb-like breasts with cherry red nipples.

"One of the women is wearing a black veil and she looks like you," Anna tells me.

"What do you mean?"

"A brunette, with a sweet, sexy smile." She winks.

Anna's flirting with me and I don't know how to take it. I feel myself blush and hope she doesn't notice.

"The other one," she continues, "doesn't have a head. Where the head should be are two arms that emerge from the inky background of the painting like crabs legs and hold her nipples like pincers."

She tells me that the other painting is so odd that it's difficult to describe. At first, it looks like three female bodies in fishnet stockings engaged in a ménage à trois. When you look closer, male body parts are mixed in with the female ones. Sex organs and limbs sprout from places they shouldn't. Phantom hands push and pull and grope. It's all a little disturbing, Anna says, as if she's looking at one body made up of many and of indeterminate sex.

As she tells me about the painting, I start to think that, all this time, Marcus's sexuality has been a mystery to me but I never ever questioned his orientation, never even considered.

"Is Marcus gay, or bi?" I blurt out.

"Oh, no," Anna says, "I don't think so. He's just really, really strange."

It sure sounds like it. A home with no furniture, no food, but books and papers and erotic art. As if Marcus finds comfort in austerity. Or that his brain's so busy he doesn't have time to take care of his body. That's fine with me, because I only want to be fucked by his brain.

Anna says that whenever they meet, which is twice a month, the same thing occurs between them on every single occasion. Marcus has every detail planned and expects it to be carried out to the letter, like a ritual.

She is told to arrive at a specified time.

"I can't be late," she says. "Not one minute, not even thirty seconds. I'm always right on time for his private sessions. And I have my own key to the apartment, so I let myself in."

Now I understand why she's always late to Marcus's class.

Just to fuck with him.

"Marcus is already in place when I arrive," she continues. "In the back room. In the closet. With the door closed. And he's so silent, so still, that you wouldn't even know he's there, that there's anybody else in the room. The curtains are closed and the lights are off. It's dark, but still just light enough to see."

She says the closet has two holes in one of the doors, like two knots of wood fell out of it. One small. One larger. One at head height, the other lower down.

"Marcus swears it was like that when he bought it," says Anna. "But I don't believe him."

When Anna arrives, she's meant to be wearing the uniform that Marcus has told her to wear. The same clothes every time.

"How does he make you dress?" I say.

"Guess," she says.

"Like a nurse?" I say.

"Nope," she says.

"Like a schoolgirl?"

"Uh-uh." She shakes her head.

"A whore?"

"Not even close," she says.

"OK, you have to tell me."

"Like his mother." She giggles.

I just look at her in surprise, and Anna can't wait to reveal more. She tells me that she has to wear a loose flowery sack dress, flat-heeled dress shoes, flesh stockings, and really, really large underwear that looks and feels like a chastity belt made of polyester. She dresses like Marcus's mother, in clothes that used to belong to her. Clothes that Marcus's mom owned since the fifties and wore up until her death, but still look perfect and new, as if they'd come off the rack the day before.

"Is this getting freaky enough for you? Too much?" she asks, smiling.

"Getting there...," I say. Because now Marcus is sounding less like Jason Bourne, which is a good thing. He's sounding less the way I imagine Jason Bourne would fuck. With the lights off and his socks on. In the missionary position. Like a real man.

And he's sounding more like Norman Bates, which is even better, because I've had a huge, huge crush on Anthony Perkins since the very first time I saw *Psycho* and fell head-over-heels in love with his clean-cut, buttoned-up preppy look. The thin, bony face. Those cheekbones. The neatly trimmed, perfectly sculpted, shiny jet black hair. Those dark, smoky eyes. That smile. So hot. Just knowing that, underneath it all, he was a screwed-up psycho killer made him seem all the more delicious. It seems Marcus is completely in thrall to his mommy fixation, just like Norman Bates or Charles Foster Kane.

"So let's recap," I say to Anna. "You're in the room, dressed like a prim fifties housewife from an episode of *The Twilight Zone*, and Marcus is in the closet with the doors closed and his eye pressed to one of the holes, watching you."

"Right," she says. "And I do exactly what he's asked me to do. I turn my back to him and I start to undress, taking off each item of clothing in the order he's asked me to."

"Exactly the same way every time?" I ask.

"It has to be," says Anna. "Choreographed to the second. I feel like an air stewardess demonstrating safety procedures. I've done it so many times now that I've made it my own, adding little flourishes, things I think he'd like."

Anna's not shy with the details and as she talks I can see it all happening in my head.

First she takes off the sack dress, which she unbuttons at the back, slips off her shoulders, one by one, and lets fall to the floor. She looks over her shoulder and down at her feet as she does so to make sure the dress doesn't catch on the shoes as she steps out of it. Then she unhooks the bra, hiking it up her chest so her breasts fall out to their natural position, bouncing a little as they do. She hunches her shoulders forward so the straps drop off them.

"He likes to see the bra slide down my arms," she says. "Then watch me catch it and swing it free of my body."

I imagine Anna naked from the waist up, standing in dress shoes and flesh stockings held up by suspenders, my gaze lingering on her round, curvy ass and breasts with salmon pink nipples.

There's only one thing wrong for me about this fantasy, Marcus's fantasy. Anna is wearing an old-fashioned girdle that covers just about four-fifths of her ass, giving a slight peek of those large polyester panties with the broad gusset seam that firmly grip and hold her cheeks like rubber. Which is just the way Marcus likes it, but next to useless as jerk-off material for anyone else.

"He likes me to extend one leg out and bend over it as I unhook the suspenders," Anna continues, "all the way over, so he can see my tits hang. I let the suspenders ping up around my thigh, one by one, then wiggle my tush as I slide the girdle off and step out of it."

Then she peels off those large, ungainly underpants, but slowly because she says, "Marcus is an ass man and, for him, it's all about the long tease."

That's as far as she's meant to go. Marcus wants her to leave the stockings and the dress shoes on. And a long string necklace of pearls, alternating black and white, that hang down between her breasts. "His mother's pearls," she says.

While she's doing all this, she's not allowed to look in his direction. "Marcus is very firm about that," she says. "I snuck a glance at the cupboard once, out of the corner of my eye. And I saw this large eyeball pressed right up close to the door, framed by this ragged knothole. And I think he caught me because it didn't know where to look.

"The eyeball got embarrassed. It moved from side to side, up and down, frantically scanning the room, looking for somewhere to hide. And it wasn't Marcus. I didn't register it as Marcus. It was just an eyeball in a long narrow wooden slit. And I was so weirded out that I never looked again."

"So he likes to look but not be looked at," I say.

"It's the only way he can get fully erect," she says.

I think of Doctor Alfred Kinsey. From what I know about him, he could only get off one way too. That's the bit they left out of the movie, the part where Kinsey sticks things in his pecker. Stuff that didn't belong there. Objects that didn't always fit. Items that didn't appear anywhere in the data he meticulously compiled, ordered, tabulated, and analyzed. Grass, straw, hair, bristle. Anything long and flexible that tickled.

Thinking about Kinsey and listening to Anna's story about Marcus makes my little fantasy of fucking Jack in his boss's office seem so tame. But Anna hasn't finished yet.

Once she's stripped down to her underwear and neatly folded her clothes on a chair, and only then, Anna says she's allowed to turn around and look.

What she sees is Marcus's erect penis slowly inching its way out of the lower knothole in the closet, like a snail emerging from its shell.

"I gasp," she says, "the way Marcus told me to—the perfect combination of horror, surprise, and delight."

She stays there, rooted to the spot, staring, open mouthed, until almost the entire shaft has presented itself and his balls pop out from the hole and hang over the door.

"When his cock starts to twitch," she says, "as if it's beckoning to me, I sit down and lick it the way you lick melted ice cream that's dripping down the cone."

"This is just foreplay, right?" I ask.

I just want to be certain, because it all sounds so involved.

"Yes," says Anna, "just foreplay."

Even though she's on the other side of the door from him now, Anna says, Marcus doesn't make a sound. She can't even hear him breathe. No little gasps of excitement to let her know she's doing the right thing, just little twitches in his cock as it bobs away from the attentions of her tongue. "Like the way your knee shoots out when the doctor hits it with his little silver hammer," she says.

"How do you know when to stop, so he doesn't come?"

"The door opens," she says. "It's kind of creepy."

I imagine a door creaking open in one of those really old black-and-white haunted house movies that play on TV at the dead of night and there's no one and nothing behind it, just an inky blackness.

"That's my cue to step inside," she says. "And I can feel my heart beat faster every time, even though I know exactly what's going to happen and who's behind the door."

Anna steps inside the closet, closes the door behind her and can't see a thing, because Marcus has plugged the holes with tissue paper so no light can get in.

"It takes a while for my eyes to adjust," she says. "Even then, all I can see are shadows in the gloom that move like vapor trails and feel like hallucinations."

"How big is the closet? Doesn't it feel claustrophobic?"

"It's big enough so that my feet are the only part of my body touching the sides," she says. "It's scary how quickly I lose track of the space and time. It's super hot in there too, a steamy-wet dry heat like in a Turkish bath. Because Marcus has already used up so much of the air, I feel myself starting to sweat almost as soon as I've stepped inside."

"What happens next?" I say eagerly.

"Then I feel his clammy hand on my breast. You'd think that'd feel real creepy," she says, "but it actually turns me on.

Really turns me on. Being touched like that, by someone I can't see, in a confined space."

It makes all the other stuff worthwhile, she says, the annoying preliminaries that Marcus insists on being carried out to the letter.

"And anyway," she says, "once we're in the closet, in the dark, with the doors closed, and he's initiated physical contact, there are no more rules. He's not shy anymore. Marcus fucks like a madman, like a beast, like a different person entirely. And the closet rocks on its feet."

"How many ways can you fuck in a closet?" I wonder aloud.

"You'd be surprised," says Anna. "We must have gone through the entire Kama Sutra five or six times by now," she says.

"One time," she says, "he was fucking me so hard the closet fell over onto its side. Onto the door. We were trapped inside. Marcus didn't care. It turned him on even more. We fucked for hours. Then he punched out the top and we crawled out, naked and bruised."

After they emerge out of the closet, there's one final duty Anna has to perform. They move to the bathroom and she has to wash him.

Anna says it's a really old bathroom with a tiled floor and paint peeling off the walls from damp. And Marcus has one of those old-fashioned ceramic tubs that looks like a dinghy, with a shower hanging from a long steel mast that extends up from the spout.

"Marcus only ever takes a shower, never a bath," says Anna.

"Why?" I say.

"He told me people drown in bathtubs."

I let the comment pass but I wonder if Anna realizes he was quoting Cassavetes.

Once they're in the shower, Anna soaps and lathers Marcus, vigorously scrubbing his back, his chest, around his thighs, under his arms, and behind his balls. She towels him dry and then he walks out of the bathroom without saying a word, leaving her there alone, to dress. When she's done, she lets herself out again.

"That's the way it always is," she says. "Without fail. Never any other way.

"Did you ever fuck in a closet?" Anna asks, matter-of-factly.

I have to admit to her that, no, I never did. And, after hearing all this, I feel so depressingly normal.

We sit there under the tree for a few minutes, in silence. And a line of dialogue pops into my head that Marlon Brando says in *Last Tango in Paris*, one throwaway line that I've always loved from the monologue he delivers to his dead wife, as she's lying in the casket in front of him:

"A little touch of mommy in the night."

And if that's what Marcus likes, I'm fine with that. Because a lot of great men had mommy complexes.

I'm taking in everything Anna's told me. I take a sip from my coffee and wince when I realize it's almost gone cold because we've been here so long.

"Did I ruin all your fantasies?" Anna says. "I hope not. Underneath it all, Marcus is really rather sweet."

"Oh, no," I say. "Absolutely not."

Now I want to know even more. Now it feels like I can read Marcus like a book and find out something new about him with every turn of the page. And I wish Marcus could teach me what it means to be freaky.

But then I realize Anna could teach me a lot about being freaky too.

The more I get to know her, the more I start to think of Anna as the best friend who understands you and everything that goes on inside you. I can tell her anything and she can tell me exactly how I'm feeling and why. It's like we're two heads with one brain and a shared consciousness. Sometimes she can even finish my sentences before I've started them.

We complement each other perfectly. You could say we were made for each other. People say we could be sisters. I can't see it myself. Anna has the jump on me in most things. She is everything that I'm not.

She's the beauty. I'm the brains.

I'm the smart girl. She's the popular one.

She just makes me laugh. She doesn't have the filter between her brain and her mouth that most people have. She can look at some random guy in class and, apropos of nothing at all, will say cute inappropriate things like,

"I wonder if he's cut or uncut."

And, "I'd say he hangs to the left."

Or, "I bet his come tastes of lemon jelly."

But she doesn't think it's at all inappropriate. Just something that needs to be said at that particular point in time. She's so pure and uncomplicated and free in that way. Sex is as natural as breathing to her.

I'm so into Anna, and everything about her, that I contrive an excuse for Jack to pick me up from class so we can have lunch together. Because I want him to meet my new best friend. I introduce them to each other proudly. But it doesn't quite go the way I planned. Jack is so intimidated by Anna, he can barely bring himself to look her in the eye or utter more than a few words. Then he just stands there while I do all the talking. It's awkward. He quickly makes an excuse to leave.

When I get home, later that evening, I play our game, determined to draw out what he really thinks of her.

"Did you like Anna?" I say.

"She's nice," he says.

"Do you think she's cute?"

"I guess," he says.

"If you weren't with me, would you be with her?"

"I don't think I'm her type," he says.

"You didn't answer the question," I say.

"Yeah, I did," he says.

"But is she yours?"

"She could be," he says.

"She has nice tits, don't you think?"

"Sure," he says.

"Do you like her firm, round ass?" I say.

"Where is this going?" he says, frustrated.

"Well, would you like to fuck her?" I tease.

"Maybe," he says.

But it's not the answer I want.

5

Marcus has set, as homework, a screening of *Belle de Jour*, the Luis Buñuel movie that stars Catherine Deneuve.

I've never seen the movie before. I know nothing about it. I have no idea what to expect.

I sit down in the theater on campus and I'm not alone but, when the lights go down and the darkness closes in around me, I might as well be. This is how I like to experience movies. In a theater, in the dark, as a one-on-one communion between me and the screen. As something approaching the quiet contemplation you feel when standing in front of a great painting that awes you into silence.

I sit down to watch a movie and expect to be transported on a flight from reality into another world. I expect, at the very least, to be entertained, maybe enthralled, even appalled. The last thing I expect is to see myself up on the screen.

Bear with me, I'm not completely deluded. I know I'm not the star of this movie, even if I do share a name with the lead. I'm not even a supporting character. But somehow, some way, something about it connects with me deeply. Even if I only have one thing in common with its protagonist, a frigid, upper-middle-class French housewife who harbors secret masochistic desires about sex.

Her name is Séverine. Latin for "stern." Imagine going through life, your entire life, and having people decide they don't like you before they've even met you. Just from hearing your name. Séverine. Severe. Stern.

Imagine lumbering a kid from birth with a name like that. You might as well call it "No fun."

No fun at all.

And it's not as if that name doesn't suit Catherine Deneuve's character in Buñuel's movie. In fact, there isn't another name that suits her better because, to be honest, she isn't a whole lot of fun. She's icy-cold and dispossessed of every quality that could make you like her, stripped of almost everything that makes her human. Everything except her morbid fantasies of humiliation and punishment. Because you're not meant to like her or even identify with her.

And yet, somehow I do.

Séverine. No fun. No fun at all. Married a year and she's never let her husband fuck her. Married a year and she won't even let him sleep in the same bed. Married a year and he hasn't even seen her naked. Her husband; devoted, protective, dependable, and so, so understanding.

Séverine. A virgin in reality, but a whore in her imagination. And it's her imagination that leads her astray.

Remember. Plot, always subservient to character.

And Séverine, always in thrall to her desires, never in control of them, floats through the movie in a trance. Floats through her life like it's a movie. Until a friend of her husband's, an older man, devious and sleazy, who seems to see right through her, implants the idea in Séverine's head that there is a place where women like her—repressed, immoral, insatiable—can fulfill their fantasies in private and maintain their reputation in public.

A brothel.

He even gives her the address. And so she visits the brothel and she's given a new name, to disguise her identity. Something that sounds exotic. Not Séverine. Something that will entice the clients.

Belle de jour.

A cute French phrase that sounds like nonsense in English any way you cut it, which is probably why no one bothered to translate the title of the movie for the foreign market.

Belle de jour.

Literally, beauty of the day. Or, today's beauty.

Makes me think, "today's special."

Maybe that's how Buñuel meant it too. The woman who has everything and wants for nothing, reduced to the dish of the day on the menu in a whorehouse. Buñuel's little joke. His little humiliation. She's always dish of the day, every single day. The special that never ever changes, that's not really special at all.

The only thing special about her is her beauty, which, although divine and transcendent, is ultimately worthless, because the only purpose it serves is to ease her passage into whoredom, to cheapen her.

She's liver and mashed potatoes. Every single day.

Liver and mashed potatoes.

Makes me think, Kim Kardashian.

Liver and mashed potatoes. Dressed in Hermés and Gucci.

And pretty soon, in that brothel, marked down and cheapened, Séverine submits to her desires, every single one of them, her dreams now superimposed on reality. And pretty soon, her dreams supersede her reality.

And that's where I come in.

I'm sitting in the theater watching the movie, and I recognize myself.

I have no ambition to be a whore. Not even in secret. That's not what I meant.

What I mean is that I recognize something inside Séverine, as unlikely as it seems, that's also inside me; as far apart as we are in background, temperament, and character, there is something that connects us.

I'm not a prude. And I'm not a masochist—at least, I don't think I am—but Séverine's fantasies touch a nerve. Her reality, less so.

I'm sitting in the theater and my imagination takes over. I'm watching the movie and filling in the gaps. And pretty soon I've lost track of where the film ends and my fantasies begin.

When the movie's over and I emerge from the dark into the mid-afternoon sun, I feel like I'm walking a high-wire. Teetering on the edge of a precipice, struggling to maintain my balance. I'm shaking inside. I don't know what's happened to me. I'm so confused. I can't work out whether I've been overcome by delirium or have given in to mania. I only know that I don't want the fantasy to stop. I've never imagined myself being pleasured in this way, and now that I have, I want more.

I walk home in a trance, navigating on autopilot, running the scenes back in my mind. I forget where I am and I realize I'm back in the movie.

I'm underneath the sweeping branches of a pine, held there against my will by the man I adore. Restrained, beaten, and brutalized on his order by two savage men, while he watches, indifferent to my suffering.

My hands are hitched together with coarse rope and hauled so high above my head that the muscles in my arms stretch and burn. My feet claw at the ground as it swings beneath me. My dress has been ripped at the seams and sags from my waist like a wilted petal. My bra hangs loose from my shoulders, the underwire clipping against the nipples and hardening them.

Leather whips bear down upon my back, biting into the flesh, one and then another in quick succession, beating out a vicious rhythm that holds me in its thrall. I hear the crack of the lash, and then...the sting. The crack. And then the sting. As inevitably as lightning follows thunder, so pleasure follows pain. The intensity ratchets up and up and up with every stroke, until both, the pleasure and the pain, are all too much to bear. Adrenaline courses through my body.

I turn a corner.

I'm not even halfway home and I'm horny as hell.

I turn another corner and I'm back in the movie, now in the brothel, preparing to be inculcated into the pleasures of criminal desire by a ruffian with a cane and gold teeth who carries himself with a rough, primal swagger.

If clothes make the man, then this man is a study in contradictions. He has fashionable patent leather Chelsea boots worn down to a dull luster and socks that are threadbare, with large, ragged holes where the heels once were. A metal signet ring inset with a huge, finely cut diamond. And those gold teeth that gleam when he bares them and push his top lip up into a sneer. His hair, his leather overcoat, his pants, his shoes, all black as night. Everything else, mismatched and fanciful. A purple waistcoat and a loud and lurid patterned tie.

When he takes off his shirt—a white shirt, the only thing pure and uncomplicated about him—there is a lean, hairless torso, as delicately contoured as a marble statue. Skin that's pale and unblemished, until he turns around.

On his back is a large scar that curves underneath the shoulder blade, a ridged crescent of damaged tissue, even paler than the rest of his skin, although that doesn't seem possible, an intimation of terrible violence.

He looks at me with an affected aristocratic aloofness. I

look at him and I think of Marcus, but younger and rougher and more disheveled, dangerous and unpredictable where Marcus is soft and diffident. I look at him and I think of how I want Marcus to be, of how I want him to treat me.

With disdain.

I start to take off my underwear. He looks me hard in the eyes and says, "Leave your stockings on."

An order, not a request. He unzips his pants, still looking at me, and adds, "A girl tried to strangle me once."

I wonder if maybe this is a warning. I wonder if this is what he intends for me. A chill runs through me.

But it's too late for second thoughts because he's already taking off his underpants, which are white like his shirt and his naked torso.

I lie on the bed, on my front, and turn my head to look at him over my shoulder.

I think of Marcus and his cock, snaking along the leg of his too-tight brown suit pants. And then I don't have to wonder anymore because it's there, right in front of me, long and thin and majestic, curling upward in a perfect curve, like a crescent moon at the end of its cycle, like the scar on his back and the blade of the dagger that made it. And he crawls up onto the bed, his long limbs craning over me, a spider closing in on the fly. He kicks my legs apart and lowers himself down between them. I can feel the swell of his cock resting against the crack of my ass. I can feel him raise himself up in a sawing motion.

His hand is flat against my neck, his fingers curving around it, the span between them so broad that he can almost reach all the way around. He squeezes slightly and the pressure feels so good. I wait for him to slide it down and hit all the pressure points on my neck and along my back. Instead, he tightens his grip and puts all his weight behind it, slamming my head down into the mattress.

I cry out, more in surprise than in pain.

I feel him pry open the cheeks of my ass with his one free hand and I prepare to cry out again, this time in pain more than in surprise. Because I know what's coming. And it's too late for second thoughts.

Then there's a horn blaring in my ear. The squeal of brakes from a cab that's come to a hard stop not six inches from my body, which is not two paces from the curb, where I've stepped off the sidewalk and into the street on a green light.

I'm shaking. Shocked out of my stupor. Thrown out of the screen and back to reality. And I do know the difference. I do know which is worse and which will cause more damage—being fucked up the ass by a thug, or fucked up the ass by a yellow cab.

I turn the key to the apartment, and the door's not even halfway open before I call out,

"Jack...Jack?"

He steps out into the hallway and I don't say, "I love you. I missed you. How was your day?"

I say, "I want to fuck you so bad."

And I'm on him in an instant and have him pinned up against the wall before he even knows what's hit him. My mouth on his, kissing him hard and deep before he can say a word, before he can even catch a breath.

My hands are up inside his shirt and all over his chest. Running my nails down his torso. Pinching the nipples till he moans. And I don't hear it, I feel it; the gasp of a low moan that escapes from his mouth into mine.

I'm a woman possessed. And all I can think about is holding his cock inside me and never letting go. I want to be controlled by his cock. I've never felt this way, I couldn't be more certain, and I've never been this turned on.

I reach down and feel his crotch. And this is what I love about Jack. I never have to wait for him to get hard. Never have to waste time teasing a limp cock into action. As soon as I make a move, it's always there, ready and waiting and willing, as if through auto-suggestion, and so fucking hard.

I yank off his pants and underwear in one frenzied motion. I have it in my hand now and I disengage my mouth from his, but only so I can look him in the eyes and say, "I want your cock. I want to fuck your cock with my mouth."

And I'm not seeking his permission.

I'm not asking; I'm telling.

I'm not begging; I'm taking.

And he doesn't have a choice.

I slide down his body, still holding him, only letting go to change my grip. I'm on my knees in front of him and I pull his penis down firmly, like a lever, so it's at a perfect right angle with his body, and perfectly level with my mouth.

I sink the head into my mouth, ever so slowly, the whole head, closing my lips around it, tight. I withdraw and tease him with my tongue. Then take him into me again, a little deeper this time, advancing along the shaft. Then withdraw. Teasing.

And I tell him what he wants to hear.

I tell him, "Your hard cock feels so good in my tight little mouth. It tastes so good. It feels so fucking good, doesn't it?"

And I don't wait for an answer.

I push his cock up flat against his belly and hold it in place as I lick from the bottom of his balls, all around the sack, flicking his balls with my tongue, sucking one and then the other, then lapping along the shaft, like a brush stroking a canvas, until I get to the tip. And I lick it, and spit on it, and pump it with my hand, looking him right in the eye. I can see that he's overwhelmed and I know that he's at my mercy.

I open my mouth, wide, so I can take him all the way, drawing in enough air to fill my lungs, as if I'm about to dive underwater, drawing his length into me slowly, curling my tongue around to cradle the head, stroking the underside of his cock as it slips inside. As I do, I can feel myself getting wet.

I hold him there until I feel him quiver, and then withdraw. He's still connected to me by a thick pearly string of sputum that hangs between us and coats the tip of his cock like a snow capped mountain. I look at the spit that joins us and imagine my pussy opening like a flower and the sticky white juices adhering to the lips.

I come up gasping for air and pump my hand hard and fast along his shaft, sheathing it with a film of spit while I catch my breath, and I prepare to go under again.

I bob forward in rapid little movements, open my throat and spear myself on his cock, feeling his engorged fleshy head press against the back of my throat, his cock filling my mouth. I imagine it deep inside my hot wet pussy and I can feel that my panties are soaked all the way through.

I feel his hands slip through my hair and I wait for him to clasp the back of my skull, holding it steady as he thrusts— one short, sharp, final thrust—deeper into me. This is what I want to happen. This is what I imagine ahead of time.

I'll hear him groan as he unloads into the back of my throat. And he'll be at a loss for words.

Except, "fuck."

And, "yeah."

I'll take hit after hit after hit, hot and thick and sugar-sweet, sliding down my throat. And his come, it won't stop. I'll feel like I'm going to drown.

This is how I have it all planned out in my head. But that's not what happens.

He slips his hands through my hair but he doesn't push into me. He pushes me off him. It's as if I've been woken abruptly. Jerked out of a dream.

I look up at him and say, "What's wrong?"

I'm confused and hurt. I don't try to hide it. He can hear it in my voice.

"What's wrong with me? What's wrong with you?" he says.

Throwing it back in my face like that just makes it worse.

"What's gotten into you, Catherine?"

He has many names for me—silly little nicknames that he

makes up on the spot—Kitty, Cat, Trini. He only calls me Catherine when he's pissed.

Nothing's gotten into me. Nothing at all. That's the problem. Can't he see how horny I am?

He's made me feel stupid and cheap.

"I'm working," he pleads. "I don't have time for this now. Maybe later."

And when he says that I know there won't be a later. I know he'll work late and keep me waiting.

And that's exactly what happens. I'm in bed, ready and waiting and willing. And I can hear him outside but he doesn't come in. I'm left with only myself for company, my fantasies for comfort, and all these strange images from the movie swirling around in my head.

I am tied to a tree that's sheathed in ivy. My arms are bent back around the trunk and held in place by a thick coarse rope that's crisscrossed over my body and binds me tight.

I'm in the middle of a wood but my head is filled with the sound of the ocean. It's broad daylight. My body is bathed in the warmth of the sun. I hear only the sound of the crickets that sing in the night.

There is blood at my temple. But no wound. It has streamed down my cheek like a drip of paint, oily and thick. Like a tear that shows the color of pain.

And I don't feel afraid because my lover is with me, standing in front of me. He puts his hands on my shoulders and I feel comforted. He caresses my body with his eyes and I feel desired. He doesn't say a word, doesn't make a sound, but I am bathed in the warmth of his love. He kisses me tenderly, with lips so soft. He glances up at the blood, traces a finger through my pain, and kisses me again. And his kisses are sweet, but that's all.

6

This is what I've always wanted to know, pretty much since the first time I ever had sex:

Why do they call it "cum"?

What's wrong with "come"? Isn't that sexy enough?

Cum just sounds silly, cheap, and disposable. It sounds like a brand name.

Spam, Tampax, Alpo, and Cum.

Or a branded additive in another product.

Porn—now with added Cum.

If you ask me, cum is a perversion of the English language. One I just can't abide. Call me curmudgeonly if you like, but it just doesn't sound right.

While we're on the subject, if you feel the need to splooge, jizz, spunk, nut, or cream, do so by all means, but not in my face, or anywhere near, but if you're going to skeet or shoot your wad, then I'm your girl.

And I'd rather have a cock than a prick any day. Wouldn't you? I'm no size queen but prick just makes me think "pin-prick" or "just a little prick"—which really doesn't turn me on.

Boast all you like about your wang, your schlong, or your dong, just keep it right where it belongs. In your pants. Because it's not coming anywhere near my pussy. And whenever I hear a guy talk about Dick, Willy, Johnson, and Peter, it just makes me think of a bunch of dudes circle-jerking in a men's bathroom.

I don't want a cock with a name. I want a man with a cock.

It doesn't have to be big, but it definitely has to be hard and operated by someone with a license to drive. Because there's no point in banging hard on the accelerator if you don't know how to apply the brakes, turn the wheel, or shift gears. And that gear stick? If you want to put it in my box, you better know how to use it.

You see, a penis is all well and good, but a cock feels so much dirtier and more poetic. Cock makes me think of a cockerel. And a cock struts and crows. You can cock your head, your arm, or your bat. Or you might be the cock of the walk. And that all sounds like sex to me.

Don't think I'm a prude, because I'm really not. And I don't mean to be reductive or prescriptive because I guess everyone has their own personal preference if we're talking sexual vocabulary. So let's not argue over semantics. I'm just going to state this here for the record. For me, it's "come" over "cum" all the way.

★   ★   ★

You'd think an educated young woman might have more profound things to spend her time thinking about than the most satisfying way to articulate ejaculate. I'm not so sure about that.

I mean, you can search all you want for the deeper meaning of existence; you can look for the physical proof of God. You can read as many books as you like on the subject, on any subject—books on religion, on science, on philosophy, on nature—but I guarantee you will never, ever find an answer that satisfies you. That really satisfies you, deep down, giving you a sense of well-being that you finally know your place and purpose in the world.

Why?

Because the answer is already right there, in front of you.

Come.

You don't believe me?

I'll prove it to you.

Let's start with a statement we can all agree on:

Sex is the engine of life.

Because without sex there is no life. And equally, without life there is no sex. They are inextricably linked, like the chicken and the egg. Likewise, sex without come is like a Big Mac without the special sauce. It's the magical essence from which we all, well, come. Because every single thing that exists in this world needs to reproduce to survive. Even the common cold. Existence itself relies on the reproductive process.

From the birds to the bees, the flowers and the seeds, the

same exact process is repeated over and over and over—from micro to macro. I don't really need to say this. It's all basic science and biology. But maybe it bears repeating, because I think we forget.

The Big Bang created a universal body made up of solar systems—giant wombs, incubators for the planets, which are cosmic eggs waiting to be fertilized with the seed of life, which is:

Come.

And that, in essence, is my sexual theory of life, the universe and everything. The only string theory I'll ever need.

And for all you people that are more spiritually inclined, all I can say is, you weren't paying enough attention in Bible class, or reading the good book closely enough, because if there's something that the Bible is not short of, it's sex. You can barely turn a page without finding someone wondering when God will come, when Jesus is coming, when salvation cometh.

You say, don't be silly.

I say, we're taught to take the Bible literally; I'm doing exactly that.

If the Bible really was intended as a guide for life, why would the people who wrote it want to play semantic tricks with language and hide its meaning?

Isn't the Bible meant to make people feel good about themselves?

What can make people feel better about themselves than sex?

Let's take a random passage. Say, Luke 17:20–21. The

Pharisees ask Jesus when the Kingdom of God is coming. And what does he tell them? He says, "The Kingdom of God is within."

I'd say that's pretty self-explanatory. No real mystery there. I'd say he could only be talking about one thing.

Come.

And what is that if not a synonym for God.

Here's another thing I'm going to state for the record:

I'm a true believer. I worship come.

But I'm a relatively new convert to the cause. I wasn't always this way. In fact, precisely the opposite.

If I think of the word "cum" and visualize it, it shouldn't be any great surprise why even the thought of letting a guy "cum" anywhere near me, or on me, used to be one huge turnoff. It's just not sexy at all. It doesn't speak to me of the transcendent rapture experienced during the human orgasm, whether female or male. It sounds like what's left over when a man's done using you. Or the used rubber you drop in the trash afterward. So, to me, "cum" was always something dirty and obscene. It disgusted me. I didn't want to see it, I didn't want to feel it, and I definitely didn't want to taste it.

Right out of high school, I had a boyfriend who was constantly trying to finish on my face. That was his thing and he wanted it to be my thing too, so he'd have an excuse to do it whenever he chose to. One second we'd be fucking, the next I knew he'd pull out and would be scrabbling up my body, trying to straddle my face, like a puppy trying to paw at a door and then pouncing into its owner's arms when it's been left alone for too long. Except, he was just a pathetic boy who'd watched way too much porn and didn't have the slightest clue how to please a real live girl. I'd bat him away, like a puppy that won't stop humping your leg, and the closest he ever got was my belly. But even that didn't feel right. Not the texture, the temperature. It just didn't make me feel good inside. Just the idea of it made me feel sick to my stomach.

After him, I dated a college football player. All-star body and a face to match. But when the lights went out, so did our sex life. His personality was as nonexistent as his imagination in the sack. I always tried to climax before him, because once he did, it just killed the mood for me. When he reached orgasm he would whine like a little boy on the verge of crying. I always wondered if he was on steroids and never could tell if he had any real desire to fuck me or was just faking it.

Then something changed. You could say I had a revelation, whether through the call of love, or lust, or maybe a combination of both. But I remember it vividly, as if it happened this morning.

It was the eighth time Jack and I had sex. And it felt so special. Jack was really the first guy who even made me feel comfortable being naked around him. I was on top, riding him, we kissed passionately, and just as he was about to come, he looked me right in the eyes and asked…he actually asked me if he could come in my mouth.

I panicked at just the thought of it, but was so overwhelmed with this new love-lust that all I could do, all I wanted to do, was smile and nod my approval and give my permission. He asked. I was in control. He cared to ask, and that alone made me want it.

From that time on, I lost all fear of the sticky substance associated with that dirty word. I was no longer even afraid of what it might taste like. I just wanted it. It turned me on. I loved it. I was fascinated by it. I craved it, just as I craved Jack's tender arms wrapping themselves around me, his lips giving me soft, sweet kisses. Sex was just one big disappointment before I met Jack. I guess it was all down to finding the right person, the one who would open me up, show me the way and teach me how to find pleasure in sex.

You know that line by William Blake about "the world in a grain of sand"? Well, I can see the universe in a grain of Jack's come. When I think of Jack's come, I think of how it got there, how great the sex was, and how I never wanted it to end. When I think of Jack's come, he's always with me and it's like we're never apart.

I like to feel his come. I like to feel it shoot into my mouth. I like when he shoots it into my hair and makes it thick and sticky and matted, the way you feel when you walk into a cobweb.

I like to tell him to come on my tits so I can smear it around in messy circles, the way a painter mixes paint on his palette. He is the paint. I am the painter and the canvas too. I like to paint with his come on my body so I can feel it dry, harden and contract, pinching the skin as it does. I like the way it flakes away in scales as I brush it. I like to hold a flake of his dried come on my finger and look at it the way you look at a snowflake, trying to discern the crystalline pattern of nature within.

I like to look down and see come gush from the head of his cock. First spurting in long, gloopy arcs of ever-decreasing reach and volume. Then pouring slowly, inexorably, like foam from a can of beer that was shaken too much just before it was opened.

I like when it pools in my belly, drowning my belly button and spilling across my waist like cream soup spilling from a plate. When it rains down on the small of my back in big, thick drops, like hot rain, like hot milk, like hot lava. When he pulls out and shoots it all over my pussy and into my bush, where it hangs in thin strands like cotton caught on hedgerows.

I like when he shoots inside me and I feel full and satisfied and calm, as if I've just eaten a good, hearty meal. And then feel it slide out of my pussy, leaving a thick pearly trail that gathers in the bud of my asshole. Sometimes it will ooze out, hours later, when I'd long forgotten it was even there. When I'm walking around campus or sitting in class, or sitting on the bus, or standing in line at the checkout and, all of a sudden, the crotch of my panties is wet with slime and I remember the moment he thrust inside me, letting out that cute pained little groan a split second before he let out his load. And I relive it, as if he's fucking me, ejaculating inside me, right then and there, on campus, in class, on the bus, in the supermarket.

I like when he comes on my face and it feels like I'm completely at his mercy, like he's humiliating me with his come. When I close my eyes and feel it splash onto my face. When he shoots come onto come onto come and it feels heavy and slides down my face. Filling my pores, dripping down my cheek, my forehead, hanging off my chin. And it feels like my face isn't big enough to take all his come. His endless semen.

I like to wipe it off my lips and cheek and stretch it between my finger and thumb like snot, then slurp it back into my mouth, roll it around, and mix it with my saliva, into a cocktail of my fluids and his, and slurp that down like an oyster. Then I open my mouth, wide, and stick out my tongue to show him it's all gone. That I've been a good girl and taken my medicine.

I like to guess what he's had for breakfast, lunch, dinner, and in between from the way it tastes and the way it smells. Salty, bitter, sweet, sour, and smoky. Beer, coffee, asparagus, banana, pineapple, chocolate. From the texture and consistency. Sometimes it's runny like half-cooked egg whites, sometimes thick and lumpy like semolina, sometimes both of those at the same time. And sometimes it's smooth like cough syrup, which is how I like it best, because it goes down so easy.

I like to lick his cock after he's come inside me, when he pulls out and his penis is slick and shiny with his come and mine. I want to savor the flavor of him and me together, our sweat and passion. I want that taste to linger in my mouth until it starts to turn rank on my breath. I love the smell of his come when it starts to ferment on my body.

And then I like to wash his dried come off my body in the shower and feel it reconstitute itself as the water hits it, almost as if it's come back to life from the dead. I like to watch that water, his come, swirl down the plughole, and think about the journey it's about to embark on.

The places it has been and the place it will end up. From inside Jack's body onto mine. From my body all the way to the sea.

Born from nature and returned to nature. The way of all things.

The way it's meant to be.

7

Marcus is leaning against his desk, dissecting *Belle de Jour* scene by scene. He is talking about Séverine's need to submit to her desires, completely and absolutely, until her fantasy and her reality are merged and she is unable to distinguish one from the other. And I am on my knees in front of Marcus, licking his outstretched hand.

I am on my knees. I have a collar around my neck with my owner's name on it. It tells me:

I am the teacher's pet.

I am Marcus's dog.

He is my master.

I'm balanced on my hind legs with my paws resting on his torso and my head buried in his crotch. I am a bitch in heat and I can smell my master's sex. I am rubbing my nose in the crotch of his pants, snuffling his aroma, drawing it into me. The secret musk that tells me I belong to him and only to him. It fills my nostrils, fills my head. I am in a cloud of love and there is nowhere I would rather be. I pant and bark to show my delight.

I look at his crotch and cock my head as I trace a crease in his brown suit pants with my eyes. I lap at his crotch, tracing the crease with my tongue, and feel it swell and bulge against the fabric.

I am staining the crotch of Marcus's pants with my tongue and he pushes me off him, roughly, without warning. He pushes me away so violently that I fall hard on my side and sprawl across the floor. He barks his displeasure at me, admonishing me.

Bad dog.

I look up at him and cry out, pathetically. And it just makes him more angry. My master hates my guts and I feel sad. I feel like I want to curl up and hide in a corner and chew on a nice, tasty bone.

Marcus is talking about the secrets we keep in dreams, about the secrets we keep that threaten to consume us.

I am on all fours on top of the desk with my head resting on my front paws and my ass stuck up in the air as high as it will go. Marcus has two fingers deep in my pussy and his thumb lodged in my asshole, like he's standing on the highway trying to hitch a ride. I'm wagging my behind and whimpering with pleasure. And all is forgiven.

I am my master's bitch.

Anna is late to class. Anna walks in and all the men stand

to attention. Marcus stands to attention. And Anna is on her knees in front of him. She has her head buried in his crotch. She is sucking in the secret scent that was known only to me. She is lapping at the place where I once was. But I'm not jealous. I'm not worried that I've lost his affections to another. I'm happy to share my obsession. Happy to share my master with my best friend.

Marcus is talking about Séverine's need to annihilate herself through sex. And I am my master's slave. I will do anything he demands. I will submit to his desires and make them mine. I want to annihilate myself on his sex.

But my master has other ideas. He wants to save Anna for himself. He wants me for all the others.

Marcus is directing all the men in class to form a line. One by one. Two by two. Like the animals in the ark. He directs me to turn around, to face away from class, away from the men who wait in line, standing at attention. He tells me to face the board.

On the board, Marcus has written HEGEMONY.

He tells me to say it out aloud, over and over and over, until the word means nothing, until the word just is. As I do so, he instructs the men to take me. One by one. Two by two. And I'm happy to share myself for my master. If that's what he wants.

Marcus is talking about the unknowable limits of female desire and I think I understand what he means.

I'm sitting in class and I don't know who I am, what's come over me or why.

I'm sitting in the front row, as always.

Dressed for Marcus, as always.

But everything else has changed.

I've changed.

Marcus is leaning against his desk talking about erotic hallucinations and the capacity of the human mind to process fervent emotional states into phantasmagoric experiences that feel completely and utterly real, indistinguishable from reality itself.

I'm convinced Marcus is talking about me.

He's talking to me. And only to me.

How does he know?

Marcus is talking about how film can act as a direct portal to the subconscious. How art can stir our unconscious thoughts and desires, often in ways that seem as fantastic and unreal as art itself. How, in extreme cases, our reactions to art can stimulate physical symptoms. Like the way teenage girls used to lose control of their bowels in the presence of the Beatles. Or how in the thirties they used to say that at the end of a Valentino movie there wasn't a dry seat left in the house.

He's talking about Stendhal syndrome, an actual documented phenomenon whereby people experience high anxiety, fainting, and even mild psychosis in the presence of great works of art.

Stendhal syndrome. Sounds like the kind of thing a chronic hypochondriac would come up with if they were to look up "art" and "psychosis." The way chronic hypochondriacs always look up their symptoms, intentionally fuzzy on the details, in the hope of diagnosing some atrocious, incurable malady—the worse it is, the better to calm their anxiety. Stendhal syndrome almost sounds as bad as it gets.

And here I was thinking it was just the name of a movie. A horror movie by Dario Argento that I once saw and never forgot—*The Stendhal Syndrome*—about a young female cop, played by Dario's daughter, Asia, who while investigating a series of brutal murders, chases her prey into an art gallery and is stopped dead in her tracks by the majesty of the works she finds herself confronted by. Botticelli's *Birth of Venus*, Caravaggio's *Medusa*, one work of divine beauty, another of sheer terror.

And she is transfixed. Her field of vision telescopes in, toward the painting, until she can see nothing else. Until she finds herself, not looking in from the outside, but inside the painting looking out.

Like Alice through the looking glass.

I wonder if this movie holds the key to what I'm experiencing. And I realize how silly that sounds, as if anyone looks for answers in a horror movie. Or any movie at all, if it comes to that. As if art is capable of doing anything except raising more questions.

I have so many questions and I don't know which way to turn. But I do know who to ask.

I corner Anna after class and we go to the cafeteria. Lunch is over and it's almost empty. We sit at a table that's far away from everyone else. I want to tell her everything, but I know if I do, it'll sound insane, like the ravings of a lunatic.

Instead, I tell her I've been having these really intense dreams.

"About Marcus," she says.

Not a question, a statement. How could she know?

"Yes," I say. "About Marcus."

Anna claps her hands together and giggles, giddy as a child at Christmas.

"I want to hear all the juicy details," she says. "Don't leave anything out."

"Have you ever felt so turned on that you thought you were going insane? That you were losing your grip on reality and might never get it back?"

"In my dreams?" Anna asks.

"Yes," I say. "Or any time."

"In reality," she says.

I nod.

Without saying a word, she draws up a large hinged silver bangle decorated with ornate swirls that hangs down on her left wrist. Underneath it, there is a ring of deep patterned livid bruises, like a fossilized imprint woven into her skin, almost as if the pattern on the bangle has been branded onto her wrist.

"Isn't it beautiful?" she says, tracing her fingers lightly across the grooves, as if in a trance.

It looks grotesque. And painful.

She has such pretty, delicate wrists. They look swollen and deformed.

"What happened?" And I try not to sound shocked, but it's hard not to.

"They tied me up," she says, as if it's the most obvious answer in the world. As if she expects me to know.

"Who's they?"

And Anna tells me everything. She tells me all of her unbidden secrets. She tells me things about her that I'd never have guessed.

She tells me about the website she models for.

"It pays really well," she says. "All my tuition, all my bills."

The reason why the money's so good, she says, is because the site "caters to a very select group of people."

"What kind of people?"

"People who know what they like," she says. "People who want to see a particular type of girl in specific kinds of situations. Pretty, willing young girls restrained, tied, chained, disciplined, and kept."

I try to imagine who those people are, what they do, and why they would want to see something like that. I look at Anna's wrists and imagine what she could possibly get out of it, other than severe bruising.

I wonder if she self-harms, or if she used to, like the cutters I knew at high school. Those weird intense loner girls from good families who were so screwed up about their bodies and everything else that they harm themselves even further, beyond repair, inside and out.

And I wonder if this is what cutters do when they outgrow

their teenage obsessions and move on to adult ones. I can't imagine any other reasons why someone would submit themselves to that. For all the college tuition in the world.

"It's not about the money," Anna says, almost as an afterthought, as if she heard what I was thinking. And I almost believe her.

I look at her wrist again and then notice two large yellowing bruises on her upper arm. She's wearing a sleeveless blouse, so she couldn't hide them even if she wanted to. And I don't think she does.

"Did those come from the same place?" I say.

"These?" she says, stroking them lovingly with her index finger.

"No." She smiles, as if recalling some pleasant memory. "Fuck bruises. You know?"

I don't, but I can probably make an educated guess.

Anna tells me she has a boyfriend. Actually, she tells me she has many boyfriends, other than Marcus, and they all provide something different; they all satisfy a different part of her. But this one guy, he likes to treat her rough and leave his mark for others to know where he's been. And that's fine with her too.

"I love to feel them on my body," she says. "As long as I can see them and feel them, I remember how they got there. I remember how he put his hands on me. How he fucked me. And I like to watch them fade. From red to black to green to gold. And when they fade away to nothing, I know it's time to hook up with him again."

Out of all her boyfriends, she thinks she likes him the best of all, because he's the only one who thinks the way that she thinks. Who believes, like her, that "sex and violence are two sides of the same coin"—who not only believes it, but also acts upon it.

"You know how at school they tell you they're going to teach you about the birds and the bees?" Anna says. "Well, they don't tell you everything, not the whole truth. They only tell you part of it. Only the stuff they want you to know. About the birds. All the fairy-tale stuff about courtship and mating rituals and raising children. They don't tell you about the bees."

"Sure they do," I say. "They tell you how bees go from flower to flower and spread the pollen."

Anna shakes her head and rolls her eyes.

"So it should be the birds and flowers then," she says. "Not the birds and the bees. Do you know how bees fuck?"

"I guess I don't," I say. I don't think I ever even thought about it.

"It's violent," she says. "Really violent."

When bees fuck, Anna tells me, it's like rough sex but the boy bee gets the hard end of the bargain, not the girl.

"When he puts his penis in the queen, it turns inside out," she says. "And when he comes it's like a firework going off. It's so explosive that it rips his cock off and sends him flying. And a few hours later, he dies from the trauma.

"If a guy ever hits on me too hard, or he's being a pain in the ass, or I'm just not into him, I always tell him about the birds and the bees," she laughs. "They never ever know about the bees. And, afterward, they wish they never did."

She giggles.

"One fuck and it's all over," she marvels. "If it was like that for guys, think how different the world would be? And if we learned about the bees at school, and not just the birds and the flowers, think what kind of sex we'd want to have later on."

Listening to Anna talk about sex makes me feel like a virgin all over again. No, that's not right. She makes me feel like I did on my first day at elementary school, freshly graduated from kindergarten, so proud and thinking I was an adult now—the way you do as a kid every time something significant happens, like attending a new school or getting your first bike—when I really knew nothing. Nothing at all.

That's what I feel like now. Like I've been playing doctors and nurses all this time and I've only just worked out how sex works in the real world. I'm trying to digest all this information, but Anna hasn't finished yet.

She says she remembers why she started telling me about the bees. That when the boy bee dies, its castrated penis stays stuck half-in and half-out of the queen's vagina, like a cork in a half-drunk bottle of wine, as a cue for other boy bees to impregnate her—like a mating sign.

"That's what these are," Anna says, as she rubs her hand slowly over the bruises on her arm again. She wears them like a temporary tattoo because she wants everyone to know what she's into—the way people wear badges of their favorite bands on the lapels of their jacket—so others who are into the same thing will recognize and respond.

"And if they don't?" I say.

"I guess they just figure I'm really clumsy." She shrugs.

I'm looking at Anna, at her bruises, and I see her in a completely different light now. But she hasn't answered any of my questions. Just left me with a whole set of new ones.

8

I'm thinking about everything Anna told me about Marcus, herself, and the birds and the bees. About fuck bruises. And I want to know what it's like to feel Jack on my body. Not just his come. His mark. I want to know if that's what's missing from our sex life. Rough sex.

Jack is fucking me in bed. He's sitting on his haunches with my legs resting against his chest and my feet over his left shoulder. He's holding my ankles and fucking me like he's playing the cello. His cock is sawing back and forth in my pussy. His balls are slapping against my ass, his hand is spread across my lower belly and down to my crotch, his thumb is plucking at the hood and button of my clit. He's running through all the scales, pushing my passion up by octaves and I'm singing for him.

I'm singing for him and I decide I want to hit a higher note.

I say, "Hit me, Jack. I want you to hit me. Hit me hard enough to make me scream."

I say it on the spur of the moment, and because I'm feeling good and I like the idea. But it doesn't quite work out that way.

He stops mid-thrust.

"What?" he says.

"I want you to hit me. I want you to hurt me."

He pulls out and sits at the end of the bed, just looking at me.

It's dark and I can't see his expression clearly, but I know it's not good.

"What's the matter?" I ask.

There's a long silence.

"What did you say that for?" Jack says. "Why would you even ask me to do something like that to you?"

"I'm sorry, I didn't mean to...I thought..."

And I give up, because I can't really think of any good reason why. It wasn't something I planned; it's something I felt and acted upon. So I don't have an easy answer for him. I don't have any answer at all.

"Even if I did it, I couldn't pretend to like it," he says. "I can't pretend I even want to do it. I just don't. Why would I want to hurt you?"

And I can hear in his voice that he's not just upset and confused; he's angry and fuming.

He gets into bed, all the way over on the edge of his side, and wraps the covers around him.

I'm left feeling frustrated, unsatisfied, and deeply confused. I feel clumsy and dumb, so dumb, to even think that Jack would be into it.

We're lying in bed. Together, but so remote, as if there's a wall between us.

I start to hear Jack's breathing getting heavy, but I can't sleep.

I go into the living room, sit on the couch with my laptop, in the dark, and pull up the porn website Anna works for. I've been thinking about it all day, ever since she told me, and I want to see for myself how those marks got on her wrists and what she does.

I'm going to hold up my hand here and admit something embarrassing. I don't have a whole lot of experience with Internet porn. Porn movies, yes. Internet porn, no—two different beasts. And, yes, I do know it's almost impossible to avoid, but it's just never been my thing. Maybe Kinsey was onto something after all with his little theory about women and visual stimuli.

When I think of Internet porn, I think of video games, Star Wars figures, Marvel comics and science fiction, and all the things that geeky virgin teenage boys develop obsessions with as a cover for their one overriding obsession:

Jerking off to search terms on Google Images.

I think of geeky adult men who never outgrow their

obsessions, just upgrade them. From toy cars to real cars, action figures to pussy-in-a-can. From Google Images to YouPorn.

I think of all the billions of guys, in every country of the world, who are jerking off to Internet porn at the same time. Or maybe not even Internet porn. Maybe just Kim Kardashian's website. Jerking off over badly retouched and barely titillating photos of the Kardashian sisters. I think of all the billions of men ejaculating gazillions of spermatozoa simultaneously over images of Kim Kardashian's digital ass.

I think, what a waste of good sperm.

What a waste of precious energy.

If only someone invented a way of tapping that energy at its source. Or found a way to turn the billions of come-stiffened Kleenex tissues discarded daily into a source of fuel. If someone discovered how to do that, most of the world's energy problems would be solved in a snap. No more wars for oil. No more carbon footprints. No more nuclear waste.

No more wasted tax dollars needlessly spent trying to achieve cold fusion.

Just billions of hot, sweaty guys sitting in front of their computer monitors with their pants around their ankles, furiously jerking themselves off over Internet porn and Kim Kardashian's ass, day and night, night and day.

Without ever feeling guilty.

So I guess what I'm saying is this: when it comes to Internet porn, I'm on the fence. Not a user myself, but I can definitely see the potential benefits for everlasting world peace.

But this porn site, Anna's site, even with my limited experience of the genre, must be the strangest porn site I've ever seen. Starting with the name.

Sodom.

Or rather, SODOM, all caps. Because the last thing anyone requires from pornography is subtlety.

Sodom. And not Gomorrah. Not because it's too subtle, but probably because it's too hard to spell and sounds like an STD. Because pornography and STDs, well, let's just say they're never going to be the best of friends.

So, SODOM. An acronym of sorts. For the words splashed across the home page, also in caps.

SODALITY OF DOMINANTS.

Whatever that means.

I'm looking at this website and I can't make head or tail of it. This isn't pornography as I know it or understand it. For a start, there's no sex on display. None at all. At least, none that I can see. Just a gallery and a search engine.

I don't know what to search for and am afraid of what I might find if I do. I scan through the gallery instead. An endless scrolling collection of girls, in portraits that look like yearbook photos, all exceptionally pretty, almost every one college-age. I scan through the gallery looking for Anna, half-expecting to recognize someone else I know too.

I wonder how many girls there are like Anna who pay their way through college like this, in porn. If I'm the only college-age female who doesn't. I wonder why pretty girls, whose looks give them such a natural advantage in life, choose to turn what they have to their disadvantage.

I think of Séverine. Who had everything, wanted for nothing, and how that wasn't enough. Séverine, who, more than anything, wanted to *be* nothing.

I think of Anna. And then I see her.

I click on her picture. It brings up another gallery. All of Anna's scenes, each one illustrated by a thumbnail. I scroll through them. There's a lot, too many to count. And the thumbnails, they look like minutely detailed tableaus of medieval torture from an illuminated manuscript.

The movie clips don't have titles. Anna doesn't have a name, not even a porn name. She's been reduced to a number—a generic ten-digit number. It feels like I'm flicking through a Sears catalog of sexual aberration and torture or that I've clicked open a window into Pandora's Box. I wish I'd never seen it because now I can never un-see it.

Where should I start?

How about the drilldo? Seems as good a place as any. The first clip I click on features Anna, a toilet, and a drilldo. If you don't know what a drilldo is, I'll tell you.

It's exactly what it sounds like. A drill with a dildo where the tip should be.

The next question is, how does it work?

And the answer to that is, do you really have to ask?

Ever had to drill holes in the wall to put up a set of shelves?

Then you already know that once it gets going, an electric drill will slice through plaster like butter. And it will keep going until it hits that outer wall of concrete and stone. Then it starts to shake the shit out of you. You set it to "hammer," hoping to chisel away a little further and, when it hits stone again, your drill has a kick like a .45.

Now, imagine putting that inside you.

I'll stop there for a second to let that sink in.

An ordinary household electric drill, put to uses its manufacturer never intended, never even considered as part of its recommended usage. A power tool turned into a sex toy.

Not just any sex toy.

The .45 Magnum of sex toys.

Call me naive but I had no idea such a thing existed. I had no idea vibrator technology had advanced to the degree that the battery-powered rabbit was now as outmoded as the Sony Walkman. That vibrator technology had evolved into the realms of body horror, dragging female sexuality kicking and screaming along with it.

Two thousand years of culture and seven ages of man, all leading up to the moment when some genius came up with the idea of combining a dildo and a power drill. As if that's exactly what the world was waiting for, a sex toy that can punish the insides of a woman to orgasm at twenty-four hundred revolutions per minute.

Not just any sex toy.

The Maserati of sex toys.

Built for women, but designed—and could only have been designed—by man. As if women haven't already been punished and tortured enough by the designs of man. Someone had to invent the drilldo. Now imagine watching this thing punish the insides of your new best friend.

I'm looking at Anna tied to a toilet, on a concrete plinth in the middle of a large, dark, dank, dirty, creepy warehouse. There's no setup for the clip, no explanation, no plot, no dialogue. Other than Anna you never see a single other person. No shadows lurking in the background. No voices off-camera. It's as if she has been abducted, locked up, and left there. And maybe that's the point. Anna told me that the site had a specific audience and now I understand why she said it. The movies are edited so that you can see only what whoever made them wants you to see.

When Anna told me what she did, when I saw the welts and bruises on her wrists, it unnerved me. But my first instinct when confronted with this is to laugh. It looks so silly. But also strangely beautiful.

Anna's soft, pale, ruddied flesh is set against the hard white enamel of the toilet. She's slouching against the toilet, head and shoulders against the cistern, lower back resting against the seat, her legs extended vertically, in a v-shape, held by ropes tied around her ankles, like the strings that hold up a marionette, so her pussy and ass are on show. Ropes above and below her breasts reach behind and around her, anchoring her to the bowl like a hat strapped to a lady race-goer at the Kentucky Derby.

She looks like the kind of thing Marcel Duchamp might have come up with if he'd only ventured into porn.

A woman tied to a toilet.

Every plumber's fantasy.

The drilldo.

Joe the electrician's favorite tool.

Put them together and what have you got?

The ultimate in handyman porn.

And this drilldo, it's pounding away at Anna's pussy like a jackhammer and her eyes have rolled into the back of her head. Her body is trembling the way your hand trembles when you're holding an electric drill. Her whole body. Like she's strapped to a chair in a wind tunnel.

And she's screaming. The way you scream when the car of the roller coaster tips over that first big curve and all you can see is that long drop racing toward you. A scream of pure pleasure and sheer inexhaustible terror. But her scream doesn't stop; it just merges into the remorseless electric roar of the drilldo.

I have the volume turned all the way down, but somehow it still doesn't seem low enough. Because a scream sounds piercing at any volume. I'm scared to turn off the sound because I'm certain that, without it, everything will just look ten times worse.

I glance at the bedroom door.

I really hope Jack's asleep.

I'm trying to imagine why any woman would want to submit to that. I ask myself why Anna would want to submit to that. And the answer is right there in front of me.

Her eyes have glazed over. There's a strange kind of ecstasy written on her face. A look that says, "gimme more" and "no more." Both. At the same time. A look beyond the limits of endurance. A look I'll never forget. I can't stop looking. I'm afraid to look away. I don't know whether I want to fuck Anna or save her.

I don't hear the bedroom door until it's open.

Until it's too late and Jack's standing there, naked and rubbing sleep out of his eyes.

I stab at the keyboard, frantically.

Turn off the volume.

"What time is it?" Jack says, sleepy-voiced. He's woozy, but still a little sour.

"You frightened me," I say.

Did he hear?

Hide the browser.

I'm flushed with the fear of being discovered. Paranoid it shows on my face.

Pull up the word processor.

"What are you doing?" he says.

He heard. He knows. He suspects.

"Essay," I say, and sigh, just a little too dramatically.

No more questions. Please, no more questions. I'm not good at this. The guilt thing.

He goes to get himself a glass of water in the kitchen, and walks back through the living room.

"Don't stay up too long," he says, standing above me, looking down.

"Soon," I say.

He doesn't know; he didn't hear. I can hear it in his voice now. I feel stupid.

The guilt of doing wrong replaced by the guilt of being dumb.

And then I'm distracted by his cock. Right at eye level. Early morning cock, fat and fleshy. His balls hanging full and low. Sometimes I think I could tell the time of day by the shape and size of his cock at any given moment, like the shadows on a sundial that lengthen and recede. I know if I could put Jack's cock in my mouth now, I could suck all the disappointment out of him and make him forget anything happened between us at all.

He goes back to the bedroom and closes the door behind him. I wait to make sure he's not going to come out again. I wait as long as I can. I wait thirty wasted seconds staring at the blank page of an essay I have no intention of writing. Then I pull up the SODOM website and start again.

I'm looking at Anna in an iron cage that's been cast in the shape of a dog, standing on all fours. It fits the curves of her body so snugly it seems like it was custom-made. Only her rear end and her head are not encased by metal.

From what I can tell, the whole cage is electrified because there are cables connected to it that trail off, out of shot, and every time Anna knocks against the bars, even slightly, she howls in pain. Just like a dog is supposed to.

The clip is shot so it never cuts, just tracks around and around and around Anna, ever so slowly, just so you can soak in all the details.

It tracks past Anna's rear end and I can't help but notice her labia squeezed plump between her thighs, entirely and expertly shaved, with not a razor bump or burn in sight, but coated with thin beads of sweat. She's completely smooth and hairless, except for a neatly trimmed bush, dirty-blond and downy, in the shape of a rabbit's foot.

Sticking out her ass is a large, shiny aluminum butt-plug that looks like an H-bomb. And sticking out of that are several black cables that are clamped to the bars of the cage.

The lips of Anna's pussy are held apart by metal clips. They look like bulldog clips, but they have screws in the top with copper wire around them, which hangs slack, all the way down to the terminals of a car battery placed nearby on the floor. It is jury-rigged with dials so that the juice can be turned up and down.

I figure it must have been done for effect because even I know it's pretty hard to get an electric shock from a car battery. A mild buzz, maybe, but nothing lethal. Even so, there are more electrical cables clustered around Anna's nether region than the backside of an office mainframe. And it makes me nervous.

To look at Anna—sweet, sexy, fun, and carefree—you'd never suspect what's underneath. It's as if this Anna, the one I'm watching, is a different person. Not the Anna who sits behind me in class. Not even the one who pulled up her sleeves and showed me the deep welts and livid bruises on her wrists and arms.

This Anna deliberately puts herself in harm's way. Not knowing exactly what she's getting into or how she'll react. Whether she can take it or if it will break her.

Even so, I find it absolutely compelling. I can't stop

watching. I'm glued to the screen. I need to see what will happen next. I'm drawn to it the way I'm always drawn toward things that scare me. I see myself in Anna, just as I saw myself in Séverine. And I want to understand why.

9

Today at school a girl killed herself. Her name is Daisy. Was Daisy.

Pretty girl. Sweet girl. And smart. I didn't know her, but Jack knew her. She'd worked at the campaign office.

The whole campus is in a state of shock. You can almost feel it in the air. When something like this happens, it affects everybody, brings them all together. College campuses are like villages. Everybody is connected to everybody else by no more than two or three degrees of separation. So everybody knew somebody who knew Daisy. And they all need to understand, want to understand, to make sense of the senseless, so they can deal with it, move past it, and get on with their lives. But death has a way of making its presence felt long after the fact. It tends to linger.

And, anyway, this keeps happening.

Daisy wasn't the first. She was the third this year. The

second this semester. All girls who seemed to have everything going for them. And decided they had nothing.

I can tell Jack's really shaken. But he keeps saying he's OK. He's so macho in his own way. Refuses to show his weakness, wants me to think he can handle it, and I know he can but I worry all the same.

Bob DeVille has closed the campaign office for the night, out of respect. Not an easy decision to make with an election less than two months away, but the right one. The staff have decided to hold an impromptu wake for Daisy. Bob is going to make an appearance to say a few words, lead them in prayer, and rally the troops. A natural leader in a time of mourning.

Jack always jokes he'd make a great president. I always tell him he's thinking too far ahead. Bob hasn't even made government yet. But Jack has high hopes; he looks up to Bob as a kind of father figure, and who am I to dissuade him. Maybe he's right.

I want to come with Jack tonight. I want to be there for him and support him.

"No," he says. "You didn't know her. It's better if I go alone."

And I understand why, but I'm worried about Jack. I want to help him. He's not letting me in. He's shutting me out. I'm frustrated. I just want to be by his side and he's spurned me. And it tears me apart.

When Jack leaves, I feel abandoned. I don't want to be here, all on my own like this, with my thoughts. All he needed to say is, "Come with me." But he didn't. It's his call. I don't want to be angry with him but I can't help but feel upset. The only way I can stop driving myself crazy by thinking about it is to call someone.

I call Anna. She already knows what happened to Daisy.

"Did you know her?" I say.

"No," she says, "but we had a mutual friend. A guy."

I want to talk to Anna but I don't want to talk about Jack. I want to talk about anything else but Jack, so I blurt out the first thing that comes into my head.

"I looked at that website," I say, "the one you told me about."

"SODOM?" she says.

"Yeah. I've never seen anything like it in my life. It didn't look like porn, at least any porn I've seen. It looked scary."

"It's not about what it looks like," Anna says. "It's about how it feels. It's not about the scenario, or the situation, but the effect it has on you. About what happens to your body and your mind. And if it's done right, it feels really good."

Anna wants me to understand what it feels like when you're suspended in the air with no means of support other than the ropes that bind you, or constrained in a cage with no means of escape.

"I feel completely helpless," she says, "and I just let go and it's the best feeling in the world.

"I feel hyper-aware of my body, of every muscle and sinew, of every inch and pound. I can feel even the slightest shift and movement in my body weight. And I become sensitive to every stimuli. Every movement in the air around me. Every movement in the ropes, as they scratch and burn at my wrists, my ankles, around my breasts."

"Isn't it painful?" I say.

"Everyone has their limit," she says. "Mine's pretty high. When I'm tied up, at first, I feel this tingling sensation all over my body, like an electrical current going through it. My fingers and toes slowly go numb from being so tightly constricted; then this intense burning heat spreads along my arms and legs. Just pain on pain. Until I can't bear it anymore. And the pain turns in on itself and turns into the most intense pleasure I've ever felt.

"Everything becomes inverted. Pain becomes pleasure. Pleasure becomes pain. And I will do anything I can to increase it, to make sure it never ever stops, because it feels so good.

"I've had the most intense orgasms I've ever had while tied up," Anna says. "Orgasms so intense I passed out, woke up still hanging there, and then the whole thing started all over again."

She says you lose track of time so quickly when you're suspended or restrained, like someone's put you under hypnosis.

"It's like I'm in a trance," she says, "an erotic trance. Like I've been there for minutes, but it could be hours. I'm outside time and it all feels endless. And I'm afraid of what might happen when it does."

It's at that point, Anna says, caught between the fear of wanting and not wanting, that she feels she might go insane.

"But I feel so alive," she says. "More alive than at any time in my life, and at peace. I feel transcendent."

I've never heard Anna talk like this before. She's normally

so giggly and carefree. Now she's serious and I can hear that she really means what she says.

I remember that look on Anna's face. Now I understand what she was feeling. Now I want to know even more. I want to know what it feels like to be in Anna's world.

Anna thinks she's said enough. I know this because she trails off and goes strangely silent, then abruptly changes the subject.

She says, "What are you doing now?"

"Not much," I say.

"I want you to meet Bundy," she says, slightly mischievously.

"Sure," I say.

And I don't even give it a second thought. I know it'll be a few hours at least before Jack gets home and I don't want to sit here stewing all on my own.

10

Bundy says, "Take a look at this."

And he swipes through a series of photos on his phone so fast that at first I can't make out what I'm looking at, except a blur of clashing colors and close-ups taken at extreme angles.

Bundy's swiping through the pictures on his phone like a rookie salesman so nervous about giving his first PowerPoint presentation to a room full of important clients that he forgets to let go of the remote and races through all his slides at once.

The slides he's been up for three days non-stop without sleep to get finished in time for this, his first big sale.

All gone, in less than half a minute.

And he's left standing there, looking up at a big blank screen before he's even finished talking through the first slide, hoping he's still going to make his commission this month.

Bundy's not nervous; he's just excited. But he is trying to sell me something. He's trying to sell me on the idea of snorting a line of cocaine racked out along his penis.

This is what the photos are of mostly, I realize, when he lingers on one just slightly longer than the rest. A portfolio of girls doing exactly that. And this is his pitch to the unwary. Not an easy sell, but he's giving it his all.

We've only just met. Actually, we've only just been introduced, by Anna. Bundy doesn't say "hi" or "nice to meet you." He says, "Take a look at this." And out comes his portfolio of conquests.

This is what Bundy does.

He trawls clubs, bars, clothing stores, fast-food outlets, supermarket checkouts for cute girls. But it's not enough for them to be cute. They also have to be willing.

He calls it "making new friends."

Proof of these encounters appears daily on his website, Bundy's Got Talent, for a worldwide audience of bozos.

Sounds innocuous. It's anything but.

In the armed forces, they call it "mission creep." When a military campaign oversteps its original boundaries and shifts objectives.

This is porno creep.

When pornography oversteps its boundaries and pretends it's something it isn't.

Almost as soon as Bundy's new "friends" have made his acquaintance, he pulls out his camera and tries his damnedest to encourage them to do one of three things, right there and then.

Flash tits. Parade pussy. Suck cock.

On a good day, all three.

On a bad day—and, it has to be said, most days are bad days—Bundy will take anything he can get. He'll settle for less because less is better than nothing at all and Bundy's really not fussy. On a bad day he'll get what's known in the biz as a sneak shot, a photograph taken of the subject unawares. A photograph that comes in a number of specific subcategories: the down-blouse, the up-skirt, the crotch shot, the nip-slip, the pussy-slip, and so on.

Bundy seems to fancy himself as the Simon Cowell of Internet porn. A curator of adult entertainment, a Svengali of sexual talent—because that's what he likes to call the girls who have submitted to his dubious charms. Talent.

This is more of what Bundy does.

He buys access, relationships, patronage to people, places, and things through his extensive portfolio of girls in explicit poses. To him, it's a case of supply and demand, the logic of the market. He's a true capitalist.

But he has far too much pride, and too large an ego, to call himself a pornographer. Bundy considers himself an artist. A fearless chronicler of sex and the single male—himself—in the modern age.

In reality, there's a vast gulf between what Bundy thinks he is and what he really is.

A photographer by trade. A pornographer by default.

A paparazzo in theory. A sexual predator with a camera in practice.

Bundy likes to call himself an Internet entrepreneur and social media engineer.

I'd lean more toward calling him a bottom-feeding hipster.

You hate him already.

Don't.

Anna tells me Bundy has lots of great qualities. They're just not immediately obvious. But they are there, if you look past the smirk, the leer, and the extreme cynicism that colors anything and everything he does. Because he's Anna's friend, I want to like him too. At the same time, I'm more than aware that Bundy's the kind of guy your mother always warned you about, the one she told you was "bad news."

At least with those kind of guys, like with Bundy, there's no pretense to be anything else. What you see is what you get. And Bundy's certainly driven. Just possibly in all the wrong directions.

I'll give him this. He's great fun to be around. And you never know what's going to happen, where you'll end up, or with whom.

We're in a bar. One of Bundy's haunts. The Bread and Butter, a regular corner bar named like a soup kitchen. There's dirt on the floor, dirt on the walls, cracked vinyl seats, chipped glasses, and a toilet that doesn't flush; grime and dysfunction accumulated over years that conveys a certain authenticity to people who have none—Bundy's kind of people, who have invaded this once-unpretentious local drinking establishment and made it their own.

The Bread and Butter is tended by a guy who's only got a first name, Sal, a grizzled Italian-American war veteran who's been here since the place opened and really resents the way the neighborhood's changed, especially his bar. So Sal's decided he would much rather insult his clientele than serve them drinks. He insults their appearance, their manners, their parents and, if that doesn't work, suggests they're the product of incest, anything to get a rise out of them. And these people think that's part of the charm, which just makes him even more mad. But Sal has had to bow to the inevitable, because he's making more money now than he's ever done. He's making money hand over fist, even though he doesn't understand how because, as far as he can tell, none of these kids have a job.

Sal treats his customers like shit, but has a soft spot for Bundy. The reason why is pretty simple. Bundy gives Sal free publicity by featuring the talent he finds there on his website. In return, Sal gives him free drinks. And, I have to admit, Bundy's really got this down to an art.

Using free drinks to score free pussy. To score free drinks. To score free pussy.

Technology being what it is, he can post the photos as content right from his camera. They go live almost the second he takes them.

This is Bundy's philosophy.

Submit first. Ask permission later.

Because Bundy already considers the act itself informed

consent. And anyway he's going to make her a star before she's even gotten round to wiping the come from the corners of her mouth.

Bundy says, "You're not like all the other girls." And I know he's spinning me a line that's probably worked a thousand times before. But not this time.

"How so," I say, "because my mouth is connected to my brain and not your cock?"

He pretends not to hear.

Bundy gets us both a drink, me and Anna. He gets mine wrong. I ask for orange juice. I get a Screwdriver. He thinks I wouldn't notice.

Cute trick.

I figure he thinks, she's drunk already. What's the harm of one more. More will loosen her up. And he'll make sure that the refills keep coming thick and fast. Then the photos will come out again and they won't seem so dumb and abusive. And so it goes. The gradual wearing down. I can see it coming.

What Bundy doesn't know is this:

I don't drink.

And the last thing I want is to end up on his website as bait for some loser trolling the Internet for jerk-off material.

Bundy's Got Talent is just one of his many websites. The flagship site for a stable of publications that glorify Bundy's fucked-up view of life, sex, sexuality, women, and himself.

He likes to think that each site expresses a different aspect of his personality, the way people wear a different pair of glasses according to their mood. Only, like glasses, what you see is essentially what you get. The only thing that's really different is the color of the frames. And Bundy's personality only comes in one shade.

So Bundy's websites, they're all essentially interchangeable. Different titles. Same content. More opportunities to sell advertising.

"The thing about Bundy is," says Anna, in that dreamy, ditzy, completely endearing way of hers, "you'd never know it, but he's kind of a genius."

I'm not convinced.

Bundy's version of genius came up with a website called Red Hot Cherry Poppers, to cater to his predilection for young girls, dumb girls, girls who don't see him coming.

He came up with one called Caramel Candy Cotton Coochies to express his cutesy romantic side. His girly Hello Kitty keychain side.

And not forgetting NFA—aka, No Fags Allowed. To express Bundy's fear of seeming gay. Not just casual homophobia. Homophobia disguised as irony.

As if there's any difference.

All part and parcel of the hipster credo to which Bundy subscribes to.

Racism as social commentary. Intolerance as a badge of pride. Misogyny as a lifestyle choice. Irony as a fashion statement.

You know how gang members who've committed a particularly grisly murder get a teardrop tattoo inked under their eye, a clear warning to all their peers that they've earned their stripes and are NTBFW—Not To Be Fucked With.

Well, Bundy doesn't have a tear. He has a tear-sized Krispy Kreme doughnut. With a swirl of pink frosting.

In Russia, convicted members of criminal gangs, bored out of their minds sitting in isolated gulags, bide their time by tattooing a trail of tears, misery, and violence on their bodies—skulls and knives, severed heads and crucifixion scenes—that purport to tell the true tale of their bearer.

Well, Bundy's tells the story of his personality, and it's not a pretty picture either. Like a parody of body art. A parody of a parody of bad body art. As if God set out to make an example of him, a walking, talking tattooed fool, covered in tattoos that are embarrassed to call themselves tattoos.

Not least, Bundy's pride and joy. The ink that makes you think that maybe, just maybe, Paris Hilton might not be the dumbest string of DNA to walk the planet. Or else, maybe the kind of genius Albert Einstein always aspired to be.

This tattoo is truly the secret of Bundy's success, if you can really call it that, with the ladies.

But not with me.

Bundy's already decided I'm a lost cause and he's looking for fresh meat. He's descended on a girl who looks like she might have potential. A pretty, geeky hipster girl with square-rimmed glasses, black lipstick, and a Mayhem T-shirt. Trying to be black metal but failing miserably.

Anna says, "Just watch."

And I get to see Bundy in action. I get to witness the routine. And it's simple, really. And I realize Anna's right. So simple, it is almost genius.

Bundy's talking to this girl, and he knows he's got her where he wants her but she's still playing hard to get. And so he pulls his trump card.

Bundy says, "I promise that once you see my cock, you're gonna want to put it in your mouth. I guarantee it. I double guarantee it."

He says it in the cutest pussycat voice he can muster. And, just to be sure, he's also making puppy dog eyes. Because he knows that if they've come this far, if they're still standing in front of him, listening to what he has to say, if they've fallen for this, then they'll probably go all the way, and they won't need a whole lot more persuading.

And Bundy pulls out his cock. Leaves it hanging there out of his pants for this pretty-geeky-dumb-wannabe-black-metal-but-failing-miserably-hipster girl to work out exactly what it is that she's looking at.

The head of Bundy's penis.

With EAT tattooed across the top.

And ME inscribed on the underside.

Like the mushroom in *Alice in Wonderland*, except it doesn't make any difference which side you take a bite of.

And I don't know who I feel more sorry for.

The tattooist who had to put it there.

The girl who's about to put it in her mouth.

Bundy.

Or his parents.

His poor parents.

Bundy's parents were yuppies.

You hate him even more.

Don't. Let me finish.

Bundy's parents were yuppies who made their money in a banking boom, back in the days when yuppies, AIDS, Madonna, and crack were the biggest things going. But "were" in the operative sense. Shortly after Bundy was born they lost everything. In crack-fueled shopping sprees, acquiring crap they couldn't possibly need and certainly didn't want. Crap they later sold at rock-bottom prices for rocks of crack that, as inflation goes, cost more than a large uncut diamond smuggled out of Sierra Leone. So yeah, growing up, Bundy had something of a hard luck life. This is what he tells me, in one final ploy, to play the sympathy card.

All this happened sometime in the eighties, but if you were to ask Bundy, he'd be a little vague on dates, not so hot on those important little details, like when he was born. The most I can get out of him is this.

"It was after eight-track tape and before CDs," he says. "When The Police were still cool and before they sucked. Somewhere between blockbuster albums, possibly after *Thriller* and before *Purple Rain*. Or maybe the other way round."

Bundy says he can't remember because he was just a baby. MTV was on all the time and he was planted in front of it in his bouncy inflatable crib while his parents were doing lines of coke the size of Cuban cigars off a stained glass coffee table through monogrammed silver coke straws.

But MTV at that time was just a blur of big hair and eye-liner, of Linn drums and Roland synths, and it was hard to distinguish Duran Duran from Kajagoogoo or Mötley Crüe.

Bundy says, "It was after Martha Quinn and before Downtown Julie Brown. No, wait…between Adam Curry and Kurt Loder."

He's trying to make me think he's got Asperger's and a savant-like recall of all the VJs on MTV in the order they first appeared. But I've got no idea who he's even talking about because when I was born, VJs on MTV were all but a thing of the past and MC Hammer was making his ill-advised comeback as a born-again gangsta rapper.

From everything he's told me, I can deduce three things. Bundy is much older than he looks. Too old to look like he does. And definitely old enough to know better.

Bundy's parents also gifted him with a middle name, Royale—with a superfluous "e"—thinking it would confer kingly status on their firstborn, when all it really brings to mind is a deluxe flavor of Ben and Jerry's.

Cherry Garcia.

Cherry Garcia Royale.

Bundy Royale Tremayne.

And there you pretty much have the root of all Bundy's problems. Charles Foster Kane had his mommy fixation. Bundy Royale Tremayne has his name. Given to him on a whim the night after the morning before his parents went on a massive bender. And feeling terribly sorry for herself, that's when his mom decided to kick drugs.

This was sometime into her second trimester. This was her

big idea. That maybe a steady diet of crack cocaine, Hostess Twinkies, cheese whips, and Beaujolais Nouveau wasn't so good for her unborn baby's future health.

For Bundy's folks, this was such a momentous decision they decided to commit the night to memory by naming their firstborn. Crack cocaine not being that conducive to long-term thinking, they named him after whatever was on TV that night. They named him during an ad break in a true crime documentary, after a particularly odious serial killer and some cheap marketing gimmick dreamt up to sell junk food to junkies.

And the Tremayne, even though it sounds like the name of a doctor on *General Hospital*, that was just part of the deal.

As if all that isn't going to lead to a massive personality crisis somewhere down the line once their sweet baby boy starts to walk and talk and shit and think for himself.

To say that Bundy was born with a handicap is a massive, massive understatement. But I have to say, he's coped with it admirably. He's achieved a lot, given the circumstances.

He's almost famous. Certainly notorious.

The world is at his feet.

And slutty girls with low self-esteem are on their knees before him.

Bundy's on to victim number three in less than an hour. And he's warming up now, so it doesn't take long, maybe ninety seconds, before his cock is already hanging out of his zipper, tattoo ready for inspection.

From what I can see, from where Anna and I are sitting, at the bar, Bundy's cock looks like one of those boiled German sausages, the ones made of a very pale sweet meat spiced with herbs and stuffed into a thick rubbery skin, like a pigskin condom. You don't eat the skin and you wouldn't want to. To cook it, you leave the sausage in a pan of hot water that's been taken off the boil; then you lance the skin and peel it off.

Or else you hold the hot sausage ever so gingerly between the thumb and forefingers of both hands, put your lips to the tiny hole at the top, and suck and suck and suck, until the skin slips back and the meat pops into your mouth.

Bundy's cock looks like one of those sausages. Short, fat, stubby, and pale, with a head that's flat and wide, like an oyster mushroom, or a paper hat at a party that somebody sat on. And it has EAT ME carved around it in thick, black gothic script.

If that sounds pretty unappetizing, if it sounds like the kind of thing you wouldn't want to put in your mouth, then that's about right.

It's not the kind of thing I would want to put in my mouth. But it didn't stop any of these girls.

It didn't stop them snorting cocaine off it either. Maybe they figured that was an easy compromise to make. So they wouldn't have to find out if it tastes as unappetizing as it looks.

And I feel sorry for them. Not because they've compromised themselves. But because they did it for so little reward.

Not really even a line.

More like a bump.

★　　★　　★

What is it about guys with small dicks anyway?

They always have something to prove, always want to show you what they're made of. They always have to tell you how big their cock is. How women always tell them how big it is. And they get away with it, for one reason and one reason only.

Because "big" is such a relative term.

When you finally get to see it, after all that hype, it couldn't fail to be a disappointment and you try not to show it on your face. Because, in actual fact, "big" is no bigger than a cocktail sausage with one of those tiny bows of skin at the end.

And the ones who don't want to tell you how big it is, the ones who think they're smarter than that, they'll try and show you instead.

They'll pull out a bunch of badly composed, self-shot Polaroids of them fucking a girlfriend and pretend it's an art project.

Big guy. Tiny cock. Something to prove.

Because they've only just worked out what everyone in Hollywood, everyone in the porn industry, has known for years and years and years.

Everything looks bigger on film.

Everything but everything.

Whether it's Tom Cruise.

Or a three-inch penis.

Because, despite what you may have heard, the camera always lies.

Or else they might try and show you photos taken on

their phone of some random lonely girl they and their best bud picked up in a bar one night and plied with drinks using their dad's credit card until she was almost totally shit-faced. Then they dragged her back to their apartment, virtually unconscious, propped her up on the couch, and both face-fucked her. First in turn. Then at the same time.

They face-fuck her until they both come. Simultaneously. Both telling themselves it's not because they were rubbing up against their best bud's cock in the same girl's mouth.

But because she gave such good head.

Or else they face-fuck her until she wakes up, realizes what's happening to her, and vomits.

Whichever comes first.

Bundy has a website for that too: What Girls Want.

No irony intended.

Devoted entirely to Bundy's personal archive of girls, in various stages of undress and inebriation, chowing down on his penis.

Even though I can't imagine it has much of an audience, other than Bundy. And the women who appear on it, who only check it out as a memo to self:

Never accept free drinks from strangers in bars.

The bar is starting to get pretty full now. Bundy's hardcore army of fans have already worked out where he is from the GPS data on the photos he posted not thirty minutes ago. He's starting to draw a crowd. Things are getting out of control.

This poor girl is pumping Bundy's cock with her pretty

little mouth, and there's a crowd of jocks standing around them. A bunch of jocks in a hipster bar looking terribly out of place. They're slamming shots of Jäger and Jack Daniel's and pumping their fists in the air, chanting:

BUN-DEE.

BUN-DEE.

BUN-DEE.

And it cramps his style. As it would.

So Bundy gets a few shots off, because that's all he needs, uploads, and pulls out.

He slings his camera around his neck, dashes over to Anna and me at the bar, and says, "Let's go."

And we split.

11

It's early when I crawl to bed. Three, at least, maybe close to four. I didn't expect to be out this long. The room is dark and still. I think Jack's asleep.

I've barely laid my head on the pillow when he says, "Where were you?"

"I'm sorry," I say.

He says it again. "Where were you?"

I can't tell him.

"With Anna," I say.

Only half a lie.

I wait for the conversation to continue. It doesn't. He's not happy. I know he's not happy.

"Jack," I say.

No reply.

"Jack?"

I reach over and touch his arm. He recoils and turns away from me sharply, rolling onto his side and out of reach.

"Jack, I'm sorry," I say.

What else can I say?

Still no response. The silence is deafening. I want to scream just so I can drown it out, just so he'll have to react.

The room is dark and still. For the longest time.

Then he says, coldly, "We'll talk about it in the morning, Catherine."

We don't talk about it in the morning. I oversleep and Jack's already gone. I hate waking up and he's not there. Some people are afraid to go to sleep alone. I'm afraid of waking up, never knowing whether the new day is going to greet me with an empty bed, and no one there to hold me.

I call his name. "Jack?"

No answer.

I know he's not happy. I feel rotten, laden with the dread of a whole day of not knowing if his anger will have eased off by the time he comes home. And what will happen if it hasn't.

Jack's anger is like the raging ocean; it whips itself up, with no concern for the destruction it wreaks, no remorse for whatever gets caught in its path, and there's no way to avoid it, no way to placate it. It's not a violent anger, but a quiet rage, a misalignment of the passion that drives everything he does. And so the only thing to do is to wait it out, until the wind dies down, until it abates and subsides. Until calm prevails. But that doesn't make it any easier to bear.

I do what I usually do to quell the anxiety, to quiet the voice in my head that won't stop talking. I masturbate.

I close my eyes, slide my fingers between my thighs, and think of Jack, still sleeping, as if none of this had happened. As if he had never woken when I came to bed. As if he was completely oblivious to the time. Whether it was four or three or two or one.

I wake him with a kiss on the forehead, my sweet prince, and watch him slowly rouse from slumber. He looks up at me, still woozy, and says, "I waited up, but I was so exhausted."

He doesn't say, "Where were you?" Cold and accusatory.

But, "When did you get back?"

And I lie. A full lie this time, but a white lie, so he's none the wiser.

And he smiles. "I missed you."

He starts to kiss me, softly, sweetly, tugging at my lips with his.

He cups my breast, brushes the nipple with his thumb.

I reach down and stroke myself where all the sweat gathers, where the smell of my sex is strongest. I stroke it and then lick my fingers and stroke it some more.

He gently bites my top lip, sucks it. Tugs at my nipple, rolling it between his thumb and forefinger.

I feel it harden.

I feel him harden.

I feel myself getting wet.

I wet my finger, run it up the lips of my pussy and imagine it's his tongue, wetting the wings of my labia, feeling them flutter and spread, circling my clit and flicking it. Blood rushes to my head, to my clit. I feel dizzy.

I feel the head of his cock bouncing against my thigh as he crawls over me, positioning himself above me, poised to enter. And I turn on my side to accommodate him, bending the top leg at the knee, like a dancer doing the Can-Can, to give him a clear view of the runway as his craft comes into land.

He takes his cock in his hands, guides it toward my pussy, toward the hole, where the wetness gathers. He pushes into it, just enough to wet the tip. Pulls out and slides the head up my pussy, making me slick with my own juices.

He pushes into me again, just enough to bury the tip. And holds it there. Not in, not out. Just waiting. Teasing.

And my finger probes around the hole, scooping up my juice and spreading it up toward my clit, wetting it, brushing it, feeling it throb.

He pushes into me.

I push a finger into me. And moan.

His cock stretches my hole. And I feel my pussy close around the head.

Two fingers now.

And he slides his length in slowly. Teasing. He slides in all the way until he's pressing against my pelvis. I can feel him hard, pressing against my wall. And he holds it there. Teasing.

I'm up to the joint now, and moving toward the knuckle, sinking my fingers as deep as they will go. My fingers are slick with juice, thick and sticky, and white as snow.

He shifts his weight, rotates his hips slightly, like he's piloting a ship, inching the wheel around so the rudder shifts. And I can feel his cock move inside me, brushing ever so slightly against the soft fleshy wall.

And suddenly I can feel that I'm about to come. I can feel a surge building up inside me and I can't stop it. I don't want to. I want to be overwhelmed. I can feel him inside me and I want to come.

I'm going to come.

And as I come, I call out his name. Because I want him to hear, even though he's not there.

Jack. I'm going to come.

Jack, I'm coming.

I'm coming, Jack.

Jack…

And I judder and buck as the orgasm shocks through me. My pussy tightens its grip on my fingers and I can feel the sheets, wet underneath me. But I'm not finished yet. I'm not satisfied.

My pussy is like a cat that's hungry all the time. A cat that doesn't know when to stop eating. My pussy is hungry all the time. And I can't stop myself from feeding it. So another scenario.

This time, Jack comes home, still roiling with anger. And I just want this to end; I want this to be over.

Now.

So I wade in; I give him an excuse and let the waves crash over me. And when it's over we both feel cleansed; we both feel raw and emotional and connected again. We both want to fuck.

Because there's nothing like makeup sex to fill the void and heal the wounds. Rough, angry and frantic, like it's the first time you ever fucked. And might be the last.

Not in the bed, anywhere but the bed. Maybe up against the wall. Me facing the wall, hands above my head like I'm holding it up, trying to stop it from falling on top of us, my skirt bunched up over my ass, my panties around my knees, standing on my tiptoes. Jack slamming into me from behind. And all I can think is, fuck me harder.

And he must have heard me, because he does. I raise myself up higher on my toes so he can hit me deeper, and it feels so good that my legs almost buckle underneath me.

I'm bent over the coffee table and Jack's fucking me from behind again. Not doggy style, but froggy style, resting on his haunches, with his hands pressing against my lower back to support himself, fucking me deep and hard. And it feels as if his cock is going to bore through my pussy, right into the table, like a human drilldo. And we'll be stuck there. Screwing and screwed to the table.

We're fucking on the kitchen counter. My knees are hooked over Jack's shoulders. And he's standing on tiptoes now so he can get just the right angle. I'm sliding back and forth on the counter as he thrusts into me and I'm afraid I'm going to fall off. I sweep my hands behind me for something to grab on to. My hands find the wall, they find the spice rack attached to it, and I think, that'll do. But it cracks off almost immediately and comes away in my hands and the spices spill all over the counter. Jack's fucking me and my ass is being rubbed in cumin, ginger, garlic, salt, and pepper. I'm marinating in my own juices and my ass is ready to be cooked, but I come multiple times before he's ready to leave his yeast in my oven. And as I come, my asshole puckers and snorts a pinch of chili. The pain is excruciating. My asshole is burning and my pussy's on fire. And the flames consume my body and lick at my brain. We're both burning up in the heat of our love.

I'm lying on the hard floor, on my back, and my arms and legs are wrapped around his, like a baby monkey clinging to the underside of its parent. And Jack's pounding into me so hard that I want to scream, but instead I dig my nails deep into his back and draw them all the way up until I reach his shoulders. I feel like I might have drawn blood and he must be into it because he slams into me with thrusts that are even more powerful. And by the time we both come, we've moved the length of the entire hallway, from the front door all the way to the bathroom, and I have friction burns all along my back.

I fast forward through all these scenarios in my head, as if I'm flicking through hotel porn channels, trying to get off on the previews alone. And I switch back and forth between them while I frig myself into a stupor. I stuff myself until my fingers ache and my pussy's sore. Until I can't take any more pleasure. Until I feel broken.

I'm lying there, sprawled on the bed, all tangled up in soaking wet sheets, my body exhausted, my mind floating somewhere between half-sleep and unconsciousness. And I remember that, last night, I had the strangest dream. At least, I think it was a dream. But I can't be sure and have no way of knowing. All I have is the memory, the sensation of knowing.

I remember that just before I fell asleep, I heard a drum. The beat of a big bass drum, slow, insistent, reverberating like the sound of the ocean. I hear it far away, then closer, and closer, until it's on top of me, moving across my body, from my feet up to my head.

Vibrations pass through me in waves, leaving in their wake a warm, tingling feeling. In my fingers and my toes, along my arms and legs, whirling around my belly.

And then the drum is inside me, a steady throb at my crotch, a pounding in my head that gets louder and louder and louder, until a galaxy of stars explodes in front of my eyes. And I'm flying through them, spinning like a gyroscope, jerking in one direction, then another. Or they're flying through me, because I'm fixed to the spot. I can't move. I'm inside my body and out of it at the same time. I am a galaxy of stars.

Then everything goes black. Pitch black. Like someone turned the lights out on the universe. I am in a space with no beginning and no end. No light. No sound. I am numb. I am immobile.

And I can feel someone tugging at my pajamas. I don't struggle; I don't feel afraid. I let them fall away from my body.

I am being carried, naked, in the arms of a man. Being carried like a baby in arms so large they seem to wrap themselves around me completely. Arms so hairy it feels like I'm swaddled in a coat of feathers. In these arms, I am pitching and rolling like a boat on the ocean, but I feel safe—safer than I've ever felt before—and warm.

And the warmth, I realize, is not the warmth of the hair on his arms, not the warmth of feeling safe and secure, but the warmth of the sun. A brilliant, late afternoon sun, still burning bright, and bearing down on me. A white light, blinding me. A white heat, enveloping me.

And I can feel the steady throb at my crotch again, but my head is clear. Absolutely clear and alert and aware. I can hear voices all around me. Voices taunting and mocking me. And I suddenly feel utterly exposed and ashamed of my nakedness. I desperately want to cover myself and disappear. But there's nothing at hand, nothing except the sun. So I grab it and wrap it around me like a towel. Everything goes black again and I shiver.

I woke up with a start from the dream and Jack wasn't there and I felt terribly sad and alone and anxious. And I touched myself.

Jack doesn't come home until near midnight. I'm sure it's just to spite me. I run to greet him when I hear the door open. I try to throw my arms around him but he brushes me off.

"Catherine, we need to talk," he says impassively.

A wave of dread washes over me. He's still angry and I don't know what's coming next.

He walks into the living room and sits over on one end of the couch, leaning forward with his hands clasped in front of him. I sit at the other end, like a child waiting to be scolded.

"I think we should take some time off," he says.

He won't even look me in the eye.

I feel like I've been punched in the gut. Like my world's collapsed around me.

"I don't understand," I say, and I can hear my voice crumbling. "Why?"

"You've been acting weirdly," he says.

"What do you mean?" I say.

"You know what I mean," he says.

I really don't know what he's talking about. I'm starting to panic because he's cut me off cold and I know there's no way to get through to him.

"What did I do?"

"If you don't know, there's nothing more I can say," he says.

"Please, Jack. Don't be like this," I say.

Tears are welling up in my eyes but I'm trying to keep it together.

"Can't we just talk about it? What have I done wrong?"

"I'm going to be away a lot for the next few weeks," he says. "It's a good time to put a little distance between us."

And he says it because he's already made up his mind and doesn't want to give me an opportunity to reason with him.

"Jack, please..."

I'm crying now and pleading with him through my tears.

He doesn't move.

"I'm going away tomorrow," he says.

It's the first I've heard of it.

"For how long?" I sob.

"A few days," he says.

That's all he's going to tell me.

"We're not splitting up," he says. "I just need some space."

"OK...," I mumble. I don't like it but I don't have a choice. And I don't want to push him and make things worse than they already are.

"I'm going to sleep on the couch tonight," he says.

I don't want to sleep alone but I know there's no way to persuade him not to.

I cry myself to sleep and, when I wake up, Jack's gone.

And the apartment feels so empty without him.

12

If you've never heard of the Fuck Factory, you probably wouldn't know that it, or even a place like it, existed.

And even if you've already guessed from the name what kind of place it is—which, let's face it, probably isn't too hard—you likely wouldn't have any idea what goes on inside.

Not in your wildest imagination.

If you never knew it existed, you had no idea what went on there; you're probably better off not knowing. But you got this far so, what the hell, I'm going to tell you anyway.

It's a sex club. The most notorious underground sex club of its time.

If, by some slim chance, you have heard of the Fuck Factory and wanted to go, but don't know where it is, don't try looking for it because you will never ever find it.

*   *   *

Anna and I are standing outside an abandoned, half-demolished warehouse in a section of the city that I've never been to before. That I had no reason to ever come to. That no one has any reason to come to.

Even the cabdriver who brought us here had no idea where he was going and drove around in circles for twenty minutes trying to find exactly the right derelict warehouse, when there's nothing else but warehouses, rows and rows of them. For some reason, the streets around here don't have names. No streets or avenues, no North, West, East, or South. Just a string of numbers, like the girls on Anna's website.

But we're here now. The moon is hanging low in the sky, there's a chill in the air that's pretty unusual for this time of year, and I'm freezing my ass off in a denim shirt, knotted in the front across my midriff, Daisy Dukes that are riding so far up the crack of my ass I might as well be wearing chaps, bare legs, and stiletto heels that make it next to impossible to maintain a steady footing on the rubble under my feet. I'm standing on a street corner, looking like a hooker, and feeling pretty damned exposed.

Jack and I are on hiatus. To me, that just sounds like a fancy way of saying "we're breaking up." But it's worse. It hurts like a breakup but without the closure.

Anna calls and asks if I want to come with her to the Fuck Factory and there's no one to stop me. What does Jack expect me to do? Sit at home and feel sorry for myself? That's not me.

The Fuck Factory is Anna's favorite club. The only place where she says she really feels at home, at peace and among her own kind. She says she wants to take me there so that I'll understand her a little better and why she does the things she does.

Tonight, it's Black and Blue Night, which Anna had to assure me three or four times wasn't the way our bodies would look by the time we walked out of there.

She told me, "It's a dress code, silly."

Leather and denim. And strictly nothing else. No cotton, no rayon, no polyester or spandex.

But I cheated.

I put on a bra and panties underneath the denim.

And Anna doesn't know. Or if she does, she's not letting on.

She came over to my apartment. We got ready together and she brought something for me too, because we're about the same size. And Anna was adamant that I had to stick to the dress code. She said, "You've got to play by the rule. It's the only rule there is."

And I was adamant that, dress code be damned, my modesty would prevail. So I put them on when she wasn't looking.

She made me look at myself in the mirror, while she stood behind with her hands on my hips and a satisfied smile on her face that said, job well done. All I could think was, I look kind of cheap and slutty, like the way young female movie stars have to dress if they want to make the cover of *Maxim*, but Anna looked at me and said, "I'd fuck you."

Right after that, I made an excuse to go to the bathroom and that's when I put my underwear back on—a thong and my demi-cup bra. I checked my ass in the bathroom mirror to make sure the panties couldn't be seen and did up one extra button of the shirt, so the cleavage was still visible but its support was not.

Anna played by the rule. She picked out a black leather catsuit that fits her like a second skin. It has a zip that runs from the neck all the way down the front and disappears between her legs. She couldn't wear underwear even if she wanted to, because it would show and ruin the effect. And anyway, she has it open almost all the way to the navel and her tits are half-exposed.

As she touched up her makeup, I asked her what I should expect.

"It's not a society ball," she said. "It's a place where people go to fuck. You look around, you scope out what's going on, what you like the look of, and you get into a scene. It's no big deal."

Anna tells me the Fuck Factory is legendary. It's been around since before she was born. And busted more times than Lindsay Lohan and Paris Hilton combined for almost any health and safety statute you'd care to mention, even the most minor infractions, anything that could provide a pretext. And every time it's busted, the club moves to a different location and starts afresh, farther away from the rest of polite society, farther away from civilization, where it can exist without fear of harassment or prosecution.

Now it's moved here.

*   *   *

If there was a place called Nowhere, this is probably what it would look like. A war zone. Like those photos you see of some battle-scarred city in some territory on the other side of the world that seems to be in a permanent state of conflict. Or the long-forgotten ruins of a lost civilization. A city that's long been abandoned. Streets that are empty. Buildings bombed-out and barely standing. No inhabitants. No sign of life.

That's what it feels like here. Spooky and eerie. We're two girls standing on a deserted street at the edge of the city. There's nothing to indicate that there's a club here. No signage. No people. Nothing to suggest there's anything here at all. Except something that looks like graffiti. As primitive as a Paleolithic cave painting. Or something someone might have drawn on a bathroom wall.

A cartoon penis and balls, spurting four large teardrops of come.

White stains on a dirty black wall. Below that, a pair of legs raised in the air, in a v-shape, like devil's horns. It reminds me of the way Anna's legs were strung up when she was tied to the toilet in that video. And between the legs, a hole. A crudely drawn vagina. With teeth. Lots of small sharp pointed teeth. Below that there's an arrow, pointing down, to a steep, stone staircase that leads below the street.

As we head down the stairs, into the gloom, I imagine what it must smell like in the Fuck Factory. Maybe like an old basement dive bar, wet and moldy and sweet from all the alcohol consumed in such a confined space. With every step, I can feel an air of mystery and deviance brewing around us.

At the bottom we're confronted by an unmarked black door, like the door to the underworld. Anna knocks twice, then pauses and knocks again three times. And it opens. And when it opens there's not a whole lot more light inside than out. Just a half-light so dim that your eyes need time to adjust to it. A shadowy, hulking figure, the kind of man mountain you always find working the door at a club, ushers us inside without saying a word.

I follow Anna down a long thin corridor, with walls so close that we can only walk in single file, like a passage in a catacomb, then down two more flights of stairs. We're under the city now. And it feels like we're so far down that we've burrowed through the earth into a section of hell.

We're in front of a large steel door painted dirty green. Anna knocks again and it swings open, held by another man mountain.

The first thing that hits me is the smell. And instead of the faint smell of alcohol and mold, this place smells like sex— the smell of hot bodies colliding and combining.

The second thing that hits me is the heat. Wet and humid. The kind of heat that makes you break into a sweat the second you step into it.

The third thing is the sound. Techno. Because what's a club without techno and, specifically, German techno. German gabber techno at ear-destroying volumes. The perfect sense-disorientating, high-velocity fuck music.

We walk into a large rectangular room with brick walls, a bar all along one side and a ceiling so low it seems as if I could reach out and touch it. It's packed with every kind of freak you could imagine, those who are freakish in appearance and others who are just freakish by nature, in behavior, all congregating and in some form of congress, whatever that may be. It feels as if all the social misfits of the world have been drawn here. They don't know why. They just know that this is their place. Where they won't be judged or condemned or looked at strangely. Where they can indulge in whatever their particular peccadillo is.

Two large cages sit on either side of the bar, the kind you'd keep a hamster in but larger, much larger. One contains a naked girl, the other a guy. There's a tray for food and a feeding bottle attached to the bars, both empty. A midget, wearing a top hat and nothing else, is standing on the bar throwing peanuts through the bars of the cage at the girl.

Opposite the bar there are several arched passageways that lead off into other areas of the club.

"That's where all the real action goes on," Anna tells me. "But once you leave this room it's like a labyrinth. You can easily get lost and it feels like you'll never find your way out."

I look around and I tell myself that this is like every club scene you've ever seen in a movie. There's loud, pounding music; it's dark and populated by freaky-looking people who don't look like regular people, who barely even look human. And the protagonist is frantically searching for something or somebody vital to their quest but clearly doesn't belong there. Clearly doesn't even want to be there.

And that character, it's almost always a man—someone uptight, repressed, and staunchly heterosexual. Like a male version of Séverine.

And the club is like Séverine's place of employment, the brothel. The club represents a place where sex of all types and persuasions and perversions are allowed to flourish and play out unchecked by laws, by morals, or by man. And it's a huge threat to his masculinity, to the semblance of order in his life.

But he's not going to be fucked. He's going to be allowed to leave without his manhood being impugned.

Just toyed with a little.

And, at the same time, this is a club scene like you've never seen in a movie, like you will never see in any movie. Because club scenes in movies are made by people who have likely never set foot in a real club. They've just re-created one for their stupid movie so the hero can wander through it looking totally weirded-out by the strange freaks with no fashion sense whatsoever, who are dancing like loons to some of the worst club music you've ever heard in your life.

The people who make club scenes in movies have likely never set foot in this club, or any club like it. The Fuck Factory is a place where people are defined only by their kinks, their fetishes, and their desires. Nothing else matters. Nobody cares whether you're young or old, who you are or what you do in the real world, whether you're a janitor or a CEO.

Anna says, "I want you to meet Kubrick," and she pulls me toward an older man leaning against the bar. Kubrick is the manager-proprietor of the Fuck Factory. Not Stanley, Larry—but everyone just calls him Kubrick. He is short, fat, Jewish, camp, and bald. Because if life's going to deal you one bum card, it's probably going to deal you the whole deck. But Kubrick doesn't seem to mind. He's happy as Larry.

Kubrick has a friendly smile and a tactile manner. He looks pretty harmless. He has a long snow-white beard, a curtain of downy white hair all over his body—down his arms, over his chest, covering a belly the size and shape of a beach ball, not flabby but hard and taut like muscle. He looks like Santa Claus. If Santa Claus had ditched the big red fur-trimmed coat for a black leather jerkin and had the word SADIST carved into his bare chest.

Kubrick has the word SADIST carved into his chest and it looks like someone put it there with a can opener. It's written in large jagged letters that stretch across his torso, between his neck and his nipples. And I wonder if he really is, or if he just got his wires crossed, because it must have hurt like holy hell.

The Fuck Factory is Kubrick's place, his creation, his happening. A pansexual laboratory of carnal pleasure where anything and everything goes. There are things going on in here that, hard as it is to believe, you won't even find on the Internet.

If you're going to name your club the Fuck Factory, you'd better make pretty damn sure it lives up to its name. Kubrick seems pretty confident it does because he welcomes me, saying, "I'm telling you, sweetheart, this is the greatest sex club in the world. The greatest sex club there's ever been."

Kubrick calls me sweetheart. He calls Anna "this one."

Kubrick's big meaty arms are wrapped around Anna's waist and he's pulling her into him so her breasts smoosh against his chest. He has upper arms like hambones and fore-arms like Popeye. On one arm, I can see a faded blue sailor tattoo; on the other, some strange-looking sigil or pictogram that, try as I might, I can't work out what it is.

He gives Anna a squeeze and says, "This one, she doesn't know when to stop."

Then he laughs and casually slaps her on the ass. And she's not expecting it so she jumps with a start and then giggles.

Anna puts her hand on my chest and says, "It's Catherine's first time."

"It is?" says Kubrick, in mock surprise. Then, looking at me, "You've got nothing to worry about, sweetheart. We're all friends down here."

I'm not so sure about that, but Kubrick sounds sincere.

"Just look within yourself," he says, "follow what your heart desires and your body craves. And you will find it."

Kubrick's suddenly come over all Zen and he's giving me life advice like a New Age guru. He has his hands clasped together in front of him as he talks, so he's even starting to look like a guru.

"There's no big secret," he says. "All you need to know in life to get some head is that everyone needs to fuck or be fucked. That's it."

It's not exactly Deepak Chopra, but I think I get his drift.

Kubrick's philosophy, simply put, is this:

Come one, come all.

Fuck one, fuck all.

Fuck whomever you want, however you want.

And that is the whole of the law.

"Just one word of caution," says Kubrick, leaning into me and indicating behind. "Stay away from the midget."

I look over Kubrick's shoulder at the midget, who's now on top of the cage, on all fours, growling like a dog. And the girl is curled up in one corner of it on a bed of straw.

"Why?" I say, "He looks harmless enough."

"He's really horny," says Kubrick. "And he may not have much to work with but that doesn't stop him trying.

"The thing about midgets is they're all super-macho and never do anything in half-measures. So they usually either want to beat themselves up because they're so small or they want to fuck the world. And this one, he's a real sadist."

I look over again and now the midget's holding himself up with one arm, like he's about to do one-arm press-ups, holding his cock with the other, and pissing through the bars of the cage. The poor girl is scurrying back and forth on her hands and knees trying to avoid the spray and not doing a very good job of it.

I must look shocked because Anna says to me, "Don't worry, that's part of her kick. She wouldn't be there otherwise."

"OK, kids," Kubrick says, clapping his hands together like a summer camp counselor, "I have a club to run and people to fuck. Have fun."

He hops down off the bar stool and we watch him scurry away, off down a passage like the White Rabbit.

Anna turns to me and says, "You'd never guess what Kubrick did before this."

"I have no idea," I say.

"Guess," she says.

"Life coach?"

"No."

"Fitness instructor."

Anna shakes her head.

"Librarian."

"Nope."

"Anesthetist."

She laughs.

This is pointless, I think.

"I give up," I say. "What?"

"Accountant."

I try to imagine Kubrick in a three-piece suit poring over ledgers in an office. And fail miserably.

"Not just any accountant," she says. Then leans into me and whispers, "C–I–A."

The way Anna tells it, back when Kubrick was an accountant, he was living a pretty normal life. House in the burbs, married. Healthy, regular sex life, no kids.

But Kubrick had a secret. He used to sneak off to the garage and jerk off over beefcake mags. It's not that he was pretending he was straight when he was really gay, or that he was more of one than the other. He just found himself bored of the sex he had with his wife and was looking for a new kick.

He started thinking about what else could get him off. He decided to let his imagination really fly and see where it would take him. He started collecting catalogues.

Not underwear catalogues. That would be far too obvious, too easy. Catalogues of garden furniture, of seeds and cereals and grains, of dental instruments, of woods and metals and concrete. He followed his whims and collected whatever tickled his fancy. He would look at the photos and he found out that he was pretty adept at constructing detailed sexual fantasies around inanimate objects, the more mundane the better, because Kubrick was training himself to sexualize the world around him.

He figured that was a world that would be a far more exciting place to live in, that it would take him out of the drudgery of his government desk job, his normal suburban life. It would be far more exciting than even beating off to beefcake magazines in the garage after dinner.

This is how Kubrick found his calling. As a fetishist.

One thing led to another and soon Kubrick had a whole library of the most bizarre beat-off material anyone's ever seen. A library that to anyone else just looked like the kind of eccentric collection of books you'd find at a flea market or Goodwill. Soon there was no more room in the garage to house the collection, but it meant so much to him that, instead of moving it or paring it down, he decided to sell his car.

One day, Kubrick got to talking with one of his co-workers about his collection and they both realized they had something in common. They both realized they were living a lie. They decided to start a club to pursue their interests.

At first, they would meet in a room deep in the recesses of the building after work hours. There were only a handful of them and they would just sit around with a beer, each discussing their fantasies in turn for the others—like group therapy but for sadists and perverts. It was all very sedate and civilized. Until, one evening, as Kubrick was relating a particularly lurid sex fantasy involving a hosepipe, a sprinkler, and a pile of manure, a guy sitting opposite him, who was new to the group, pulled out his penis and started to jerk off in front of everyone else. Instead of stopping to tell him to zip up, Kubrick carried on, incredulous. Now he had a new challenge. He wanted to see if he could get this guy off.

As he continued, the other guys in the room also started to unzip and soon Kubrick found himself in the position of trying to help them all, stimulating them to orgasm solely through the power of his imagination. And, to him, this was like the greatest kick of all. Way better than simply beating off over catalogues of cleaning products and jewelry and power tools.

The next time they met, a few of the guys brought their secretaries and interns. As Kubrick sat in the middle of the circle and told them stories, they started doing a lot more than just jerking off in front of each other. Kubrick's little gathering very quickly turned into a support group for sex addicts where more sex was encouraged, not less. People started bringing props and dressing up. The scenes they acted out became more elaborate and involved.

As word got out and more and more government employees wanted to join, things started to get out of hand. It was getting harder and harder to keep it a secret. Around the same time, Kubrick decided he'd had enough of cooking the books for the government so they could prosecute dirty wars in far-flung territories across the world, then point at the accountants and claim plausible denial. He decided he wanted to devote his energies to his real passion, helping people to discover and activate their kinks.

I can't quite believe what I'm hearing so I stop Anna there and say, "Are you telling me that's how the Fuck Factory started? As an after-hours sex club in the Pentagon?"

"I guess," says Anna. She doesn't say anything after that for a few seconds, as if she's deep in thought. Then she says, "You know, the strangest people work in government."

Kubrick still has pretty good connections, Anna tells me.

"You wouldn't believe the kind of people that come here," she says.

I wait for her to tell me who but she doesn't, and I don't ask because I'm not sure I want to know. It's not just the combination of those two statements that unnerves me, but the totality of everything she's just revealed to me about the executive branch and what really goes on behind closed doors of government.

I'm inside the Fuck Factory and I feel like Al Pacino in *Cruising*. I'm Al Pacino pretending to be gay. And giving off all the wrong signals.

Yellow rag in the left back pocket. You like to piss on.

Yellow rag in the right back pocket. You like to be pissed on.

I'm giving off all the wrong signals, without even realizing I'm giving any off at all, and I clock this guy staring at me from the other end of the bar. Young, blond, bare-chested, muscular, and obscenely good-looking with a page boy haircut that would look ridiculous on anyone else, but on him, with a body like that, seems just perfect—the way male models can pull off the most outrageous look and be so self-possessed they still command your attention. He's lean-ing with his back to the bar, his elbows on the counter, legs at a forty-five degree angle in front of him, the better to show off the huge bulge in his leather pants.

He's really not my type and I'm not even into blonds, but he carries himself with such supreme confidence and poise that I can't stop looking. And I can see that's exactly what he wants.

He looks at me coldly, like a lion watching its prey wait-ing for the time to pounce. He's hunting me without mov-ing an inch. He wants me to know that he's there, that he's affecting me, controlling me with his look.

And I want him to know that I'm not easy, that I'm not alone and have backup, so I turn around to talk to Anna. But she's not there anymore. I scan the room frantically, but I can't see her anywhere. I look back. He's still staring at me and now he knows that I'm defenseless and have nowhere to hide. Before he makes his move, I decide to seek refuge in the bathroom, hoping I might find Anna there too.

Now, ordinarily, this would be a great move because a ladies' room is like a convent, a sanctuary offering protection for the fairer sex, where confessions can be made, secrets can be aired, and men are definitely not allowed.

There's only one problem. This bathroom is unisex. And

it's not so much a bathroom, as an excuse for water sports and anonymous sex. In the center there's a trough tailor-made for people to either piss in or bathe in or both—and that's exactly what's happening. Bathroom stalls line each side of the room, something like twenty or thirty of them, and they all have holes in the doors—like the holes in Marcus's closet—and body parts either sticking through or pressed against them. It takes me a split second to look around, take this all in, and realize this isn't the kind of refuge I was seeking.

I step out of the bathroom, into the dimly lit corridor that leads back into the main room of the club, and he's there, waiting for me, in a recess shrouded in semidarkness.

I don't see him at first but as I pass, his hand shoots out and grabs my forearm.

He pulls me into him. I don't resist. I let him take me.

And he whirls me around so I'm up against the wall.

His hands are on my waist, holding me, his lower body pressed against mine.

He kisses me on the lips, while his hand glides over my body, around my back, and up to my shoulder.

He leans in to nuzzle me and somehow finds this magic spot, right on the ridge of my neck, almost midway between the collarbone and the ear, an erogenous zone that opens me up like a puzzle box. And it feels so good that just before the dopamine hits my brain, I catch myself thinking, How did he do that?

He buries his nose behind my ear, drawing in my scent. His lips, soft and moist, fix themselves to my neck, the tongue circling, searching, then slowly tracing the curve up to my ear, and curling down inside the rim, leaving a thin sheen of saliva in its wake. Teasing beneath the lobe, then flicking it and biting down just enough for me to feel the sharpness of his teeth.

I let out a moan. He's in my ear, whispering, "You like that." But it's more of an observation than an inquiry, because he already knows what he's doing, where he's taking me, and how to lower my defenses, one by one.

He plunges his tongue deep inside the crevice, thrusting, probing, making it wet. And I moan again, now dizzy with pleasure and abandon, my body trembling with anticipation for the next touch.

Instead, he makes me wait as he maneuvers me farther back into the alcove. Back where it's dark and private and we can't be seen. And he lifts me up so I'm perched on a thin shelf that runs along the back wall at waist height.

My feet are barely touching the ground. My heels scrabble to find a hold and I have to brace myself and lean against the wall to stop from falling forward.

The wall is wet with sweat. As if all the heat and humidity has become trapped in this one little pocket of the club. But it's also cold and clammy and I stick to it and it feels so good because I'm burning up inside.

And now he has me in a place where he knows I'm vulnerable and my resistance is down. I can sense his ardor increasing. He's becoming bolder, less decorous.

His lust is off the leash.

His mouth is on mine again and his kisses are more forceful now. Using lips and tongue and teeth.

His hands are all over me. One running up through my hair, the other up inside my shirt, reaching for my bra. Kneading and squeezing one breast through the cup. Fingers brushing and pinching the nipple.

I can feel the blood rush in. Tightening and hardening it. Making the nipple so sensitive that I have to stop myself from crying out as the cotton grazes against it.

I can feel my breath getting shorter. Hear my fervor as I moan. And it makes me even more excited.

He kicks my feet apart, parts my legs with his knee, and slides his thigh up against my crotch. His groin is up against my thigh. And I can feel his hardness pressing into me. I raise my leg and slide my pelvis forward so he can move deeper between my legs.

I'm right on the edge and the shelf is cutting deep into my ass, and it hurts so much, but I don't care because he's riding me with his thigh now, pressing it hard against me.

I put my hands flat on his chest and brace myself so I can grind down harder. And it feels so good that I think I'm going to lose my mind and I know I've lost control.

Instead, I think I must have blacked out from the heat and the pleasure and the pain. Because suddenly, I can see myself. I can see him on top of me. And I am outside my body.

The knot of my denim shirt is undone and hanging open.

My bra is unclasped at the front and hangs loose from my shoulders.

My breasts are exposed and slick with sweat. The nipples pink and swollen.

My shorts are hanging off one leg. The other is curled around his back.

His hand is in my panties. I'm wet and squirming to his touch.

And then it feels like I've just woken up because everything is fuzzy and indistinct, and the music sounds so distant.

But I clearly hear him say, "Not such a good girl after all."

He's telling me something I don't want to know about myself. And I think he's mocking me.

The laugh that comes in its wake sounds smug and leering, a slap in the face, and I come crashing back to earth again. I'm fully in my body. I'm naked and ashamed and I don't want it anymore, not here, not now, not like this.

I raise my head to look past him, over his shoulder, and that's when I realize that we're not alone anymore.

There are eight or nine leather boys, and when I say leather boys, I mean leather boys—the kind you'd see in a seventies gay porn film. Inordinately beautiful men, slim and toned. They are crowded into the entrance of the alcove, two or three deep. The ones at the back are craning their necks, pushing and shoving to get a better view.

The three at the front are leaning back into them to hold their ground, to hold the distance between us and them. They are all stripped to the waist with their pants hanging open at the crotch, their balls hanging obscenely over the fly of their pants, below thick, black, bushy curls of pubic hair, and their big rough, sweaty hands defiantly stroking hard, indelicate cocks.

I'm totally thrown and really freaked out because I can't work out if they're jerking off over me or over him.

"I can't do this," I say, and push him off weakly. "Really, I have to go." I can hear my voice crack with emotion. "I have to find my friend."

And it's like when a director yells "Cut" and the scene breaks. I've killed the mood; they all start to peel away in search of another scene, one that will be more satisfying, and I quickly dress and right myself and push past them, wordlessly.

I hurry down a passageway, shaking and exhausted and excited all at the same time, trying to make sense of what the hell just happened. Part of me wanted to go all the way but I just couldn't let myself go and I got scared, like when you get on a white-knuckle ride at an amusement park and you suddenly realize where you are and tense up, and the thrill turns to fear.

And now, like the hero in every club scene you've ever seen in every movie, I'm searching for someone. I'm searching for Anna.

I think I'm heading back to the main room, back to the bar, when I'm going in the opposite direction entirely. And I realize Anna was right; this place is like a labyrinth. All the passages look the same. Two, three turns and I'm utterly lost. I keep on the same direction, thinking that I'm going to recognize some feature or other, then realize that I don't. And then just as I think I'm never going to find my way back, I turn another corner and I see Anna. I could hardly miss her. I've walked into a large cavernous room teeming with people, all moving as one, all thinking as one, acting on instinct as they cruise and watch and fuck.

And there's a film projected on the entire back wall of the room, maybe thirty foot high and forty foot wide, of Anna. One of her clips from the SODOM website. At least, I assume it's from the website because it's not one I've seen before. She's topless and blindfolded with a black T-shirt tied around her head. But it's still unmistakably Anna. I recognize the same shoulder-length blond hair; I recognize her body—voluptuous, curvy, pale, and easily marked.

She's sitting on a bench that's little more than several planks of splintered, unvarnished timber nailed into each other with no concern for comfort or stability. Her arms are extended along the back, in a crucifixion pose, tied along its length by loops of thick rope, and more tied tightly around her body, one above her breasts and one around her waist.

I don't know what happened in the video before this, but Anna's torso is flushed red, as if she's been whipped. Her head is slumped forward, her jaw is hanging open, and she's drooling. A long, thick gob of spit hangs lazily from the corner of her mouth and hangs down between her breasts, where the lashes look red and raw and really painful, and her chest is heaving up and down like she's just run a marathon.

I'm looking at Anna on the screen and I see Séverine, blindfolded and tied to that tree, and I realize that they're one and the same—two fatal blondes chained to their desires.

I turn away and I see Anna again—the real Anna—crouching naked on a platform in front of her video image. She's a star of stage and screen. And the reason I didn't see her at first is that she's surrounded by a swarm of guys, all trying to get near her like autograph hunters crowding an ingénue at her first big movie premiere. Instead of offering her paper and pen, they're waving their cocks in her face as she grabs at them, making sure that all of them get what they came for and none of them are disappointed.

Anna's body glistens with sweat and come. Her face is radiant and alive. She has that look on her face again, the one I saw in the video of her with the drilldo, that same look of ecstatic pleasure.

I'm standing there, taking all this in, and it's one thing to see this stuff on video. It's something else entirely to see it in front of your eyes; you're watching this happening to your best friend and it's like you're watching it happen to yourself.

That's what I think of when I see Anna hemmed in by all these frenzied horny guys, stripped of her clothes, her defenses, her boundaries. I recognize myself. Anna looks so comfortable and relaxed, without a care in the world, entirely assured of herself and her body, her capabilities. In the midst of chaos but completely in control. And getting off from it. I'm getting turned on just from watching her. I finally realize that's where I want to be too, that from here on in, nothing will ever be the same. I'll never be the same again. I've finally crossed over.

13

In my dreams, I am brave. In my dreams, I replay what happened in the Fuck Factory all over again. And I don't run away. I stay exactly where I am, rooted to the spot, my ass wedged against that shelf, my legs wrapped around his waist, and I let him take me.

I let him take me while the others wait their turn. I watch them spit on their hands and stroke their cocks, watching me, as they edge closer and closer.

And I feel like a race queen, in the pit, surrounded by grease monkeys stripped to the waist, fingering dirty wrenches that glisten with oil. The roar of revving engines fills my ears. I'm dizzy and intoxicated by the fumes. I am ready to be consumed by their lust.

And, pretty soon, they decide with their hive mind that they don't want to wait any longer, and they all advance toward me at once, swooping around me. A wall of men, crazed, unstoppable, all demanding attention. Pecking at me with their peckers. All of a sudden, I've got more cocks than I can handle. More than I really know what to do with. And I'm overwhelmed, but so, so turned on.

This is what I've come to realize:

In my dreams, I'm more like Anna.

Willing.

I wish I could be more like Anna.

Voracious.

And, from this point on, I determine to be more like Anna.

Free.

Two days later, Jack comes home to pick up a fresh set of clothes. He's been gone for such a short time but it already feels like everything's changed and a stranger walked into the apartment. He's frosty. I don't know how to break the thaw. And I keep my distance because I don't want to antagonize him. He's in and out within half an hour.

We barely talk. Or rather, he makes it clear he doesn't want to talk to me, other than to tell me he's heading right off for another weeklong trip, all the way to the other side of the state to help set up an important campaign stop for Bob. Some backwater town where poverty is the norm, voter registration is low, and Bob needs to get the word out for every vote that he can get. A place he needs to make a point of visiting to show that he cares. When the irony is it's the kind of place a politician will only ever go when they care about needing your vote. And you'll never see them again until the next time they're up for reelection. And, as far as I'm concerned, Bob's not much different.

No matter how much Jack looks up to Bob, no matter how successful Bob is, no matter how much he represents "new" politics and rails against the old, he has to play the game like all the rest of them, in exactly the same way as it's always been played. Because the rules were set in motion such a long, long time ago that they might as well be set in stone.

If you're ambitious and determined, like Bob, you might get away with bending them a little, or you might get away with bending them a lot. But no one politician is ever going to change the rules for fear of upsetting the apple cart or collapsing the whole deck of cards, because then it's every man for himself. That's a losing game for everyone. Because politics is all about advantage.

This is where Jack and I differ.

When it comes to politics, he's an idealist. I'm a realist.

In real life, he's a pragmatist. I'm a fantasist.

They say opposites attract. But, right now, that feels like the very reason why we're poles apart.

And I've been compensating for my frustration by hanging out with Anna, which isn't helping, because I know Jack doesn't approve, even though that too remains unspoken. I know he doesn't like how quickly I've become close to Anna. And it's compounded by the fact that he knows he can never be a part of the intimacy we share.

It's not because he doesn't like her. I know he does. I think Jack, like every other man who's met Anna, secretly wants to fuck her. And I don't blame him, because if I was Jack, I'd want to fuck her too. If he was curious and told me that's what he wanted, I wouldn't kick up a fuss; I wouldn't stop him. I'd encourage it.

And I'd want to watch.

I'd want to watch how Anna seduces a man with her body. My man.

I'd want to watch how Jack fucks her. So I can be an outside observer onto my own sex life.

I already know what it feels like to be fucked by Jack. Now I just want to see it. I want visual proof of how it feels.

I can see them together now. Alone. Naked. In our bedroom, mine and Jack's. And I can feel Jack's nervousness, because he's never been with anyone like Anna. Someone so self-possessed and sure of her body and the power it holds. He's never been with anyone so confident of their sexuality.

And I guess that anyone is me, but it's not like I'm some naïf when it comes to sex. When I look at a penis, I know which way is up. I know which way to hold it, what to do with it, and what comes out the end. I know Jack's body inside and out. Every millimeter, every crease and fold. I know what he likes and exactly which buttons to press, and when, to make him feel good. But I still think I've got so much to learn and I can learn it all from Anna, by watching her every move.

Jack is lying on the bed, on his back. He's already hard, as always, and his whole body is rigid and tense, not just with the anticipation of being with Anna, but because he's shy and embarrassed.

Anna is crawling over Jack, the way I sometimes imagine Marcus crawling over me. She straddles his legs and leans forward, putting one hand on Jack's chest to steady herself, then makes a show of licking the index and middle finger of the other, and rubbing them between her legs to lubricate herself, while looking Jack right in the eye.

She puts both hands on his chest, raises herself up, and shifts forward, sliding her pussy up along the shaft of his cock, then slowly back and forth a few times, until the lips part and his cock settles into the groove and soon becomes slick with her juice.

She slides forward until she finds the spot where the ridge of the head of his cock meets the hood of her clit and she quickens her movements so she can get herself off too while she's doing the same for him. She presses down on Jack's cock and swivels her hips in a circular motion, grinding hard against it. He can hear her exhale and let out a series of quick little moans. He can feel Anna getting wetter and wetter. Her juice is collecting at the base of his cock, spilling over his balls, running down between his thighs.

She leans down, puts a hand on his cheek, and plants a kiss on his lips, slides her hand down his neck and a nail down his chest. Her caresses are so delicate, so sincere in their devotion, that she soon dissolves his anxiety and makes him feel at ease. And the dynamic between them starts to change. I can see Jack return to himself. His boldness and his decisiveness, two of the qualities about him that really turn me on, make themselves felt in the way he touches her, the way he maneuvers her into precisely the position he wants her in, so that he can take control.

I'm watching them and it's as if I'm some omniscient observer because I can see them fucking from every single angle simultaneously. I'm inside the action—present within each of their bodies, feeling everything they feel, switching between them at will—and outside of them at the same time.

And now Anna is bent over on the bed and Jack is standing on the floor, riding her from behind. He has her hair all bunched up in his left hand, the way an expert rider holds the reins of a horse as it prepares to incite it from a trot into a gallop—tight, in one hand, with a crop ready in the other.

Jack is pulling Anna's hair so hard that it's taut against her skull, as if she's scraped it all back into a ponytail; her head is locked in an upright posture and her spine is bent back and arched into an impossibly perfect J-curve. He's slapping her ass in broad, sweeping, powerful strokes that crack like the snap of a wet towel in a men's locker room.

I can see her ass flush and redden as his hand moves away, swinging back in preparation to land another. I can see her ass ripple as he slams into her. And his balls, wet and sticky with his sweat and her juice, are slapping against Anna's clit, which is large and swollen. His steady pounding is so hard and precise that she's mewing like a bird in distress.

Jack has this expression on his face that I've never seen before, of pure concentration and unswerving determination, like he's set on riding Anna into the ground. Like he wants to fuck her until her body gives in and collapses underneath him.

Even then, he will continue to pound away, with no letup and no mercy, until her body is prostrate and completely still. And only then will he withdraw his hard cock, wet and quivering and triumphant, and start to jerk himself off, sliding the skin back and forth across the shaft, slamming his fist hard into his balls.

I've never seen Jack like this. I've never seen him so dirty, so animalistic and predatory. He's fucking Anna in a way that he's never fucked me, as if she's unlocked some part of him that was locked up deep inside—the way she helped unlock part of me.

And now I've seen all I want to see. I've had enough of just watching. Now I want to join in.

I can see myself there with them. And this isn't like the three-way you'd see in a porno, the typical bullshit male fantasy, where the super-stud with the magnificently tooled penis and a tongue like Gene Simmons is somehow satisfying two women at once, like a circus strongman who can hold up two girls, one sitting on each bicep. Or its equally ludicrous opposite, where two hyper-sexed succubi set upon a guy, overwhelm him, smother him, fuck him into submission, and steal his essence.

No, this is different. This goes beyond the cliché. This is real.

I see myself with Jack and Anna and we've formed a perfect circle.

We're all lying on our sides with our heads buried in each other's crotches. I'm sucking Jack's cock, while he eats out Anna's pussy and she's eating mine. We all have a taste of each other. We're all giving and receiving. We're like the snake that eats its own tail.

When Jack moves his mouth up to Anna's asshole and starts finger-fucking her pussy, I hear her moan as she momentarily detaches from mine, then instinctively follows suit and does the same to me. I can feel Anna's tongue slowly probing around my hole—licking it, testing it, and then plunging inside, while her thin, flexible fingers are pumping my pussy with the speed of a piston to a completely different rhythm.

It's like that trick you learn as a kid, when you rub your tummy and pat your head at the same time and try and keep them both going. And the way you do it is to forget what you're doing, move your limbs independently and instinctively. And that's how it is with sex too. Good sex. Your body moves in perpetual motion, your mind completely relaxes, gives up control, and takes it all in.

Whatever Anna's doing to me, it feels so good that I feel myself shifting position to do the same to Jack. I'm tonguing his butthole, which is something I've never done before because boys, especially the quietly macho ones like Jack, have a thing about being touched back there.

But I'm tonguing it now and he's not complaining. I can hear him moan, quietly, as if he doesn't want Anna and me to hear—but I do. And I start pulling back and forth along his shaft, giving his foreskin a little twist as I do, and then he can't contain himself, and he lets go, moaning a little louder.

We are three bodies melting into one. Free of ego, personalities dissolved. There is no distinction between Jack and Catherine and Anna. There is no male or female. We are one person, one sex. Fucking like a machine. Moving in sync. Breathing in rhythm. Moaning in harmony. In perfect tune.

When we come, we all come together, we all explode together.

And I more than get my wish.

14

I remember it all now. I remember everything. I remember the time I first became aware of sex. Not the act but the stirring. I remember it as if it happened yesterday. And this is going to sound really quaint, and might even be a little hard to believe, but I swear it's true.

When I was eleven, or twelve, thirteen—I can't remember which—my best friend showed me some dog-eared and yellowing sheets of paper she'd found in her dad's desk drawer and we lay on the floor in her bedroom while she read them out to me.

It was a sex story. A really filthy story but written as a letter. Pornography without the images. Pornography before video tapes, DVDs, cell phones, and the Internet. Pornography where the dirty pictures are inside your head.

We figured out that this letter didn't originally belong to her dad but her grandpa, who had gone overseas to fight in the Vietnam War. The only part of him that came back home was a battered footlocker filled with dank and moldy reminders of the place he'd left behind and the family that lost him. A silk slip belonging to her grandmother that still bore faint traces of the perfume she wore on their first date, some photos of her dad as a tiny baby that were old and faded and looked as if they were streaked with tears, and a bundle of peeling letters tied with blue ribbon. And this letter, the letter that told the dirty story, was one of those. It was addressed to him. But we didn't know who it was sent from because we couldn't find a signature. It seemed to be missing. There was no return address on the envelope it came in.

A few days ago, I found the story posted up on an Internet forum. The same basic story but the details were off. A couple of people commented that they thought it started as something passed around on mimeographed sheets as beat-off material for soldiers stationed overseas. And passed down through all the ages and all the wars since then until it ended up in my friend's dad's desk drawer and found its way into her innocent hands.

If I knew then what I know now, I would have told her to stop before she got to the end. I would have told her to stop before she'd even started. Put the papers back where you found them, back in the drawer. They're not ours. This is not for us. We don't need to know what's there. Not now, not yet, not ever.

Children have many beautiful, natural talents that are to be envied and admired. The one thing they lack is foresight.

For some reason, they just can't make the connection between running down the road with their laces undone and a nasty trip and fall in the immediate future. Along with two grazed knees that will sting like nothing else they've ever felt.

That if they stick their finger in the dog's butt, it will snarl and lunge and bite and might take an eye out. Because a dog is like an incarcerated gang banger in the prison shower room with soap in one hand and a shank hidden in the other. It doesn't give a fuck and a finger in the butt is as good as rape. Even if the finger belongs to a five-year-old who's only having a bit of innocent fun with Fido.

That if they poop in their pants it's going to feel unpleasant, and smell real bad. Not to mention that whole business of running to mommy and fighting to tell her what's happened through all the floods of tears. Because while a child lacks foresight, they are not without cunning. So if poop comes out one end, it must be time to turn the waterworks on at the other. If only to inspire enough pity to make the humiliating process of cleaning up afterward that much easier to bear.

So if I knew then what I know now, when my parents took me to the Christmas grotto in our local shopping mall for the very first time, as a toddler in my pretty pink frilly dress with striped candy canes stitched around the skirt, and walked me over the white Astroturf, past the creepy-looking mechanical elves who waved their arms stiffly like a grandma at a New Year's party rocking out to Katy Perry, and plopped me down on Santa's big, red log-sized knee so that he could lean in until his white beard was hanging in my lap and ask me the obligatory question about my heart's desire, I would have looked up into his rheumy, gin-soaked eyes with all the childlike innocence and wonder I could muster and said, "Gimme foresight."

It would have saved a whole lot of hassle, heartbreak, and shit-stained underwear later on. It would have saved me from myself.

And back then, lying there sprawled across the shag carpet in my friend's bedroom as she clutched those yellowing sheets in her hand and prepared to read them out loud, I might have been right on the cusp of womanhood but I was still a child. What did I know?

So I egged her on.

We were like Adam and Eve preparing to take a bite of the apple. Curiosity got the better of us; we couldn't stop ourselves and we ate the whole damn thing up in one go and almost pissed our pants from laughing at all the really dirty bits.

But the rest of the story, the stuff that was dark and weird, just seemed strange and alien to our young, still innocent and developing minds. Because we didn't understand, because we hadn't experienced anything that would give it meaning or context, it didn't affect us. Or at least, I thought it didn't. And here's something I can't really explain.

Somehow the story as I first heard it from my friend—all of it, every last word and detail—stayed with me, burrowing deep into my subconscious like a parasite, where it set up camp and made a home for itself.

And for years and years I never knew it was there.

I'd forgotten hearing not only the story but also the sequence of events that led up to it. And my friend, now she's just a voice without a face or a name and fleeting half-formed memories are all the proof I have that she even existed.

Except in my dreams.

In my dreams, I remember everything. I remember exactly how she told the story, how it went and how it made me feel.

In my dreams, I run the scenes back and forth, adding new details here and there that make it seem more vivid and believable, discarding others. Keeping some that feel as if they need to be there as a running stitch to stop the fabric of the story from falling apart at the seams.

But the second I wake up, it's gone. I lose all memory of it. Except for little strands here and there, but never enough that I can put it all together so that it would make any sense to me during my waking hours. Then, at night, it will all come flooding back again and the dream starts over.

Over the years, I think I must have slowly refined and reworked the story into a beautiful and complex patchwork of sexual desire, a catalogue of my wet dreams from puberty all the way into adulthood.

At some point over the last few weeks, something happened, something that brought the dream to light. All of it, every last bit of it has come back, invading my conscious mind. And now the story is as real to me as my own life. And my life, like Séverine's, is starting to resemble a waking dream.

And I can't lie; it scares the crap out of me to see what's been inside me for so long, gestating and growing. But it does explain a lot, at least, about the path I'm on, the things I've seen and the places I've been. About the reasons I'm drawn to Anna.

In the dream, I'm a little older than I am right now. I live alone in a large city. Jack is not there. He's not part of the dream and never has been. I haven't had a boyfriend for years and I loathe going back to my empty apartment after work. So I go for a walk at the same time every day, just as dusk is starting to draw in. More often than not, I keep to my neighborhood and simply take a stroll around the block. At other times, I catch a cab to a nearby park and wander aimlessly along its gentle, rolling avenues lined with stately elm, oak, and cypress trees, past a bandstand high on a hill that looks like a Greek temple.

On this walk, I bask in the beauty of the city and it takes me outside of myself, allowing me to escape my thoughts. And on the clearest of evenings, when the entire city seems lit by an unearthly golden twilight glow, I'm overwhelmed by an incredible sense of well-being that remains with me as I return home, making the long nights that much easier to bear.

But underneath it all I'm desperately unhappy and deeply unfulfilled. A wild passion burns deep inside me and I long for the day when I will find someone to not only share my life but also help fill the aching need to satisfy pent-up sexual desires that seem to become more frenzied and extreme as the sexless, loveless years go by.

There is someone, though—a neighbor, who lives in an apartment opposite—but we've never met; we've never spoken. When he passes me in the hallway, I try to catch his eye and he lowers his to avoid my gaze. But at night, I know he's watching me. I can feel his eyes upon my body. I can feel his longing and desire and I know he wants me. And so, as I'm getting ready for bed, I'll walk around in the nude with the lights on and the slats of the blinds on my windows tilted open to give him a good view. And when I'm in bed, I masturbate to the image of him in his apartment, pressed against the window, stroking his cock, watching me. I can see the passion on his face. But it never goes any further than this. Him watching me. Me watching him watching me. A feedback loop of carnal longing that's never fully consummated.

One particular fall evening, as I'm about to go out for my walk, my best friend calls. We talk for a while and when I leave my apartment building, it's almost dark. A cab hurtles past. Without thinking, my arm shoots out to hail it. The vehicle swerves to the curb and squeals to a halt half a block ahead. I dash to catch up to it, bark my destination breathlessly into the driver side window, and slump into the passenger seat.

The cab is suffused with a sweet chemical odor, like peppermint, as if it has just been cleaned, and the interior lights are all turned off. I'm so wrapped up in my thoughts it doesn't even occur to me that I'm sitting in the dark.

I sense a movement off to my side. A gloved hand holding

a rag appears in front of my face. I hear myself scream. But too late.

I am being carried in the arms of a great, hulking man. I feel the cool night air brush against my face. And I turn my head to see a large emerald green door looming above me. The door swings open. I see no one and nothing behind it. I'm carried beyond the threshold and enveloped in pitch blackness once again.

Then I become aware of a bright light bearing down on me from above, warm as the late afternoon sun. I wonder if I lay down in the park for a minute and fell asleep. I wonder if this has all been a terrible dream. My senses tell me otherwise.

My hands are constricted behind my head, as if I'm lying on top of them. There is a tightness around my mouth. I'm dry and parched. I hear rustling sounds, at first right beside me, then echoing in the distance. As the unfamiliar details stack up, confusion gives way to fright.

I force my eyes open and I'm blinded by the light. Shadowy figures block the source by moving across it, allowing me to make out my surroundings.

I'm in an old, old theater, looking out into the auditorium from a stage illuminated by a single spotlight. The audience is comprised of men and women dressed for a masquerade ball. They look back at me blankly through eyes veiled by Venetian masks, murmuring expectantly as if waiting for a performance to begin.

I'm reclining on some sort of gynecological chair raised up to waist height. My feet are locked into metal stirrups. My hands, I now realize, are bound tightly underneath the head-rest, with rope that scratches and burns against my wrists. I'm gagged by a red cloth. My field of vision restricted by the few inches I'm able to turn and lift my head.

I feel utterly helpless. But I don't panic. My mind is sharp and clear, buzzing with adrenaline and wiped free of emotion. Resistance, I decide, is useless. Resistance, I think, might make things worse.

Three women, the figures I saw, flutter and swoop around me like birds. They wear egg-shaped hoods made of black chiffon, cut open in a downward curve from the tip of the nose, with eyeholes the size of silver dollars. And matching caped boleros hemmed by a leather halter that runs along the chest and under the arms, leaving their breasts exposed.

One of the women produces a pair of shears and, in one quick fluid movement from neck to hem, snips the dress from my body. I feel the cold steel of the blade as a drip of ice water running from my neck to my belly. The fabric drops like a magician's curtain. My pale white skin is rose-flushed from the heat. Next, my panties are snipped at the hips. The embarrassment I feel at being exposed makes me squirm.

The first woman falls back. Two others move in to take her place, as if the whole thing has been choreographed for my benefit. One rouges my nipples, applying color with lipstick, rubbing and pinching to smooth it out, leaving them a deep crimson red that reminds me of the brilliant autumnal shades of the oak trees that flame against the silver-blue sky during my early evening walks in the park.

The other uses a pin brush, the kind used to groom dogs,

to comb the tight curls of hair between my legs. As the metal rakes my skin, blood rushes to my head and makes me dizzy.

The three women position themselves around me, one on either side, another in front, holding large sprays of peacock feathers up in front of their faces, enshrouding me. And one by one, in rotation, they lower the feathers, fan and sweep them across my body, then lift them up again. And then the next. Fan, sweep, lift. Fan, sweep, lift.

They feather my arms, they feather my pits, feather my breasts, and feather my nest. I feel my sensitivity heighten, becoming aware of every tiny filament as it dances across my skin, anticipating where the next will fall and the shape it will trace.

The vanes possess my body and all I see are the eyes, electric eyes of blue and rust and green, that stroke and flutter and lash me into a trance. Dividing and multiplying, into a thousand and more, staring down at me. Hungry eyes that want to consume me. And I want that like I've never wanted anything before.

A bell rings. The three women peel away in a flash. The auditorium falls quiet. And I'm blinded by the light again, floating toward it, in the silence, in the space that's left between wanting and being.

A man appears before me, at the foot of the chair, wearing a harlequin mask that's hooked over his ears, covers his whole face down to his mouth and extends over and around his head. It's made out of something that looks like burnt leather and molded with a nose, cheeks, and eye sockets—as if he's wearing a face on top of his face. His naked torso, his broad shoulders and powerful arms, all sharply defined and beautifully contoured, look to me as if he's been carved from stone. The Renaissance ideal of a man. My ideal of a man. What I can't see, like the statues in the Vatican, is his sex, which, I imagine, hangs there with intent just below my own, beyond my field of vision.

He steps up and there are no words exchanged, no looks, no niceties or introductions. No foreplay. He grips my legs just above the ankles to steady himself, leans back, looks down, takes aim, and thrusts.

As he enters me, there is an audible gasp from the crowd, one gasp made of many, and although I can't see the reason why, I can feel it. I can feel myself opening up to take him. I can feel him opening up a part of me that's never been accessed before. As if, in one determined thrust, he has broken through and released my desire. I find myself thinking about the bow of a ship forcing its way through the ice. And I know this is just the beginning but I'm already wondering how far I can go, how much I can take, and I want it all.

I'm distracted from his thrusts by the appearance of another man at his side. And then another, and another. Six, seven, eight, nine, forming a wall around me. All masked, naked, and aroused. And others that line up behind them.

There is no bell this time. Hands swarm all over my body, pawing at my breasts, my legs, pulling at my mouth, splashing the sweat that gathers at my belly. And the intensity of their lust startles me.

I wonder who these men are and where they come from. I look at them and imagine, behind the masks, the men

I've fantasized about alone in my bed. The men who offer friendly smiles as I pass them in the hallway of my apartment building, undress me with their eyes on the street, or steal glances on a crowded subway train.

These same men come to me as I touch myself in the deep of night when my sexual fantasies blossom, when I feel inside the deepest part of my body as if I'm being loved by them, caressing my own breast as if it's the hand of another. These hands that are upon me now are the hands of all the lovers I've never had and always wanted. The hands of the man who lives opposite, whose touch I've never felt.

What I don't know, even as this is happening to me, is that he is here too, sitting with the crowd in the auditorium, watching me. That he was brought here by a friend who, sensing his dissatisfaction, offered him a night's entertainment. A very special entertainment at a most exclusive club, accessible to only the very wealthiest of patrons.

He is wearing a mask, like all the others, to disguise his identity. His initial shock at seeing me, the object of his desire, there on stage, is soon offset by the stirring he feels at being able to cast his eyes over my body, up close and in such magnificent detail, and the swell of excitement that passes through the audience.

He wants to intervene and show himself to me but fears what might happen, fears that he might bring terrible consequences on us both, that we might be set upon and torn apart. And finally, he lets go of all those thoughts, submits to his urges, and throws his lot in with the lust of the crowd.

If I had only known there was someone I knew out there,

that he was out there, things might have been different. I might not have submitted to my fate.

The gag is removed from my mouth; the rope that ties my hands is loosened. I'm set free. But I don't cry for help or fight my way out. Freedom means something different to me now.

I'm hungry. As hungry as the feathered eyes and the hands that claw and grab me. And so I instinctively reach for something to fill my need, to fill my mouth and busy my hands. My body is red and raw from being slapped and pinched and grabbed. The same fiery red as the flaming oak leaves. And I don't mind because I feel at one with my nature now; I feel that my body was made for this.

For the first time, I'm able to raise myself up off the seat and look beyond the men who tug at themselves as they wait their turn at my side, and out into the stalls of the auditorium. I see bodies all around, row upon row, arranged in twos and threes, connected at the hip and by the mouth. Figures interlocked and moving. Like glyphs in an alphabet of desire. A universal language that needs no explanation. And I realize it's all because of me, and that's the biggest turn-on of all. It was my desire that brought me here, that created this, and I suddenly understand what it means to be maddened by lust.

And that's where the story left off on the last page. Where my dream would cut off night after night, year after year. No matter how much I thought I could mold and change it, I could not make it end. And I've dredged my mind to see if there's something I've overlooked or forgotten from the first time I heard the story, something I'd missed. And all I could come up with was this.

We sat on the floor and tried to imagine all the possible endings. Fairy-tale endings where the girl's secret admirer rushes onto the stage to rescue her like a shining white knight, and dashes her off through the big green door, back to her apartment where they live happily ever after. Because, to children, all tales have happy endings, and that's what it was to us, a fairy tale, like Sleeping Beauty or Hansel and Gretel, no more dark or frightening or unreal.

I don't believe in fairy tales anymore. I know better than that.

Happy endings are shit for the birds.

And the dream?

I'm living it now.

I know that.

The end remains unwritten.

15

Everyone's been in a situation like this.

You're at a party.

You're just standing there—or sitting—minding your own business, taking in the scene. Or maybe hanging out with a friend, talking about dumb stuff that only you and her know or care about, laughing at your own private jokes. And, out of nowhere, this guy approaches you.

You don't know who he is, neither does your friend. You don't even remember seeing him before. But it's possible you might have caught a glimpse of him when you first arrived and thought nothing of it. You might have even smiled in his direction. Not really meaning to. And he misread it as a signal, took it as his cue.

Now he's right there, standing in front of you. He says, "Hi" and introduces himself, because to him a party is where you're supposed to meet people. And he's decided he wants

SASHA GREY

to meet you. But that doesn't necessarily mean you want to meet him. In fact, thirty seconds in his company is more than enough to make up your mind that you don't. You've only just become acquainted on a first-name basis, but you already know everything and anything you could ever want or need to know about this man. And you're already trying to work out how to get away.

This is that party.

Dickie is that guy.

Dickie works in concrete. Ready-mixed. He's been in construction and aggregates all his working life. He's the chairman and CEO of one of the world's biggest building material supply companies. Concrete is his life and he is so very passionate about the subject. He's trying to convince me that the first recorded uses of cement are as important to world history as the discovery of fire. That his métier in life is as significant to the cultural development of humanity as archeology, medicine, and philosophy combined.

But he's no Mother Teresa. Dickie has offices in every conflict zone around the globe. He's making enough concrete to rebuild countries faster than they can be destroyed. "War is big business," he tells me.

Anna is talking to Dickie's pal, Freddie, a hedge fund manager. She's all giggly and she looks like she's enjoying herself. Dickie might be filthy rich but his conversation skills are as dry as the business he's in. Dickie is boring the pants off me.

If I was wearing any pants, that is. If I was, Dickie would have bored them off me by now.

But I'm not.

This is what I'm wearing: a black floral lace band that covers my eyes, white knee-high stockings, red slingback stiletto pumps, and, wrapped around me like a blanket, a floor-length cape—ruby red to match my favorite lipstick. This time I'm not wearing my underwear.

Anna is wearing a filigree metal mask shaped like a butterfly and an emerald green cape that she's draped around her curves like a fur. Together, we look like two phases of a traffic signal.

The masks and capes are part of the door policy for this little soiree. Not leather and denim. Masked and anonymous. Because this is a themed sex party. An *Eyes Wide Shut* party.

This is worlds away from the Fuck Factory. This place is different. It's exclusive and elite.

I wonder what Kubrick would make of this. Stanley, not Larry. He crafted a meticulous fable about the intersection between sex, wealth, power, and privilege, his last masterwork, the longest single shoot in film history, a movie like every movie he made, where every detail, every nuance of its construction and staging is there for a specific reason. A movie that he put so much passion and work into that it killed him and he never got to see how it was received.

Which is probably for the best. Because the one thing Stanley Kubrick probably did not foresee is that the very people he made the movie about would take the story literally. The conspicuously wealthy few whose power and privilege gives them free rein to live by their own social, moral, and sexual code, one that just doesn't apply to the rest of us, who think decadence is something you can buy with the flash of a credit card, or pick up in a showroom, would mistake it for little more than an elaborate commercial for a high-end swingers club, little more than an excuse for a place like this.

We're in the living room of a large, tastefully decorated private house filled with antique furniture and reproductions of fine art. It's somewhere in the country. Exactly where, I don't know, and neither does Anna, because we were driven up in a car service arranged by Bundy and we both dropped off on the way up, rocked to sleep by the sound of the engine, the trail of blinking taillights ahead of us, and the gentle motion of the car as it swung around the curves of winding country roads once we left the city. And the next thing I knew, Anna was touching my shoulder and shaking me gently, saying, "Catherine...Catherine...wake up. We're here."

Now that we're inside, I realize I have no idea where we are and there's no way of knowing, because it's dark outside and all the windows are shuttered. It feels like we're on the set of a movie. All of reality is focused and contained within this house.

There are large tables stacked with so much luxury food it looks like a Roman banquet. Magnums of Veuve Clicquot in ice buckets. Silver roll-top servers overflowing with Beluga caviar. Huge platters of seafood—oysters, mussels, and prawns—planted in ice like flowerbeds. Terrines of foie gras. And these people are so blasé about their wealth that no one seems to be eating it. Stoic-looking butlers in tuxedos and black eye masks pass in and out of the assembled guests serving champagne.

It's as if somebody has unlocked a door for me that's always been closed, a door to a place I never knew existed and invited me to come inside with them. And why wouldn't I want to take a look, to experience that? What life is like in the forbidden zone?

Right now, it doesn't feel like an orgy. It's all rather genteel and polite. It feels like a bourgeois cocktail party. And I look over at Anna as if to say, really? Is this what we came all the way out here for? Is this the best that Bundy can come up with? And at the same time, I'm kind of impressed because these guys are in another league entirely. And completely out of his. Way out.

Which is why we're here, me and Anna, and Bundy and his ludicrous body art are not—because he'd only stand out like a sore thumb—but he has provided the girls. And Anna, she moves between all these worlds with grace and ease. Her sexuality gives her an access-all-areas pass and I'm her plus one.

I'd say Dickie's in his sixties, minimum, possibly older, but he's at an age where the numbers cease to matter and are even harder to predict. Dickie has a shock of swept-back gray-white hair and a body like a sack of potatoes, lumpy and uneven and weighted toward the bottom. He's wearing a Zorro mask and a white satin shoulder cape with red piping, the kind priests wear. Other than that, Dickie is, for want of a better term, defrocked. He looks less like a member of the clergy, more like a retiree superhero with nudist tendencies. Captain Concrete.

Dickie's sitting talking to me, expounding on the mechanics of cement with his legs crossed. His cock and balls hang listlessly over his thigh, looking about as bored as I feel.

Freddie's a lot younger, young enough to be Dickie's son, and he seems to be wearing the cassock that goes with Dickie's cape, as if they went halves on the costume rental and flipped a coin to see who got what.

As Dickie talks, I'm overcome by an ineffable sadness, but I'm trying my best to hide it. I'm trying to seem interested and maintain a conversation. But I've never called anyone Dickie in my life and I'm not about to start. So I call him Richard instead.

I say, "Richard—"

"Dickie," he says, cutting me off for the third or fourth time, "call me Dickie." And for the third or fourth time, I pretend like I haven't heard.

"OK, Richard," I say, "so give it to me again. What are the advantages of using high slump and shrinkage-reduced concrete?"

I'm taking in just enough lingo to be able to fake it, throwing something back to make him think I'm listening.

"Pumpability, babe," he says. And once more for effect. "Pum-pa-billa-tee."

"And shrinkage reduced," I say.

"Less deformation," says Dickie. "Less curling and warping. You want it hard and straight, it stays hard and straight."

He karate chops the air with his hand and lets out a throaty laugh.

"I think I've got it," I say.

Now that I've shown a smidgen of interest, and it almost kind of sounds like I know what I'm talking about, Dickie takes it as a go-ahead to really let rip. I zone out.

On the wall behind Dickie there are a series of framed reproductions of scratchy, primitive drawings of men and women fucking in various configurations. I recognize them immediately as the drawings from a book Brigitte Bardot is flicking through in Godard's *Contempt*, the book that the vulgar American producer has given her screenwriter husband in order to help him sex up a script by German director Fritz Lang that's all arty Greek myth with zero box office potential. He's given Bardot's screenwriter husband a book of Ancient Roman pornographic art to jerk off to in the hope that it will bleed into his writing and give this producer enough bang for his buck to put asses on seats. And the pictures that are in that book and on these walls were created for a specific purpose, as a kind of instructional sex manual and erotic stimulant for the patrons of a brothel in Pompeii, which was where they were found. And I'm guessing they're here for the same purpose too.

Dickie's talking and the only words I register are "discharge," "vibrators," and "staining." I lose track of whether he's still talking cement or just talking dirty to me, but I figure that if ready-mix concrete gets Dickie hard, he's probably a man who's easily pleased. I'm just not the right person to do his pleasing.

"Staining," I say.

"Yeah, doll, staining," he says. "From impurities. In the water."

"Oh," I say. And zone straight out again. I look around the room at all the other naked men and women, of all ages shapes, and sizes, and I wonder what industries they work in.

Plastics. Biotech. Small arms. Petroleum. Pharmaceuticals. Logistics. Futures commodities.

Because all those nameless faceless bureaucrats who head corporations you've never even heard of but whose influence and decision-making extends invisibly into every corner of your daily life—from the pills you take before breakfast, to the gas you put in your car and the memory foam pillow you rest your head on at night—those people have sex lives too. They have to fuck. And I imagine this is where they do it. Right here. At a high-end sex party like this, designed to protect their dignity, if not their modesty. Wearing masks so they can be as anonymous in their private lives as they are in their public ones.

I feel a sudden urge to pee, and realize it's the perfect excuse for us to ditch Dickie and Freddie.

I say, "If you'll please excuse us, gentlemen. We need to go to the ladies' room."

We walk away as fast as our heels will carry us, to an upstairs bathroom.

We're standing side by side at the bathroom mirror, touching up our makeup, and I say to Anna, "What is this place?"

"They call it the Juliette Society," she says.

"What the hell is that?" I say.

"I don't know much more," she says. "That's just what

they call it. Let's put it like this, the Fuck Factory is for regular people. These people aren't regular people."

"I can see that," I say. "How on earth did Bundy get access to this place?"

"Oh, you know," she giggles, "Bundy's full of surprises. He moves in mysterious ways."

"How do you mean?" I ask, intrigued.

"Well," she says. "He may look low rent but he comes from money. He's got a thing for rich girls who are like him and will do anything for him. The kind of girls that have six-figure trust funds but work as strippers. He's even got a website for them."

"Let me guess," I say. "Filthy Rich Bitches?"

"How did you know?" Anna says, sounding genuinely surprised.

"Just an educated hunch."

I'm reapplying my lipstick and Anna's dusting her cheeks with blush. She's checking her face in the mirror to make sure it's evenly applied and, as she does so, she says, "You know, older guys really know how to please a woman."

Just when I think I've heard it all from Anna, she'll drop another pearl of wisdom, another gem that turns my head. She never ceases to amaze me. And she says it as if it's the most casual thing in the world.

"How so?"

"Because they're as horny as eighteen-year-olds but their bodies just can't keep up."

I burst out laughing.

"I'm serious," she says. "They go at it like maniacs until they're winded; then they have to stop to recover and build up their stamina. Then it starts all over again. That way they can keep going all night."

"But aren't young guys like that too—what's the difference?"

And as I say it, I feel like I'm back in that room with Dickie.

"Young guys always have something to prove," she says, twisting her lipstick open. "And, as a general rule, the ones who are really good-looking are so vain they have zero imagination in the sack."

"Yeah, I know exactly what you mean," I say, recalling my all-star football player ex.

"They usually want to fuck in front of a mirror so they can check themselves out from every angle," she continues, "as if they're directing their own personal porn movie. They're fucking themselves and you're just part of the set design. But old guys are more concerned with making sure you feel good. And they always want to try something new, because they've done it all before and know every trick in the book.

"And another thing," she says, while adjusting her mask. "A hard cock never shows its age. It really doesn't matter how old it is, as long as it's still fully functional. And these guys, you barely have to touch them. They pop a Viagra and they get hard in a flash."

She clicks her fingers.

★   ★   ★

I don't know how long we were in the bathroom, but when we come out it's not the same party. Not at all. The energy in the place has changed. It's as if while we were away, someone rang a bell, like the one that signals the opening of the markets at the stock exchange and, a split second later, the trading floor becomes a frenzy of activity, an orgy of keystrokes.

No one's talking now. Everyone's fucking. Partnered off in twos or threes and fours, or maybe going solo, just getting off on watching.

We're standing at the top of the stairs and I'm taking this all in and, I have to say, it's pretty overwhelming and I realize that this time there's nowhere to hide, nowhere to run. It's time to put up or shut up. I need to take a minute to gather myself, to take a breath and dive in.

"Go down," I tell Anna, "I'll join you in a minute. I just want to watch up here for a little bit."

"OK," she says, and bounds down the stairs like a lamb galloping in a field, eager to join the fray.

I'm leaning over the banister, looking down the well at people fucking in the main room, and I catch this guy across the way staring at me. And I really don't know what it is with me and strange men at the moment. I must be giving off some kind of smell.

Something draws me to the mask he's wearing, so much more elaborate than the others I've seen here. And then it hits me. He's the man from my dream, the Renaissance man in the harlequin mask who unlocks me.

I figure all this out in the split second from when I first see him to the moment he starts moving toward me. My heart starts pounding. I'm paralyzed with anticipation and he's honing in on me like a predator drone. Time slows down. It feels like I'm watching him move toward me in slow motion. I'm taking him all in, lost in the details.

He carries himself with a swagger, so cocksure and certain of his appeal. His skin is tanned and leathery but his body is taut and muscular and toned. He looks like he takes care of himself, like he works out. His physique is speaking to me and it tells me that this man knows his power and how to use it. And he looks good for his age, whatever that is, but I'm guessing he must be in his forties, at least.

Now he's so close I can smell him. He smells rich. By the time he's in front of me, I'm hooked. There's something about him, but I just can't put my finger on it. Then it hits me. Something about him reminds me of Jack.

Not Jack now. Jack later. Jack sometime in the future.

I always told myself that I wanted to grow old with Jack. Sometimes I liked to imagine what we'd be like when we're in our fifties or sixties, when we'd lived half a lifetime in each other's company. I wondered how we'd look with all that living under our belt, how we'd relate to each other, how we'd fuck.

And this guy, I've decided right then and there that he represents my fantasy of how Jack might turn out when we're older, what he'll look like, how he'll carry himself.

And I know how that sounds. It sounds like an excuse, and in a way it is. It's an excuse that my brain has come up with to explain the way my body is feeling. Because I feel an immense attraction to this man, whose identity I don't know and never will. A man who's a blank canvas to me, on whom I can project whatever fantasy I want. And live it and experience it. For real.

He offers me his hand. I take it without hesitation or reserve. When he leads me back downstairs into the main room, it feels like we're two dizzy young lovers out on the boardwalk for a Sunday afternoon stroll.

As we walk in, I see Dickie and Freddie, already double-teaming on Anna, and I can't say I'm surprised. She's on her hands and knees on this worn antique leather couch. Freddie is at her rear. And Dickie has his dick in Anna's mouth and one leg up on the couch. He has his hands placed on his lower back, just above his hips, the way you sometimes see guys posed in porn when they're getting a blow job. As if he's got lumbago.

The guys you see standing like this, fucking like this, in porn, they almost always have their socks on too. And, surprise, surprise, Dickie's got his socks on. But they're expensive-looking socks. Argyle dress socks. By Ralph Lauren.

Freddie's clearly not so particular. He's buck naked. I've got to give it to her, Anna's really going for it. She's showing those two fellows a real good time. Dickie has a grin on his face a mile wide, as you would if you had a cute young chick as filthy and willing as Anna slapping her cheeks with your penis, the way Anna's doing, and slut-talking him at the same time.

"You're a dirty old man," she says to Dickie. "A dirty, dirty, dirty old man. Dickie, Dickie, Dickie. And his filthy old dickie."

I'm not sure if she's talking to Dickie or his penis but I'd say they're both enjoying it equally.

Then she turns around to Freddie and tells him, "Oh yeah, Daddy, ream with your rod. Do it, Daddy Freddie, just the way I like it. Oh, fuck, yeah."

My masked man leads me all the way to the end of the room, as if he's parading me in front of everybody, showing me off. He motions me to sit in this oversized antique easy chair with red suede upholstery. I sit down with my legs closed together and my hands on my lap, as prim and proper as a Catholic schoolgirl. He looks at me, smiles, and taps the arm of the chair. And he doesn't have to say anything; I already know what he wants, what he expects.

I swing my legs up over each arm of the chair and slide my butt forward to the edge of the seat. He kneels down in front of me, takes my left foot in his hands, and starts kneading the sole with his thumbs, walking them up and down the way a cat tests a comfy chair before it settles down. When he reaches the top, he brushes his thumb along the base of the toes, then sweeps his finger up the length of each toe, separates them, and explores the space between.

I close my eyes so I can shut out the world and concentrate on each caress and touch and, before I know it, he's kissing the sole of my foot, sucking on each toe, circling around and between them with his tongue. And it's heavenly.

I feel him running his fingers up the inside of my legs, tracing around the crotch and brushing against my pussy, then parting the lips with his finger and thumb. My pussy is already damp and wet and sticky. I feel him lapping at my pussy with long, steady, insistent strokes of his tongue, the way a cat cleans its fur. His mask is pressed up hard against my clit and the nose rubs back and forth against it, as he works his mouth around my crotch, licking, flicking, and sucking. I feel his tongue probing around my hole. He plunges inside and it feels so good that I let out a moan and slide my hips forward so I can spear myself on his tongue. But as soon as I do, he withdraws, teasing me.

He puts his hands on my legs, clasps them together, and lifts them up so my feet are over my head, and my pussy is sticking out, wet and plump and in full view. I wrap my arms around my legs to hold them in place while he puts one hand on my thigh and gives my pussy a quick little slap with the other. I give out a little yelp, and I don't know whether it's in response to the sting or the sound, but it gives him an incentive to do it again. He slaps my pussy again and I can feel my clit throb as his hand withdraws.

Then his mouth is back on me again but this time it's fixed firmly around my clitoris, and I can feel him drawing me into his mouth, sucking hard, then flicking the head with his tongue, sweeping it across the hood, blowing on it, sucking on it again, licking it. And every time he's gone through a cycle of sucking, blowing, biting, and licking, he switches it up so I don't know what's coming next. And it feels so good that I let out a series of little syncopated pants and moans.

While he's doing this, his fingers find my hole, which is so wet that I can already feel a trail of juice dripping down to my asshole. And he doesn't waste any time; he slides his fingers right inside, probing around the soft fleshy mound behind my clitoris. He's sucking on my clit and pumping his fingers back and forth into my pussy and I can feel myself about to come and I couldn't stop even if I wanted to. I can feel the nerve endings tingle, sending shocks of electricity rushing all over my body. It surges through me. I buck against his mouth and feel his teeth, his tongue, his lips all pressing against my clit.

Then I feel him slide a thumb slick with saliva into my ass, thinking he's got me so distracted that I won't notice, and it brings me back down to earth with a bump. I look him in the eye and very firmly tell him no. If I could read his face, I'd probably see disappointment, but he consents, and I don't really care if he thinks I'm a prude. It's not about that. I'm no anal virgin. It's just that I want to keep something for myself. I want to keep something for Jack. And this isn't like the Fuck Factory. It's not a free-for-all that's every man, or woman, for himself. Here I'm in control and in my comfort zone and I can take it as far as I want.

We switch. He sits in the seat and I climb up onto the arms, crouch down, and slowly lower myself onto his cock. And my pussy's so wet it slides right in, right to the hilt, and now it's my turn to make him moan. I raise myself up off him again. Trails of thick, creamy white pussy juice slide down his cock and pool in his pubic hair. I spit in my hand and pump it along the shaft, sheathing with saliva and juice, and keep pumping it until I hear this low, insistent moan that lets me know I'm doing the right thing.

I slowly lower myself on his cock again, lean forward so my hands are resting on the arms and my ass is slightly tilted up at an angle, pulling his cock up with it. I alternate between slowly swiveling my hips and drawing back and forth and I can hear that low ghostly moan start up again. I'm sliding back and forth on his cock and his hands reach around to cup my breasts; his finger and thumb reach up to grab my nipples and hold them firmly in place.

Now that he's got me loose and wet and willing, he's got another trick up his sleeve: he wants to share me with others. And I don't know how they know, or if he gave them some kind of signal, but I'm suddenly aware that I'm surrounded. And I'm not afraid.

There's a wall of male flesh separating me from the rest of the room, as if I'm cocooned. And I feel safe.

When some peel away, others take their place immediately. And I want that. The more, the better.

I lose track of how many masked faces and anonymous cocks approach, heads bowing as they move forward, begging for attention. I grab for everything in my reach with everything that I've got and once I've got a taste I realize I'm still hungry for more. The more I get, the hungrier I am and it doesn't stop until I want it to. And I don't.

The sex just keeps getting better and better and better. The orgasms get more and more intense and just when I think I've reached the peak, another one comes along that takes me even higher and I don't want it to stop, because the pleasure is so intense.

It feels like my body is being jolted with electricity. Not just every time I come. Every time I'm touched. Like I'm being hit with a Taser, over and over and over. I experience pleasure so intense it feels like pain. Dopamine floods my brain, adrenaline courses through my body, and I lose track of time.

It feels like I'm fucking nonstop for twenty-four hours. And I figure if I want to I could probably keep going for another twenty-four. My body would keep going as long as my brain was stimulated. And here's the thing: the mind never really gets tired from physical activity; it just gets distracted and bored. That's when fatigue sets in. But if you can keep your mind focused, there's no telling how far you can go.

I go further than I ever thought I would and if I could see myself there, in that room, surrounded by all those men, I don't know that I would recognize myself. I'd probably recognize Anna.

When I get home, I'm sore all over; my muscles are aching like I've hiked over a mountain and I had to use every part of my body just to reach the summit. I feel invigorated, but exhausted and all I want to do is take a long hot soak.

While the bath is running, I take a look at myself in the bedroom mirror. And I'm glad Jack's not here, so he doesn't get a chance to see where my body is reddened from being slapped and pawed and pinched. At the same time, I'm still in a state of excitation and so fucking horny. If Jack was here, I would have his cock in my mouth in a second. I'd jump his bones and make him punish me with his cock even more.

I light a jasmine-scented candle, put some tea lights around the bath, pour in a few drops of lavender oil, and ease myself down into the water, inch by inch, until I'm all the way in and I can feel the heat start to relax my muscles, the steam seeping into the pores of my face and body, and I start to sweat it all out.

I sleep better than I've slept for a long time. I sleep like a baby. And when I wake, my body still aches but my mind is clear and focused. I'm getting ready to go out and run some errands and I write Jack a note, because he's coming back today and I want everything to be perfect, in the hope that he'll think again and we can figure something out. I write a note that tells him how much I love him. And I really mean it. I mean it more than I ever have. I want him more than I ever have.

Just before I'm about to head out the door, I rummage through my purse to check my keys are in there. Instead of my keys, I find a roll of notes. Hundred-dollar bills. And I can't for the life of me work out how they got there or when. I pick them up and just stare at them. In shock. I'm paralyzed by a jolt of realization, as if someone's just knocked me on my ass and I've come to, struggling to work out what just happened.

I should have listened to Anna. "Bundy's full of surprises," she said, and I thought it was just another one of those silly things she says. Now I get it. He turned me into the very thing I never wanted to become. I got sucked into Bundy's screwed-up reverse Pygmalion fantasy, where every female is perfection waiting to be turned into a whore. Bundy remade me as Séverine. Belle de Jour. The dish of the day. One of Bundy's bitches.

I feel dirty and used. My stomach feels empty and I can feel nausea welling up inside me. I feel so sick that I want to throw up. The nausea gives way to anger. And all I can hear is this voice in my head, raging.

How could you be so stupid?

I'm shouting at myself in my head because Bundy turned me out and I didn't even see it coming. I told myself I was in control, that I was smarter than that.

And I wasn't.

16

This is what I'm asking myself now.

What is experience worth? And what does it cost?

And they're not the same thing at all. One is concerned with meaning, the other with sacrifice.

We're so used to paying a price—for our weekly shopping, our health, our mistakes, our indiscretions, and other crimes, affronts, and misdemeanors—and never questioning how much, or who decides what that is and why. And, as a culture, we seem obsessed with what's been lost—whether it's innocence, privacy, privilege, security, or respect—rarely with what's been gained.

No one but no one can tell me what my experience is worth. No one but me. It's something only I can know and understand and feel. It's something only I can weigh up, measure, and quantify. Something I can choose to pass on to others or keep for myself. And that's my choice and my choice alone. It's my freedom to decide. My responsibility to uphold.

Let's not mince words here. We're talking about sex. About fucking. And everyone does it. Whether in public or in private. More or less. Straight or kinky. Solo or in pairs or groups. With the opposite sex or their own. And, in practice, usually several or all of the above options in combination. Our sexuality is as at least as complex as our personality; maybe more so, because it involves our bodies, not just our minds.

This isn't about science; it's about being. And that's why I don't particularly trust the conclusions of people like Doctor Kinsey and Doctor Freud, especially when it comes to women. Because how do you quantify or categorize desire? How can you make value judgments on what's good or bad for people, for individuals, based on how they feel? Based on how they fuck?

We're all freaks. In secret. Under the skin. In the sack. Behind closed doors. When no one's looking. But when someone is looking, or when someone knows, that's when there's a price to pay. A price that's put on us, like a pound of flesh. And that price, it might be called many things, when it's really just one thing.

Shame.

So consider that senior at high school who's labeled a slut or a whore simply because she's free with her affections and her body. When half her classmates are wearing promise rings as a prophylactic to contain their desires—as if that's ever going to work—and, somehow, that makes them think they're better. That she is somehow lesser, weaker, baser. Because she's already decided that she likes sex. And she especially likes sucking cock. Under the bleachers. Between biology and chemistry. Not just with the quarterback but with the science nerd and the history teacher. Sometimes one right after the other, sometimes all at the same time. Have you ever considered what she gets out of it? What she believes it's worth?

That girl, she's not like me. She's more like Anna.

That's why I refuse to condemn Anna for the things she does.

Anna is everything to every man. She can move between all these worlds. Mistress, porn star, groupie, call girl. She doesn't think of them as job descriptions, just different types of desire. She doesn't feel exploited, so it doesn't matter to her what people think. And, because she enjoys it, she doesn't have a problem with accepting money. For her, it's a fair trade.

Even though, to me, sometimes it seems like she's living on a knife edge. As if the sex has become a need, and the need is there to fill the void, a void that can never be filled. She's a smart girl so, eventually, she'll come to a realization that she's staring into an abyss. That's the future I see for Anna. And it scares me. But I'm not going to condemn her for it. And neither am I going to try and save her. Because for her, at this point in time, it's all worthwhile. She tells herself she's fulfilled. At the end of the day, that might be good enough, for her, and who am I to tell her otherwise.

And me?

That's the question.

What about me?

What am I getting out of all this? What's the price I'll have to pay?

And how could I have known? Before the fact, not after, because sex is not a supermarket aisle where you can browse all the different options and know the cost before you make your choice.

So let's assume I was fully conscious and aware of everything that I was doing and why. It's far more interesting that way, isn't it? Because there are no excuses. There's no one to blame.

I'm not just talking about the things I did, but about the things I fantasized and dreamed about. The places my subconscious led me. Because it all comes from the same place at its core. And it will all come out in the end. That's what I tell myself. It will all come out in the end.

I don't know who I'm fooling, myself or Jack. My instinct tells me he already knows, that he already suspects something about me has changed. It's not just hard to keep a secret from the person who loves you, the person who knows you the best; it's impossible. But sometimes the things that are so blindingly obvious, about the people around us, our loved ones, ourselves, are the very things we choose to ignore.

Instinct is the most powerful sense organ we have. Not the gift of sight, of smell, of touch, of taste or hearing— instinct. It's all of those combined and more and, if we learn to trust it, there is no path we can venture down that's the wrong path, no action we can take that works against us, no relationship that will break off.

I knew when I first got with Jack that he was the one for

me. Not just for now, for always. I remember that I couldn't wait to confide in my older sister about this guy I'd met and told her in a breathless rush how amazing he was. I thought she'd be happy for me. She just scoffed.

She said I was too young, that I was kidding myself, that Jack sounded too perfect and soon would come a time when I'd realize he was a jerk like all the rest. And I didn't pay her any mind, because I trusted my instinct and I knew.

As I grew up, I would watch my girlfriends go through guys, one after the other, and always find a reason to discard them, feeling dissatisfied or frustrated or used. I would look at them and realize I didn't want to be like them. And these girls, they're all single now, and it feels to me like they'll always be single, because they're always on the hunt for Mister Right. They have this image in their heads of who he is, what he looks like, what he does and how he behaves. And it's a fantasy, a total fantasy. The same line of bullshit that's been sold to women since...forever.

Prince Charming. The perfect male. Ken Doll. The perfect specimen. The Bachelor. The perfect husband. Because those guys, the impossibly good-looking ones, the charming ones, the ones that sweep you off your feet, the ones that seem too-good-to-be-true, well, they usually are too-good-to-be-true. There's another word for charmer, a more accurate description.

Sociopath.

It's amazing how many women fall for guys like that, fall for the same ruse, time and time again, and then rue the day they ever met them.

The game of love, it's one of the oldest cons going. What it really is, is this:

A shell game.

Watch the cups move round and round, and guess which one contains the perfect man. Play that game and you're going to lose. Always. It's a foregone conclusion.

No one wants to believe they've been conned, especially in love. Because that fucking hurts. Probably more than anything in the world. It hits you right in the gut. Makes you feel sick. Makes you feel stupid. Really, really stupid. And so the best thing for anyone in that situation to do is this:

Pretend they saw right through him.

Pretend they knew all along.

Pretend it never happened.

Start all over again.

And this time, tell themselves, never again. I'll never fall for the same trick again.

But they will.

They will because they don't know what they want in life and, until they do, they're destined to fall into the same pattern time and time again, destined to repeat their failures. Because they're pursuing an unattainable fantasy. Of the perfect man. The perfect husband. The perfect lover.

And life isn't like that.

It really isn't.

People aren't like that.

And this doesn't just apply to women. Guys fall prey to their own self-deception too. The sensitive ones, at least. The ones who are evolved enough to think of women as more than just a convenient receptacle for their come. Sometimes they're too evolved. They think too much. They put women up on a pedestal, idealize their perfect companion into something that no one can live up to. At least, I know I can't. And to me, that just seems like a recipe for a lifetime of disappointment, a lifetime of failed relationships. Of looking for Mr. or Mrs. Right and always ending up with someone wrong. So wrong.

This is the game of love. A cup and ball game in which everyone loses.

You say, that's cynical.

I say, it's realistic.

I'm not saying that I don't believe in love, because I do. And, if hard pushed, I'll probably admit that it's the only thing I believe in. Not God, not money, not people. Just love. And I'm not suggesting anyone lower their standards, or settle for second best. Far from it.

I'll tell you something else. My relationship with Jack, it isn't like that. It's not based on what we're not; it's based on who we are. And we're imperfect, as human beings, as lovers, as partners. And I love the imperfections, I celebrate the failings, I worship the flaws. I'm comfortable with who I am, warts and all. I'm comfortable with who he is. I'm speaking for myself here, not for Jack.

He's one of those sensitive souls who thinks too much and sometimes I despair that I can never live up to his hopes and dreams for me. And I do things that are really dumb and self-destructive, as if I want him to find a reason to hate me.

I do things like I did last night. And I can pretend all I

want that it's something else. That it's even, in some way, honorable because I was being true to myself, true to my fantasies. But the fact of the matter is this: I cheated on my boyfriend. The man I love, want to marry and spend the rest of my life with. I didn't cheat on him with my head. I cheated on him with my body. And it felt good.

But fuck it, you only live once. I can deal with the consequences of my actions. I'll mitigate the losses. But there's one thing I don't intend to lose.

Jack.

17

Jack's come home and I'll do anything for him to take me back, to make him feel he's wanted and loved, that we're meant to be together.

I cook him a meal and while we're eating I search his face for any indication that the ice has melted, because the conversation between us is stilted and awkward. And I realize that just the fact that he's here, eating something I've prepared, is a good sign.

We're still feeling our way around each other after our time apart. A week that feels like a month. But I'm so happy to have him here.

After dinner, Jack turns on the TV and catches the end of a campaign ad for Bob DeVille. He's sitting on the couch like he's watching the last thirty seconds of a football game that's too close to call, perched forward with his elbows resting on his knee, his hands clasped below his crotch. His whole body tensed and poised. I have my legs curled up under me like a cat and my arm stretched over the back of the couch, exactly where Jack's body would be if he was leaning back.

This is the closest we get to intimacy. And I'd do anything for that not to be the case. I don't know if this means we're back together or not. Jack's sending out mixed messages and it's so confusing.

We're looking at a two-shot of Bob in some sort of factory, listening intently to a young man in a work shirt and a weathered face whose short life has clearly aged him way beyond his years. He looks like he could be Bob's dad, when he's probably young enough to be his son.

Bob is looking earnest and nodding sagely. And just in case we don't get the message, he's giving that impression in the voice-over too. He says, "People are looking for a change. They're looking for someone who will listen, really listen, to their concerns and their problems and their fears. Someone who will listen, respond, and react."

He says it like he's reciting Hamlet's final soliloquy, or reading *Moby-Dick*. It's epic and intoxicating and you really want to believe him, because he sounds so damn convincing.

He's talking in sound bites that convey a message so bland it's inoffensive; so familiar, it's comforting; something that really speaks to people, goes right to the core of their being, seems to mirror their values, even as it's saying absolutely nothing—all of those things at the same time.

Sound bites are all well and good but they're just words on a page that sound real phony without somebody who can deliver them. And Bob's a natural at that.

He was born to be a politician, the way we think people are born to be artists, writers, or sportsmen. But actually that's a fallacy because people who are creative or who might excel in some particular field, although they might be born with the seeds of genius inside them, are only what they are because they've honed a talent over many years, focused in on it completely, and made it the very core of their being.

It doesn't take any particular talent to be a politician, just a particular psychopathology. So it's absolutely correct to say someone was born to be a politician. They are part of a select breed of individual who thrive on using the quirks of their personality, their cunning and wiles, rather than a specific set of skills. Who've worked out the shortcut to achieving the same goal others reach solely through hard work and discipline. Playing the game and cheating the odds to make sure they go beyond.

And I don't mean to put Bob down, because he's very good at what he does. He's one of the best and I totally get why Jack's so in awe of him.

Bob manages to pull off the trick of seeming city slick and country at the same time—without alienating either one, the city dwellers or the country folk. He speaks from both the head and the gut at the same time. I reckon Bob could sell toothpaste to people with no teeth, shoes and gloves to amputees, and life insurance to inmates on death row. He's that good.

And he looks the part as well. Bob has what I call "politician hair." So perfectly set and wet and shiny that it looks like it was made in a Jell-O mould. A strand may get loose every now and then but, other than that, it never ever loses shape. Just quivers.

The ad cuts to a close-up and it seems like I can see every pore of Bob's smooth, tanned, clean-cut face. He looks a little like Cary Grant, who I figure must be the model for the way all politicians see themselves—suave, intelligent, sexy, and vulnerable. The kind of person that men want to be, or be friends with, and women just want to fuck.

Bob is delivering his coup de grace, the killer line that's going to convince voters he's a stand-up guy, the guy they want to send to Washington to represent them. He's talking about what he's going to do for the state if he's elected. He says, "I want the people of this state to see the real Robert DeVille."

And I have to stop myself from laughing out loud, because no one ever calls him Robert. Everyone calls him Bob. It's like he's got two personas: one for the public and one for everyone else.

Bob disappears from the screen and there's just a caption that reads, VOTE ROBERT DEVILLE, and a voice stating that the ad was paid for by some Super PAC or other.

His face is replaced by Forrester Sachs, Jack's favorite anchorman.

Now, I really don't know what Jack sees in this guy, because to me he just seems like a pompous ass. But if Jack's at home, he never ever misses this show.

Forrester Sachs is Bob DeVille without any of the intellect or charm. He has a name that sounds like a corporation. And he looks and talks like one too.

All the stuff I said about the psychopathology of politicians? It applies doubly to news anchors. Anchormen are wannabe politicians whose vanity precludes them from entering into competition with anyone else except other anchormen, for more airtime, better slots, higher Nielsen ratings—all the things that really matter in life.

Forrester Sachs has the highest-rated news show on TV. He's a shark in a designer suit, with short-cropped salt and pepper hair, a jaw so square it looks like it was cast in steel, and arched eyebrows that are plucked to perfection, a look that conveys all his key values: sobriety, earnestness, youth, and wisdom. He's a sexless automaton talking straight to camera with all the mock seriousness and import he can muster. But nothing could prepare me for what's about to come out of his mouth.

He says:

"Tonight...

"On *Forrester Sachs Presents*...

"We investigate...

"Bundy's Got Talent...

"The website that drove three young women to suicide in as many months...

"And we look at the man behind it...

"Bundy Tremayne...

"The self-styled Simon Cowell of Internet porn."

My jaw drops. Now it's my turn to sit on the edge of the seat, even if I can't let on. Because I've never told Jack about Bundy. Never even mentioned him. If he knew about Bundy, he'd have to know everything. And even if I didn't tell him the whole thing, it wouldn't take him that long to figure it all out.

In the background, in the top left corner behind Forrester Sachs's smooth, strangely unlined face, they flash a mug shot of Bundy that some researcher on the show, who's far too good at their job, has somehow managed to acquire.

From what or where I don't know, but I can't imagine he was busted for anything more serious than a DUI or possession of pot because Bundy's just a jackass, not a major criminal. In the photo, Bundy looks tired and possibly a little bit worse for wear from drink and he's got hat hair.

But it's not about how bad he looks in the picture; it's about how it makes him look. As far as the viewing public are concerned Bundy's already a dangerous felon. In the thirty seconds it took for Forrester Sachs to trailer his show, he's already been arraigned, tried, convicted, and sentenced in the court of public opinion.

By the time the end credits roll, Bundy's name will be trending on Twitter with some or all of the following hashtags:

#sexpredator
#suicide
#bundyfuckingrules
#pedofile
#molestor
#nipslip
#blowjob
#deaths2good4him

#hero
#winning

Facebook pages will have been created in his honor, both anti and pro, that bear his name, age, place of birth, city of residence, sexual history, and mug shot. Each with several hundred thousand likes already. Girls will have left their phone numbers and bra sizes in the comments section. There will be as many open death threats as there are words of encouragement.

Bundy's an instant villain, an instant celebrity, a bona fide folk hero. His brand has gone global and it all seems so very wrong.

Bundy's being vilified on national TV and he deserves it. He's a jerk. Plain and simple. Even if I'm more angry at myself because I should have seen him coming. Just like all these girls should have seen him coming. But they aren't here anymore to talk for themselves and say what really happened. Instead, they have Forrester Sachs to talk for them. An anchorman who can spin their stories and their tragedy into ratings gold.

"Twenty-two-year-old Kirstin Duncan felt she had no choice," Sachs intones. "Her one-night stand turned into a nightmare from which she realized there was no escape.

"A nightmare that led her to take her own life.

"But before she did, she made this video, to let the world know her side of the story.

"And expose the sexual predator who made her feel like there was nothing left to live for."

They run the video, without any commentary or voice-over. And I have to say, it's pretty damning. Kirstin doesn't go as far as naming names. But she makes it pretty obvious. Who pushed her into it. Who was responsible.

Bundy.

The video is shot in Kirstin's bedroom. Through the web-cam on her laptop. She's sitting at her desk and, behind her, everything is white and pink, and My Little Pony, and either fluffy or lace. It looks like a child's bedroom that's been out-fitted with no expense spared.

But a child's bedroom inhabited by an adult.

She's all made up and wearing her favorite clothes. She looks really, really pretty. So innocent and sweet. She looks like someone's daughter. Not someone's one-night stand. She looks like butter wouldn't melt in her mouth. And try as I might, I just can't imagine her mouth wrapped around Bundy's penis and his semen lying on her tongue. It just doesn't seem right. Which is the whole point of this little exercise, I guess.

It's a silent video—in the age of the Internet and the smart-phone, as if talkies were never invented—with a Nickel-back song as the soundtrack. Which is appropriate, because if there's any band that should soundtrack an online suicide note, it's Nickelback.

If I was a young woman who felt there was nothing left to live for, and made a video like this, I'd probably opt for Chad Kroeger to speak for me too, as the voice I felt I never had. The voice to express my deepest inner pain and torment. The voice to say, "I'm done."

While Chad is singing, Kirstin holds up a series of cards

that she's already prepared from a pile in front of her. These are the things that she wants to say, that she wants the world to know. These are all her secrets. Written neatly in black marker pen—all caps—on eight by ten pieces of white card, albeit with no regard for grammar, punctuation, or spelling. I wonder how a girl could reach her early twenties and still be writing like a ten-year-old. And I'd hate to be the guy who had to mark her term paper.

As she holds up each card, she acts out an emoticon that seems like it might be appropriate—as if she's playing a game of charades, where everyone knows the answer before they see the mime.

She holds up the first card.

I MET A GUY

And the next:

HE WAS RILLY CUTE

She gives the thumbs-up sign and a big cheesy grin.

HE HAD A KRISPY KREME DO-NUT
TATTOO UNDER HIS EYE

Couldn't really be anyone else but Bundy.

LOL

She mimes a belly laugh.

> *I THOUGHT HE LOVED ME*
> *I THOUGHT WEED BE 2GETHER 4EVER*

She makes a heart with the finger and thumb of each hand, presses it against her chest, and grins again.

> *AND HED TAKE CARE OF ME*
> *I LET HIM TAKE PICTURES*

She shakes her head to mime regret.

> *HE SAID THEY WERE JUST 4 US*

She bites her lower lip and nods.

> *SO WEED REMEMBER R 1ST TIME 2GETHER*
> *AND LOOK BACK AT THEM WHEN WE WERE RILLY*
> *RILLY OLD*
> *AND REMEMBER HOW WE WERE*
> *AND I BELEVED HIM*
> *BUT IT WASNT TRUE*

Kirstin shakes her head solemnly. I'm looking at this and thinking, It's hardly "Subterranean Homesick Blues." And I'm not sure Bob Dylan would approve.

> *HE PUT THEM ON A WEBSITE*
> *I NEVER FOUND OUT*
> *UNTIL IT WAS 2 LATE*

She frowns and nods her head again—slowly, a can-you-believe-it nod.

> *UNTIL MY BEST FREND TOLD ME*
> *HER BROTHA HAD SEEN THEM*
> *AND HAD THEM ON HIS FONE*
> *HE TXTD THEM TO ALL HIS FRIENDS*
> *THEN EVERYONE NEW*
> *AND THEY WERE ALL TALKING ABOUT ME ON FACEBOOK*
> *TAGGING MY NAME SO ID SEE IT*

She's given up miming along. Now she's just throwing the cards up as quickly as she can, because she just wants this to be over. Because it's really embarrassing airing this stuff in a public forum. Her face is a mask of regret.

> *THEY SAID TERRIBLE THINGS ABOUT ME*
> *THEY CALLED ME A SLUT*
> *AND A HORE*
> *SAID I WAS A DRUGY.*

It seems like the more emotionally devastating the story gets, the more her spelling fails her.

AND I WISH IT NEVER HAPPENED.
THAT ID NEVER MET HIM.

That's where the video ends. I think back to the night I spent out with Bundy and Anna, watching him at work, and I decide she's missing out the details, blurring others, to protect her dignity. Only half of it sounds like Bundy. The really bad bits. And I'm not cheapening what she went through, what she felt she had to do, but the rest of it's a pretty clear-cut case of cyber-bullying, and who really knows which part was the straw that broke the camel's back.

Forrester Sachs is solemnly recounting Kirstin's final hours, with all the gravitas he might employ if relating the death of a much-loved head of state. And he begins to intone the names of all the other girls who appeared on Bundy's websites, then ended up dead.

When he gets to "Daisy Taylor" the penny drops. Daisy, the girl who worked with Jack in the campaign office. I'm not sure why I didn't make the connection before. Maybe because things you see on TV never seem real, never seem to have any connection to your own life. They just seem like all the other things you see on TV that are just pretending to be real, pretending to be about real people and real events.

But this isn't just about Bundy now; it's about Jack. I look at Jack; he's staring at the screen, stony-faced. I put a hand on his back to let him know I'm there, for him and with him. He doesn't acknowledge me, but he also doesn't move away. He's fixed to the screen, because Forrester Sachs hasn't finished yet. He's still got a few more nails to put in Bundy's coffin.

Sachs reveals something else about Bundy that I never knew. That if any of the girls who ended up on his website regretted it later, if they made a complaint, if they begged and pleaded for him to take down the photos, he said he would. But only if they paid him.

Bundy's full of surprises, said Anna. He sure is.

Photographer. Pornographer. Pimp. Extortionist. All-round creep.

It's at this point that Jack's just about had enough. He says, "This guy's a fucking jerk," with such vitriol that I'm almost afraid, because I've never seen him so angry. I never knew he had it in him. "Why are we watching this shit?"

I have to remind him that it's his favorite show.

He wants to change the channel. I tell him I want to watch it all, because Bundy's a friend of Anna's.

"Anna should pick her friends more carefully," he says. "Have you ever met him?"

"No," the lie comes to me quickly, "but I've heard her talk about him."

If only Jack knew the half of it. If he knew that Bundy tried to turn me, his girlfriend, into a high-class whore, he'd do more than just curse at the TV and try to change the channel.

That's why he can never know.

I wish I could be like Kirstin and spill all my secrets. I wish I could be as brave as she was and just come clean. Everything would be so much less complicated.

The show's producers have tracked down Kirsten's parents, Gil and Patty, to say their piece. Gil's an oil executive. Patty's a housewife. They're standing together in the driveway of their mansion, putting on a show of strength, despite being locked in a bitter divorce battle.

"My little girl would never do the things they said she did," says Gil. "I'm going to take this up in Congress. They should censor the entire Internet. Clean it of all this filth, erase those images that pervert took of my little girl."

He pauses, then decides he hasn't made a strong enough case, and adds, "So her little brother never sees them."

It doesn't sound like Gil knows what the Internet is. He's an oil executive who's completely out of touch with the real world, whose secretary handles all his emails and even switches on his computer, which he doesn't know how to use anyway and just sits there like a large, ugly black plastic desk lamp that makes a lot of noise.

It's as if he doesn't comprehend one fundamental thing: the Internet is forever. One stupid mistake and it will stay with you.

And Kirstin apparently didn't know that either—even though she used to spend eighty percent of her waking life browsing, texting, messaging, uploading—which is how she got into this mess in the first place. She met Bundy online, agreed to meet him at a bar. The rest is Internet history.

Now, she's no longer Kirstin. She's "Dirty Blonde Cocksucker #23" on Filthy Rich Bitches. She's fifteen million uniques alone during the second ad break of Forrester Sachs Presents. Kirstin has just become instant jerk-off material for several million sleazy guys who would never have linked her face to a name if Forrester Sachs hadn't done all the hard work for them. Not just in America, but all over the world. Hotlinked and reposted to porn blogs from Azerbaijan to the Cayman Isles. And it's not just Bundy's brand that's gone global; his website spiked so hard that his server temporarily went down and his ad revenue soared.

This poor girl is dead. Bundy's rich.

Life is so unfair. It really fucking sucks.

But Bundy, he's gone to ground. He's disappeared and no one can find him. And because Forrester Sachs can't get to him for an exclusive interview, his producers convince someone else to talk for Bundy.

Bundy's mom, Charmaine.

"After the break...," says Sachs.

"We talk to Bundy Tremayne's mother...

"To hear what she has to say about her son."

During the commercial, I fetch Jack a beer, and while I'm in the kitchen, I call Anna. She doesn't pick up. I text her instead.

Bundy. WTF!

She doesn't text back in the time it takes me to pull the beer from the refrigerator, so I leave my phone on the counter and lock it, in case Jack wanders in.

I bring him in his beer just in time to see Charmaine standing on the balcony of her beachside condo. The condo that Bundy bought for her. The condo that will be repossessed if he doesn't keep up the monthly payments—because

Charmaine doesn't have an income of her own. So I'm sure she jumped at the chance to appear on prime-time TV to beg for Bundy's return. Charmaine Tremayne has her own hard-luck story to tell.

After Bundy was born, Charmaine cleaned up and felt in need of something to fill the void in her life where the narcotics had been. Anna told me she turned to religion, but treated religion like everything else in her life, like being a compulsive shopper or experimenting with different combinations of pills and powders. And now, she thinks she's tried them all.

New Age, Christian, Judaism, Buddhist, Hindu, Sikh, Muslim.

Every time she found a new religion, she couldn't quite bring herself to drop the old one. So she added to it instead, adopting new rituals, superstitions, and icons. They've each left their mark on her person. She has henna tattoos on her hands, Native American charms around her wrists, and a Jesus piece around her neck. She practices yoga, chants, goes to confession, observes the Sabbath, and takes the fast. She's a walking contradiction of God's word. As if she believes in all religions and none at the same time.

Anna had also told me about Bundy's dad, Richard Savoy Tremayne, how he took a similar but slightly deviated path. He kicked drugs, got out of banking, and set up a self-help group to assist others who wanted to do the same. Without realizing it, just like Kubrick, he hit upon a rich seam of need in the financial sector. His business thrived. Junkie bankers flocked to his door, all looking to Richard for support and advice. The self-help group grew into a sect, made up of former crackhead account managers, heroin-addicted CFOs, and tweaker traders, with Richard as their figurehead and guru, and Charmaine at his side. Bundy was raised in the sect, until he reached puberty and started to rebel.

Around the same time, Charmaine briefly converted to Islam and took a Muslim name—Leila. She came to the realization that she'd only married Richard for his name because it so rhymed nicely with hers. So she left him. And he cut her off and left her without an income.

Watching her on the TV, I can tell by the look on Charmaine's face that she really doesn't get enough sex, or the right kind of sex. She's like one of those female office supervisors who's so uptight and stiff that she drives her male colleagues to distraction, and behind her back, they all say, "She just needs a good fucking."

And they all think they're the ones to give it to her. They're probably right; she probably does just need a good fucking. But at the same time, I'm not sure if it's quite that simple. I think starving yourself of sex breeds an insanity that rots your body and your mind—from the inside out—like syphilis, and eventually it shows on your face, in your skin, your behavior, and your entire manner of being.

Charmaine Tremayne has sacrificed her soul for her son. But she's only agreed to appear on Forrester Sachs to save her condo from foreclosure. What Charmaine doesn't know is that she's at a distinct disadvantage. All she knows is that Bundy is missing. She thinks she's on the show to play the grieving mother, like all the rest, pining for the return of her baby boy. When she's really there to play the scapegoat.

SASHA GREY

"I'm proud of my son," says Charmaine. She must have had a few drinks to steel her nerves before this because her eyes are a little glassy and her diction's pretty shaky. "He's a businessman. A self-made man. He's a success."

"He's a sex predator, Charmaine," says Sachs. And the words "sex predator" roll off his tongue so beautifully that he was probably up all night rehearsing how to say them with casual indifference, just a dash of righteousness and no apparent malice.

"No," she says, "no." Like she's not quite convinced of her denial. If we could see Charmaine's feet now they'd be unsteady.

"He drove those girls to suicide, Charmaine," says Sachs, and he's looking down at his notes nonchalantly as he says it, because he knows he's so fucking good at this that he could do it in his sleep. And I wonder if someone is paid to write this stuff or whether he does it himself.

"No," she says, "no."

And this time it's because she really can't think of anything else to say. You can tell Sachs isn't really interested in what she has to say anyway. That, to him, her answers are immaterial. Just dead air while he takes a breath before tossing out another volley of slander posing as inquiry, because this has all been scripted in advance. To make Forrester Sachs seem like the hero, the big man who's standing up for all the little people in the world. He's an anchorman with a Messiah complex in a Tom Ford suit, with arms so big they could embrace all the victims of the world.

When, really, he's just perpetuating the cycle, victimizing them in death as much as they were in life. Airing everybody's dirty laundry without any regard for the consequences. Sacrificing his subjects on the altar of his vanity. I wonder how he sleeps at night, I really do.

"What do you want to say to your son, Charmaine," Sachs says. "Now that you know what he's done. Now that you know that people have died."

And now Sachs is looking for the big payoff, that killer piece of footage that will end up being syndicated to every news show on every single TV channel, where it will run near-continuously as a two-second sound bite to trailer the story.

They cut to Charmaine and she's looking straight into the camera, or rather where she thinks she should be looking. She's looking at the cameraman, addressing him and not the camera, and so it seems on TV like she's staring off into the middle distance, like she's not really with it, not really there at all. And her glassy eyes are welling up with tears, her lips are quaking like she's about to cry, and she says, in a voice cracked with emotion:

"Mommy loves you, Bundy. Mommy loves you."

You can almost see the smirk on Sachs's face because he knows he's got what he's wanted. And as I'm watching all this unfold, I realize it's turning into one of those tragedies you see on TV but never ever think you'll play any part in. Blanket coverage, round-the-clock, day-in, day-out. These lives, or deaths, celebrated for a brief moment in the frenzy of a news cycle. Or if they're really lucky, maybe three or four. Maybe celebrated isn't quite the right word—

fetishized. Then just as quickly forgotten. Becoming just another nameless, faceless victim of a tragedy that probably could have been avoided in the first place.

And, at this point, I decide I've had enough too. I tell Jack to change the channel and he's all too happy to oblige. We catch the end of the same campaign ad for Bob DeVille again, and Bob's still talking about how he wants people to see the real him.

"Bob's invited us to spend a weekend at his house," Jack says, his attention still fixed on the screen, on Bob.

"He has?" I say, surprised, but delighted.

"I thought we could spend some time together there," he says.

I'm beaming inside. It sounds like an olive branch, like he's giving us another go.

"I'd like that—when?"

"This weekend," he says.

And I'm secretly delighted because it's Columbus Day weekend—a long weekend, the last public holiday before the election—and we'll be together for an extended period of time. And I'd do anything for that, even if it means playing the dutiful girlfriend to Jack in front of his boss.

18

During the journey up to the DeVilles, it feels like Jack and I are driving away from all our troubles and heading toward a new horizon, and I want to put everything behind me and start afresh. A few times, I even catch him glancing over at me when he thinks I'm not looking.

Bob DeVille and his wife Gena live in this magnificent open plan, split-level ranch house built onto a hillside, with a terraced garden, acres and acres of land, a deck, and a swimming pool that overlook a long, lush valley with a river running along the bottom and mountains in the distance. All you can see from the deck is this vast landscape that seems to stretch on uninterrupted for miles with just a handful of other houses visible to the naked eye.

When Bob takes us out on the deck to show us the view, soon after we've arrived, I'm overwhelmed.

"I want to live here," I whisper to Jack.

"Here?" he says.

"A place just like it," I say. "Just you and me, isolated by beauty."

"I guess I need to make something of myself, then." He smiles.

I don't doubt he will and I want to be with him when he does.

"This place is incredible," I add. "I knew Bob was wealthy but I didn't realize he was that wealthy."

"He's good at his job," says Jack. "One of the best. He litigates for oil companies."

This is the first time I've actually met Bob in person. The closest I've ever got to him before are those photos of him on the giant campaign placards that plaster the front of the office. Posters that look like commercials for a hygiene product. Airbrushed to perfection. And Bob, he looks rugged and handsome and slick—as if the Marlboro Man was advertising Crest—but it's all image, because he's not at all like that in person. He's so stiff that he's kind of goofy and he's a bit of a klutz as well and it makes me warm to him a little bit more.

Gena is a Southern belle with a gentle grace and bearing that could only have been the product of a private education. She looks like a relic of '60s glamour; her blond hair is styled in a flip, as if it never went out of fashion. She's wearing a turquoise pantsuit, the kind of thing you always see Hilary Clinton wear, a look that's distinguished and stylish at the same time.

Before lunch, Bob and Jack are sitting on the couch having a man-to-man talk about politics and the state of the world. I'm scanning the photos arranged on the mantel and I'm drawn to one old black-and-white photo of Gena.

I figure she must have been about my age when that photo was taken. She looks like Ingrid Bergman in *Voyage to Italy*. That beautiful, that sophisticated. But it's her eyes that draw me in, filled with a mesmerizing yearning and warmth.

"What beautiful eyes," I say aloud as I pick up the picture, to no one in particular, not realizing that Gena is standing behind me.

"Why, thank you," she says. "Bob always tells me, it was my eyes that stole his heart and he had to marry me to win it back."

And as she says it, I look from the photo into her eyes, and realize that they're not the same eyes. Gena's eyes are clouded, as if she's on too many conflicting prescription meds, and her mouth is bent out of shape at the corners, the way a nail kinks if you don't hit it straight on the head with the hammer when it's already halfway in the wall.

And I wonder what it was that hit Gena that way to bend her out of shape. I look at her now and she looks kind of crazy and lost. But, I have to say, she's putting on a good front.

Jack doesn't see any of this. He doesn't see the little cracks. He's not ready to look past the facade that Bob and Gena are putting out. He's too wrapped up in the Bob thing.

Jack's a smart guy, perceptive. But sometimes I despair. It's not that he can't see through people. He just doesn't want to. He needs to believe in them too much, to reinforce his idea of who he is and what his place is in the world. In Jack's eyes, Bob can do no wrong.

Now that I see them together, I get the feeling that Bob sees Jack in a similar way, as the kind of guy who's got a great future ahead of him. I'm pretending not to listen to their conversation but I hear Bob say to Jack, "You're the kind of guy I could use. If we take this all the way, I can find a place for you."

He puts a fatherly arm around Jack's shoulder. That's the other thing I realize, now that I see them together; Bob sees Jack as the son he never had.

They don't have children of their own, Bob and Gena, which is kind of odd when I think about it because I can't think of a politician that doesn't. Even the ones that are still in the closet, who eventually get caught with their pants around their ankles, having their asses reamed in their office on Capitol Hill by some hot piece of male fluff they picked up in a gay bar and then bent the rules to employ as their private secretary. Even those guys have a wife and kids at home.

Bob and Gena don't have kids; they have a dog instead. Some kind of terrier. And they've given it the name of the child they never had. They've named it Sebastian. And they treat it like a child too. Because this is a special occasion and they have guests, Gena has dressed it up in a doggie bow tie and tux.

Some people are cat people, some are dog people. I'm both. I love dogs. But not small dogs. And definitely not this small dog.

This dog thinks it's cute. When it really isn't. It's just a compulsive attention-seeker. Its favorite toy is a plastic dog. Same breed, same coloring, just smaller. Like a replica of itself rendered as a cartoon character. A plastic dog that squeaks. And its favorite pastime is to trot around the house like it owns it, carrying the plastic dog in its mouth and biting down every few seconds so it squeaks. It drops the drool-covered plastic version of itself at my feet and waits there expectantly until I pick it up and throw it. I throw it and within ten seconds it's come back for more and the plastic toy is back at my feet again, covered in even more drool.

Bob and Jack are still deep in conversation, Gena's in the kitchen, and I'm left playing fetch with this stupid dog and its plastic doppelgänger. After three or four rounds of this, I'm already bored. The toy is a ball of drool with plastic inside and I'm loath to pick it up because I don't know where this dog has been. Thankfully, at that point, Gena calls us all in for lunch.

We're sitting at a beautiful turn-of-the-century antique oak dining table with lion's paws for feet. It's far too big for four people. Bob sits at one end, Gena at the other, Jack and I opposite each other in the middle, and it feels like there's a yawning space between us.

The table is laid with china plates and sterling silver cutlery, and laden with pewter dishes that have been in Bob's family for generations. We're about to tuck into a traditional Columbus Day meal that Gena's prepared for us. Salted cod, sardines, anchovies, rice and beans. I never even knew there was a traditional meal for Columbus Day, except meatballs and spaghetti, but apparently there is—fisherman's food, the way they ate on the *Santa Maria*.

Bob is saying grace at the head of the table with his hands clasped in front of him and his head bowed in prayer. I have my head bowed too, but I'm peeking above my hands, like you do as a kid when you go through the motions but you don't really get it and you don't really believe. It's a habit I've never grown out of; pretending to say grace.

My family is Catholic so it's not like I didn't have plenty of practice, but I always felt like such a fraud at family dinners for faking and not believing. I'd bow my head but mumble the words so I didn't feel like I had to commit to them and sneak a peek at everyone else at the table to see if I could catch them out doing the same. My brother always did it right. But my elder sister was just like me, rebellious, and while everyone else was giving thanks to the Lord, we'd compete to see who could stick out their tongue the farthest and for the longest without getting caught. And later, when we were old enough to work out what it meant, we'd flash each other the finger as well.

I look up and around the table. Bob is saying grace the way he speaks in those TV commercials of his. Gena has her head bent in supplication, her eyes tightly shut, and this strange pained expression on her face as she repeats after Bob. And Jack, he's doing the same as me and when our eyes meet across the table, he grins.

While we're eating, the dog, who's already been fed, is trotting around and around the table with the squeaky toy in its mouth, stopping off at each place around the table, dropping the toy and looking up expectantly, waiting for playtime. When one person doesn't show any interest, it moves onto the next. At some point, it decides it's not getting the attention it deserves and the toy isn't having the desired effect.

So instead, this dog, Sebastian, it takes a dump on the edge of the dining room. It leaves a perfect little turd sitting right in the middle of this beautiful imported Moroccan rug, so that it almost looks like part of the design and it's virtually invisible.

This is this dog's idea of being cute. Leaving a turd in the middle of the room as a conversation piece. It takes a dump, without making a fuss or a scene, while we're eating—Jack and Bob and Gena and I—not five feet away, and not one of us notices. Not until Bob gets up to refill our drinks, steps right in it, skids like he stepped on a banana skin, and falls flat on his ass. And it's so comical that I almost burst into hysterics, were it not for the fact that Bob explodes in such a rage that Gena has to take him off to another part of the house to calm him down. And Jack and I are left to finish the meal on our own, feeling awkward and embarrassed as if we've seen a part of him that we weren't really meant to see. Eventually Gena reappears.

"Bob's just having a rest," she says, explaining that the campaign has really pushed Bob to the limit, because he's given it his all. "That's really not like him at all," she says apologetically.

We don't see Bob again until the early evening when he and Gena come down ready to go out for an evening commitment—a charity fund-raiser he just can't get out of.

Jack and I have been sitting out on the deck all afternoon, sunning ourselves on the loungers and taking in the view. And at one point, he leaned into me and whispered, "Bob and Gena are going out."

I smiled and gave him a look that said, And what are you saying?

But I already knew exactly what he meant. We were going to have the run of the place to ourselves. And we could do what any young couple would do when left to their own devices in a stranger's house: fuck.

Jack's really thrown me for a loop now and I can't work out what's got into him, because he's not just into it, he initiates it. We've been on this break and, even before that, I haven't been able to rouse his interest for weeks and suddenly it's like he's a new man. It's like the first time we got together, the first time anyone gets together, and we fucked like bunnies anywhere and everywhere we could.

Jack's not without daring but spontaneity, it's not really his strong suit. He always likes to be organized; he always likes a plan—even if it's concerning surreptitious sex in the boss's house—unless someone else is making the decision for him, unless it's me.

We wave Bob and Gena goodbye as they drive off in Bob's car, a beautifully kept 1968 cherry-red Cadillac DeVille convertible—what else. As they circle around the drive, Gena waves back, calling out over the sound of the engine, "Now, you kids be good and don't wreck the place."

Little does she know.

We watch them disappear around the curve of the road

and the second they're out of sight Jack starts running through the house, tearing his clothes off, and the last thing to come off are his shorts, which he drops just as he reaches the edge of the pool and dives in.

I get rid of the dog by hurling the squeaky toy into the garage and then locking the door after it races inside. Just to give it a reality check and make it realize it's not as smart or cute as it thinks. I can already hear it start to whimper as I walk off.

I get to the pool to find Jack treading water in the middle. It's a lovely warm evening and golden hour is fast approaching. Jack's hair is wet, his face is shining, he looks so beautiful, and happy, and I can't wait to join him.

I start to take off my clothes but not quickly enough for Jack, because he calls out to me from the pool, "C'mon, what you waiting for? It's beautiful."

I walk along the diving board, stand right at the end, and balance myself as I feel it give underneath my weight. I'm still in my bra and panties, because I want to tease him and take them off ever so slowly, in full view of him. I start to unhook my bra and then decide I'm going to peel off my panties first instead and then change my mind again and reach up to my bra. And, as I do, I have déjà vu.

Whenever that happens to me, it almost feels like a mystical experience. Like I've suddenly and inexplicably been made aware of a dream that's mapped out my entire life before I've even lived it. That somehow the barrier between my dream life and my real life has broken down, and I'm able to see what happens on both sides of the mirror at the same time. Real life feels like a dream and the dream feels absolutely real. And I feel like I've grasped a fundamental secret about reality that no one's ever expressed before. Then, just as quickly as it arrived, it's snatched away again, and I'm left with that horrible nagging feeling of not being able to place how or why I even felt that way in the first place.

This time it's not a memory at all; it's a scene in a movie I love that I've made my own. I'm Cybill Shepherd in *The Last Picture Show,* preparing to skinny-dip at the pool party while everyone's watching her, turning her embarrassment at getting naked into a cruel sport.

It's not like I have anything to be embarrassed about because Bob and Gena's nearest neighbor is all the way on the other side of the valley. They'd have to have binoculars trained on the place to be able to see us. But there's just something about getting naked in the open air that I've always found intimidating. Getting naked in public, no problem. I don't mind people looking at me. It's the eyes I can't see that drive me crazy.

And like Cybill Shepherd, I eventually throw caution to the wind, drop my panties and dive in. And as the cool water sheaths my skin, I forget all my silly hang-ups. I open my eyes and I see Jack's body hanging there underneath the water and swim toward it. Jack is a body without a head. Shimmers of sunlight refracted from the surface of the pool are dancing across his torso. And, as he treads water, his cock and balls are bouncing up and down like he's in zero gravity.

I reach out to grab his cock, and he must have seen me, because he darts away, swimming on his back and kicking water. He doesn't stop until he reaches the other side and then he rests his arms over the edge of the pool and just hangs there. I come up for air right in front of him and he looks so pleased with himself that he was able to outsmart me.

I put my hands on his shoulders, plant a kiss on his lips. His lips are so warm and mine so cold that I just let them linger there because it feels so good and we nuzzle. And I let my body bob up and down with the water as it laps against the side of the pool so that it's brushing up and down against his.

I hang as low as I can in the water so my crotch is touching his, and the shaft of his penis is nestled in my pussy hair. When I feel him get hard, which doesn't take long, I reach down and grab his cock and say, I got you now.

And he laughs.

I give his cock a few pumps with my hand and then I take a really deep breath and fill my lungs so full of air it feels like they're fit to burst. He looks at me as if it say, What are you doing? And I duck my head underwater, still holding his cock.

Have you ever tried giving a blow job underwater? It's not easy, but pretty incredible at the same time. As I open my mouth to take in Jack's cock, bubbles of air pour out of it and I watch as one tiny little bubble slowly rolls down the shaft of his penis and lodges in his pubic hair. I clasp my lips around the head of his cock as quickly as I can so that my mouth doesn't fill with water and suck.

Now it's like everything's happening in slow motion. My hair is swimming around me like seaweed and wraps itself around my head like a scarf until I can't see Jack anymore; I can only feel his cool hard cock as I work it in and out of my hot mouth.

I have one hand working the shaft of his penis and the other pressed against his chest to stop myself from floating away. He reaches down to fondle my breasts and I feel them wobble and bounce. Then he takes my nipples between his fingers and thumbs, holds them firmly and gently pulls them toward him. I feel the slight tug on my breasts as they shift their center of gravity and gently bump back and forth, like a moored dinghy, while the rest of my body works his cock.

It feels so good down here, and I feel so safe, that I don't want it to end, even as I can feel the oxygen in my lungs depleting and my head starting to get dizzy.

I'm working Jack's cock with my mouth, taking him in a little deeper each time and I take him in just a little too deep, because the head of his cock hits the back of my throat and I gag and choke. Bubbles pour from my nose. Water rushes into my mouth. And I come up gasping for air.

I get my breath back and we swim over to the shallow end of the pool. I sit on the second step, my upper body out of the water, my arms over the edge of the pool. Jack gently parts my legs and I wrap them around his back as he puts himself inside me and starts fucking me, slow and steady, so I can feel him draw all the way in and all the way out. And as he does so, the water laps against the bottom of my breasts. I squeeze my legs tighter around his back, to tell him I want him to go deeper.

The sun is disappearing behind the hills and casting this

brilliant burnt orange glow into the sky. All I can hear is the evening song of the birds in the trees, the water lapping against the side of the pool, my moans and Jack's moans. It feels like the perfect moment, and it seems like all of our problems have melted away: Jack's unwillingness to have sex, the barrier between us. I wish it could always be this way.

We get out of the water and traipse back to the house, still dripping wet and flushed with passion. Once we get inside, I bring a sheepskin rug down from the bedroom that Gena put us in and lay it down in front of the fireplace, while Jack stokes the fire Bob left burning for us, so we can dry ourselves off.

We're sitting side by side, cross-legged, in front of the fire, and it feels like the right time to say something romantic. I turn to Jack and say, "I want you to fuck me in the ass."

Now, that may not sound all that romantic, but maybe you had to be there because it sure felt like it at the time. Right there, right then, I couldn't think of anything more intimate than having anal sex with my boyfriend in front of a roaring fire.

I said it on a whim, because I couldn't think of anything more delicious and perverse than looking back on this weekend and thinking, We had anal sex in Bob DeVille's house. Did that really happen? And I said it as a dare because I know Jack's in the mood and I want to see how far I can push him to do something he would never suggest on his own. Not here, not now. Not in a million years.

It's not like he doesn't enjoy fucking me in the ass. I know he does. And especially because it's something I won't let him do all the time, because I don't want him to get used to it. I want it to be special. Like eating truffles or oyster or caviar, because if you ate them all the time it would lose its thrill. It wouldn't feel like a luxury anymore. And ass-fucking is the luxury food of sexual positions.

I believe nature gave us, men and women, multiple holes for good reason. To put things in and push stuff out. And I intend to use them all because, otherwise, I wouldn't be get-ting good use out of my body, and it would be such a waste.

There's just one thing missing though from this little sce-nario I'd dreamt up for me and Jack.

Lubrication.

There's no polite way to say this:

Jack's cock is just too big for my ass.

Lubrication is not only desirable, but also it's required.

Let me put it like this.

You know when you're browsing for shoes and you've fallen completely head-over-heels in love, if you'll excuse the pun, with one particular pair in a specific style and color. They're just perfect and you feel like they've been wait-ing there all this time for you to find them. But the assis-tant comes back to say they've just sold the last pair in your size and the only ones they have left are one and a half sizes smaller.

And, size be damned, you're determined that you're going to try them on anyway, because you have to have this shoe and you're not going to leave the store without them. You manage to slip it in halfway without much effort at all, but then it gets stuck just past the instep. It's half in, half out, and you tell yourself, it's really not as small as you thought. That you've gone this far so you figure another little push will do it, another push will get it in, and then the leather will start to give. It will start to stretch and mold itself around your foot and the shoe will be yours.

So you give it another push and you manage another half-inch but now it's really stuck and it's super painful. And it doesn't matter which way you move it, in or out, it sends this shooting pain all the way through your foot, all the way through your body. And you curse yourself for being so greedy and dismissing basic common sense that tells you something that big could possibly fit into a hole so small.

And if I'm not all greased-up and ready, that's what ass-fucking feels like for me. A shoe that doesn't fit. That doesn't mean to say we haven't tried.

In that scenario, the shoe is on the other foot, so to speak. Jack is the foot and I'm the shoe. And my butthole is in so much pain and his cock feels so big that he might as well be trying to put his foot up my ass. It hurts that much.

He's determined it will fit and I'm determined it won't. And the only thing I can do to convince him otherwise is to let out a blood-curling scream, as if he'd just stabbed me with a bread knife. Then he pulls out. Fast.

I'm sure there are women who like the pain, who see it as an endurance test. I figure Anna probably would.

Not me.

But I've got the idea firmly lodged in my head now. I

want Jack to fuck my ass in Bob DeVille's house, in front of his fireplace, on his sheepskin rug. It feels so deliciously wrong, and so right at the same time. And I know Jack's game, so I'm determined to follow through.

I remember that Gena told me she was big into baking and I'm pretty sure I saw a tub of Crisco up on a shelf in the kitchen, so I tell Jack to take a look and go get some. While he's gone, I stare into the fire and watch the embers glow and become hypnotized by the flames.

He comes back carrying the whole ten-pound tub and a huge grin on his face, as if he intends to use it all. As if he's planning on giving me a Crisco enema and sending an entire football team through my asshole. And I say, yeah, you and whose army?

He puts it down beside us and prizes off the lid and scoops a little dollop onto his two middle fingers, holds them up for me to see, and says, "Open wide."

I get on all fours and he kneels at my side, pulls my butt cheeks apart with one hand, and smears the Crisco around my hole with the other. It feels like cold cream and I feel my butthole pucker from the cold, then relax again as his fingers stroke and prod around it, warming me up.

I reach around and tug his cock to get him hard. And once I feel him getting stiff, I slather some grease along his shaft and pump my hand back and forth so it's covered and we're both good and mucky.

He positions himself behind me, one hand flat on my butt as he teases his Crisco-covered cock into my pussy. And it slides right in without any fuss or friction. He gets straight into gear, settles right into a rhythm, and he's sliding back and forth with the precision of a piston. He has his hands wrapped around the top of my butt. He's pulling me down as he rises up and our sex collides somewhere in the middle.

I slide my arms down to the floor and stick my butt high in the air, and he's fucking me so deep and hard that I can't help but let out a long, plaintive moan that emerges with such force and such volume that it echoes through the house. And even Sebastian hears it because, soon enough, he's howling up a storm in the garage. Me and the dog are moaning together in sympathy.

Jack's thumb is edging around my asshole while he's fucking me, scooping up the Crisco and pushing it into my hole, testing it, stretching it, and before I know it he's inside me up to the knuckle and I'm closing in around him, like a Venus flytrap closes in around its prey.

Jack has his thumb up my ass and I feel him turning it back and forth, as if he's turning a key in a lock that won't take hold. I can feel it, turning, turning, turning. And it's only turning in one direction now, clockwise, like someone's winding the mechanism and that mechanism is me.

I'm ready to go to the next level so I turn my head, catch his eye, and tell him, "I want you to fuck my ass, Jack. Fuck it real hard."

He pulls out of my pussy and slaps his cock against it, coating the shaft with my sweet, sticky white come, so he's all good and greasy to ease his entry into my tight little butt. He puts his hand on my ass to steady himself while he presses the head of his penis against my asshole. It puckers with anticipation. The head of his cock feels so big as he edges it inside my hole. I let out a gasp.

His greasy cock feels so big and tight in my butt and it's moving in deep and slow.

"Does your cock feel good in my ass?" I say.

"Feels good," he moans. "So tight."

"I want you to stretch my tight little asshole," I say. "I want your whole fucking cock inside my ass."

Jack grunts with pleasure as he slowly slides his length all the way into me and starts to pump and swivel his hips. Jack is dancing on my ass and it feels so good. Not the chicken walk. Or the bump. He's doing the grind.

His hands tightly grip my shoulders so he can slam into me with sledgehammer thrusts. And his wet balls are slapping hard against my pussy.

And it feels so good to feel my ass being stretched and probed with his thick, meaty cock that he takes me all the way. I feel like I'm going to come. I feel like I'm going to explode from the inside out.

I tell him, "Jack, I'm going to come. I'm going to come."

And, as I do, my body bucks underneath him and I let out a wail of pleasure.

I say, "Now, I want you to come in my ass, Jack. I want you to fill me up with your come. I want to feel your come dripping out of my butt."

Talking dirty to him like that seems to have the desired effect and push him over the edge. I hear him groan to signal that he's about to deliver. He gets off one last hard thrust and his gun goes off in my chamber, his come explodes in my ass, and I feel it filling me up inside. He slowly pulls his cock out of me and I feel his thick, white marshmallow come dripping out of my hole and gathering in my pussy.

We spoon in front of the fire on the soft rug, him lying behind with his arms around me.

And I think, I really don't know how this could be any better. Me, Jack, a real live fire, anal sex, and a cream pie.

It's the perfect end to a perfect weekend.

19

I'm looking at myself in a picture that hangs above a bed. It's a picture of the way I was. And I almost don't recognize myself. It feels like I'm dreaming but my eyes are wide open.

I'm standing naked. Cockle shells cover my nipples and an oyster shell covers my sex. Cumulus clouds roll above my head like waves. Waves roll over my head like dunes shifting in the wind.

I'm walking on a beach. Shells crunch underneath my feet. No matter how careful I am, no matter how lightly I tread, they crunch and break. I look down and I see they're not shells but bones. I'm walking on a beach of bones. I can taste the salt air on my tongue. I can feel the sharp edges of the bones underneath my feet, digging into the flesh. The beach is uneven and I'm unsteady on my feet, as if negotiating broken paving stones in stiletto heels.

I walk until I reach a boardwalk crowded with young

couples, glowing with love. They're all walking in one direction, and I'm walking in the other. I'm walking naked through them. They all stare at me as they pass by and I feel exposed. But I hold my head up high and keep walking.

I walk toward the end of the boardwalk, where naked men in carnival masks stand in a line along the rail, tugging at their erections. They're waiting for me to arrive. And I don't want to disappoint them. I get down on all fours and stick my butt up high and wiggle it, like it's sniffing the air, to signal that I'm ready.

The first one approaches. He puts his hands on my hips, crouches down to my level, and sinks his cock deep into my pussy, all the way to the hilt, and then slowly draws himself all the way out till I can feel the tip of his cock teasing my hole, preparing to plunge inside me again. He starts to fuck me with long, hard strokes. His balls are slamming against my clit and it feels so good that I pant and claw the ground.

Jack is walking along the boardwalk arm in arm with Anna. He doesn't notice me. He walks right past me, right past the men who are stroking their cocks, waiting their turn to fuck me. He stops maybe twenty feet away and leans back against the railing with his elbows hanging over the edge. Anna kneels down in front of him and unzips his pants, reaches inside, and pulls out Jack's penis. She holds it with her fingers around the shaft and her thumb extended along the head, the way I would hold it, licks it along the shaft, the way I would lick it, places her lips over the head and slowly draws his length into her mouth. Anna is sucking Jack's cock the way I would. I look at Jack's cock in Anna's mouth and imagine it's the cock in my pussy.

And I want Jack to look up and see me being fucked like this, on all fours, by the stranger in the carnival mask. I want Jack to know that I'm imagining him inside me. Like the men in my dreams, I want him to accept me as I am. So that we can be together.

I wake with a start, as if from a terrible nightmare. Jack's lying next to me in bed, asleep, and I grab him and wrap my arms around him, hear him gently stir, and feel the warmth of his body seep into mine. I feel safe and comforted and wanted. But I want more.

I run my hands across his chest, down his belly, and slide my fingers into his pubic hair, nudging my middle finger down so it strokes the base of his penis. I stroke it gently until I can feel it start to harden underneath my finger; then I slide my hand down farther and grab hold of his cock, meaty and thick and semi-hard. I stroke the base with my thumb and twist my fingers around the shaft. I can feel him stiffen in my hands and then his cock is erect and upright and ready for action. I let go so I can lick my hand, and I get it good and wet with saliva, then wrap it around his shaft again. As I slide it up and down and make him slick with my spit, I hear him moan, roused from his slumber into half-sleep.

I want Jack's cock inside me. I want it so fucking bad and I don't care if he's conscious or not. I swing my leg across his body, feel his cock brush against my thigh, raise myself up and straddle him. I put my hand on his chest to steady myself, look down and see him half-open his eyes just in time to see me reach back and grab his cock so I can hold it in place while I spear myself on it. I slide back and slowly lower myself down onto him. He lets out a sleepy little satisfied moan. My pussy opens up to accommodate him, getting wetter with every inch.

He's conscious now and nestled deep inside me. He starts to slowly rotate his hips. His cock is brushing back and forth inside me. And I follow his lead, riding him, rotating my hips in perfect motion with his, like we're two cogs in a machine. I lean forward over him, and he moves with me, bending his knees and arching his back so that he can brace himself to push inside of me. I hold steady to feel his cock sliding in and out of my hot wet pussy.

I say, "Fuck me, Jack. Fuck me harder."

And he does, slamming into me twice to show me his power, then settling into an emphatic rhythm. He wants to please me. I let out a long satisfied moan, breathlessly pant his name, and bury my head into the pillow, smothering his face with my tits. I run my fingers through his hair and pull his head to my breast and feel his hot breath on it as his mouth searches for the nipple.

My breast is in his mouth. He's sucking it into him and I can feel my nipple swell and harden as he teases it with his tongue, as he tugs it with his lips and gently bites down, pulling and stretching it with his teeth.

His hands grab my breasts and squish them together so he

can lick and suck and bite them, one after the other and then both at the same time. Now that he's got a taste of me, he's getting greedy. He's devouring my tits with his mouth and his cock is pounding into me. I can feel myself starting to come. And I want him to know.

I say, "Jack, I'm going to come. I'm going to come."

I raise myself up, put my hand on his chest, and grind down hard on his cock because I want to feel him deep inside me when I come.

I grind down until he's all the way inside me and I can feel his balls pressing against the cheeks of my ass. I hear his breath quicken, I hear him moan, and I know he's close too. So I grind down harder and slowly circle my hips. And he moves with me, he breathes with me, and he moans with me. We're both on the verge and I want to lead him there. I can feel myself coming and I want him to know.

"I'm coming, Jack, I'm coming, I'm coming."

And I barely get the words out before I climax.

I buck and thrash on top of him, as the orgasm surges through me, my pelvis moving in quick little powerful thrusts along his shaft. And it's too much for him too. He moans long and loud as he comes inside me. I can feel his cock twitch inside me as he fills me with his load. I can feel him judder as his body comes to rest. And I collapse on top of him, feeling his chest rise up to meet mine as we both gasp for air.

I roll off him, lie on my side. He rolls onto his, facing me. I clasp him to my breast. We both lie there, exhausted. I listen to his breathing, hear it slow down and change in pitch and I know he's asleep.

I'm lying in bed, thinking about where I've been, what I've seen, and how I got this way. And I realize something that I've always known but taken for granted:

Half of sex is the dreaming.

20

I'm sitting in class, in my usual spot, right in front of Marcus, and he's going through that climactic scene in *Vertigo*, where Judy has just revealed her secret to Scottie: that she and Madeleine, the dead blonde he's been infatuated with, are one and the same person. In doing so, she yanks Scottie out of his fantasy and forces him to confront the truth of his reality, that he's been consumed by an illusion all along. Marcus is breaking down the final shot, where Scottie is standing at the top of the bell tower where Judy/Madeleine once was. He's overcome his fear of heights to edge out onto the ledge, but now he's staring down into the abyss. Staring down at the spot where his obsession drove her, dashed on the rocks to her death.

It feels like we've studied this movie a hundred times and more, as Marcus keeps coming back to it over and over for some particular reason. Marcus is so obsessed with *Vertigo* that I think he could talk about it all day, in every class, and still find new and interesting things to say. I think it's because *Vertigo* has everything that Marcus loves about film. All the fetishes and paraphilias anyone could really want and need. Now that I know a little more about Marcus, through Anna, I can understand why.

I'm also as certain as I can be of one thing. That just like Scottie, Marcus is obsessed with blondes, the ones that will drive a man to ruin. Marcus is obsessed with Anna.

I guess Anna's influence must be rubbing off on me too, because I've found myself starting to dress more like her. Not just like her, but in her actual clothes. I'm wearing this semi-sheer white tank top with a scoop neck that shows off my bra. I asked Anna if I could borrow it, even though I wasn't sure it really suited me at all. And I'm wearing her leop-ard print Lycra leggings and stiletto sandals, the kind of look that tells a man, I am ready to eat you. Even Jack looked at me strangely this morning when I came out of the bedroom dressed and ready to leave, because he's never seen me wear-ing things like this. And when he looked at me, I wondered if my crush on Marcus had gone too far.

Now that I'm here it just seems like a lot of wasted effort for nothing because Marcus is ignoring me as usual. He's talking about Scottie's insistence that Judy dress in exactly the same manner as her deceased doppelgänger, Madeleine, the same clothes, the same hairstyle and hair color. I'm dress-ing like Anna for Marcus, but whatever I'm doing clearly isn't working, clearly doesn't make him hard. Now that I know Marcus has a thing for blondes, I'm wondering if I should just go the whole hog and bleach my hair, so that I'm as close to Anna as I can be without actually being her. I can see that Marcus isn't hard for me because he's wearing his brown suit pants again.

Marcus is telling us that everything we need to know about Hitchcock, the man, is contained in the films he directed and I figure it's kind of like the way they say that clothes make the man. I'm deconstructing the meaning of Marcus's brown suit pants—the pants he always wears—to try to get to the bottom of who he really is. And I wonder if they're the only pair he owns or whether his closet, when he's not standing in it waiting for Anna to arrive, is like Mickey Rourke's closet in *Nine and a Half Weeks*, filled with multiple pairs of the same set of clothes. The same white cotton shirt with the band collar that he always wears too, and those pants, tight around the crotch and ass, slightly flared at the legs. The kind of pants that went out of style at the end of the seventies.

I wonder if he trawls through thrift stores looking for exactly that style, with those exact measurements. The ones that hold his package firm and show it off at the same time. Then I decide that if Marcus has kept his mother's clothes in pristine condition all this time, it's probably more likely he bought them new, or almost new.

Marcus must be in his mid- to late forties, and when I do the math—and it might seem a little strange that I do math in film class, but I'm obsessed with all the facts and figures that relate to Marcus; I'm obsessed with his figure in inches and pounds—so when I do the math, it seems like he would have started dressing like that around the time puberty hit, at twelve or thirteen. Or maybe a few years later, if he was a late starter.

Those pants had probably already gone out of style by then. So I decide he must have some emotional attachment to them. That maybe they're the pants his father used to wear and, when he first put them on, they made him feel like a man, they made him feel like his dad, and he knew he didn't want to dress any other way.

I don't know any of this for sure but I figure that any-one who has a mommy complex as all-enveloping as Marcus must have issues with a father figure who was absent from their childhood emotionally or physically or both. And it makes me feel kind of sorry for him and I wish I could go right up and hug him tight and gently whisper in his ear that it's going to be alright. But that's never going to happen because Marcus always seems so serious and unapproachable in class.

Sitting in class, listening to Marcus, I have one eye on the clock because I'm waiting for Anna to arrive. Anna's late to class, as always. I'm waiting for the door to open so I can start to make a log of the times that Anna makes her big entrance and see if some pattern emerges. Marcus is forty-three minutes and thirty-two seconds into his hour-long lecture, which he somehow manages to time so that they end almost the very second the bell goes. He's covered all the relevant paraphilias and now he's onto the fetishes.

I glance again at the clock on the wall above the door. It's five minutes from the end of the lecture and Anna still hasn't arrived. She must be trying to push the envelope this time, leaving it till the last possible moment. She really wants to piss Marcus off.

My attention is fixed on the hands of the clock as it ticks its way to the top of the hour, on the crack of the door that I'm waiting to see open. I can hear Marcus's voice but, for once, I'm not really listening. The seconds tick away. The tension is unbearable. I'm sitting on the edge of my seat, the way I figure people did when *Vertigo* was first released and people in movie theaters up and down the country watched Scottie chase Judy up the steps of that bell tower to her death.

Then the bell chimes. Not in the movie, in the lecture hall. The hour is up, and Anna's still not here and I just don't understand why. She may always be late but she's never missed a class. Not once. It's so out of character.

The students start to pack up and filter out the second they hear the bell, the way that people can't wait to get up out of their seats once a plane has landed and before the seat belt sign flickers off. I stay exactly where I am, rooted to the spot, with my pen still poised to write notes on my yellow legal pad, which has a series of numbers in the top-right corner that I remember writing but I've completely forgotten the significance of. I'm wondering why Anna didn't come to class and where she could be. I sit there thinking about this until the only people left in this vast lecture hall are Marcus and me.

Marcus is slowly wiping the whiteboard clean of the words he used to illustrate the lecture, as if he's erasing all trace of his sexual obsessions. He's wiping away all the words I love to hear him say.

Scopophilia, an obsession with looking.
Retifism, a fetish for shoes.
Trichophilia, a fetish for hair.

When the board is wiped clean, Marcus turns back to his desk, collects his notes, gathers them under his arm, and looks up. He looks up and looks at me. And I realize it's the first time he's ever really looked at me. The first time I've ever met his eyes and looked directly into them. And I suddenly feel ashamed and embarrassed because I'm dressed in these clothes I borrowed from Anna that really don't suit me at all.

Marcus looks at me expectantly and I say, "I'm waiting for Anna."

"Who?" he says.

And I don't know if he's joking, but I can't imagine Marcus does humor. Too intense, too intellectual, too wrapped up in himself. And the other thing about Marcus is, there's no way to discern what he's feeling, what he's thinking, from his face or the tone of his voice. He gives nothing away. He's that closed and mysterious and that's why I'm so obsessed.

"The blonde girl," I say, "who sits behind me. Anna."

And I blurt it all out, everything she told me, because I'm so nervous that I'm here, in front of Marcus, and he's talking to me and I'm talking to him. I tell him everything I know. About Anna's visits, the apartment, the closet, his mother's clothes.

I've never had a conversation with Marcus before, we've never exchanged more than a few words, and I want him to know that I know. I want him to know that his kink is OK with me. That it's not only OK, but also that I understand. And because I understand, we have something in common. And if he likes Anna, he would like me too.

He listens to me and he doesn't say a word. He lets me speak, he lets me say my piece and he doesn't interrupt, and I'm in heaven, because I'm actually talking to Marcus, not just looking and dreaming. It's as if I've been granted an intimate meeting with the pop idol I've had a huge crush on since childhood, that I've fantasized about, held imaginary conversations with and masturbated over. And now he's here right in front of me, just me and him, and we're talking, interacting—at least it feels that way, even if it's just me talking—and everything I want to say comes out, in a breathless rush, and not necessarily in the right order. But when I'm sure I've covered everything and there's nothing I've left out, I stop.

He looks at me with this strange expression on his face that's halfway between a frown and a smile. I can't tell whether he's angry or amused. He looks at me and he says, "I really have no idea what you're talking about." Then he picks up his notes and walks out of the hall without saying another word.

All my illusions about Marcus have been shattered. Maybe he never was what I thought he was. Maybe Anna made up everything she told me about Marcus to feed into my fantasies about him. Why would she do that? I'm so confused.

All this time I thought Marcus was my Achilles' heel. But I was wrong, so wrong.

It wasn't Marcus; it was Anna.

Anna is my Achilles' heel, the fatal blonde who I'd follow to the ends of the earth.

Anna's gone. And I suddenly realize I never really knew her. That I know so little about who she is, or where she comes from. I only know what she's told me and what she means to me.

When all is said and done, how many people really know us? Know our daily routine: where we go, who we meet, what we do. If something were to happen, if we were to suddenly disappear or go missing, who would know where to look, who to ask, who to call? Friends—even the ones you think of as close friends, the ones you believe you feel a deep, abiding connection to—likely won't know. Family, probably even less.

The more I think about it, the more panicked I get, because I've texted and called and she hasn't picked up or responded; she hasn't called back—another thing that's just not like her. It seems like Anna has disappeared without a trace. Almost as if she never existed. I only know of three people who could prove that she did.

Marcus.

Bundy.

Kubrick.

For reasons I don't quite understand, Marcus has denied all intimate knowledge of Anna, of even knowing who she is.

Bundy has gone into hiding.

That just leaves Kubrick.

I give the cabdriver the address to the Fuck Factory as best as I can remember it, and the directions to get there as far as I can recall. And he looks at me as if to say, You really want to go there? No one goes there. But as I hop in, he pulls down the flag on the meter anyway, because a fare is a fare and rather him than anyone else.

We're driving around and it all looks so different to how I remember. None of it looks the same. And it's not just because it's daytime and everything looks different by day. It just doesn't look like the same place. What I remembered as derelict buildings are actually empty shells of houses that have been half-built, then abandoned. I get the driver to stop three or four times at places that look vaguely familiar so I can get out and look for the graffiti that marked the spot where the Fuck Factory was. There's nothing there.

I look for evidence that it might have been painted over or wiped off. Can't find that either. The staircases leading under the street all look the same and I'm not about to walk down on the off-chance that I find the right door. So, eventually, I resign myself to the idea that the Fuck Factory must have been busted again between now and then. Even though then doesn't seem all that long ago.

The Fuck Factory has disappeared without a trace, just like Anna.

And now there's only one option left.

I have to find Bundy.

The only person I can think of who would know where Bundy could be is Sal, the bartender at the Bread and Butter.

When the cab pulls up outside, the shutters are down. I bang on them as hard as I can with the palm of my hand. A grouchy, wise-guy voice, Sal's voice, yells from inside.

"We're closed."

Now, from the limited interaction I had with Sal when I was here last time, I just know there's little point in getting into a back-and-forth with him through the shutters. That he'd sooner insult me from the safety of his bar than help me in any way, shape, or form.

So I bang on the shutters again.

"We're *closed*."

He already sounds irritated.

I bang again, for longer this time, pretending I haven't heard.

A door opens in the shutter; Sal's grizzled mug peers out.

"What the fuck do you want, girly. You fucking deaf. Can't you see we're closed."

Not so much a series of questions, more a series of accusations and threats.

"Bundy," I say. "Where's Bundy?"

"Why d'ya wanna know?" he says.

"I'm looking for our friend," I tell him. "Bundy's friend, Anna."

"Oh, that one," he says. "Blondie."

As he says it, his voice softens, his face softens, his whole manner softens. And I think, Oh, Anna, you didn't.

Sal's face pulls back into the gloom and it looks as if he's fading into thin air like the Cheshire Cat. Then his hand comes out.

I pull out a ten-note and put it in his hand. It withdraws like one of those mechanical piggy banks. I wait for Sal to reappear. His hand comes out again.

I think, Cheapskate. Sal is the kind of guy who would spit in your drink if you tipped him too little. I can't imagine I'll ever step inside his bar again but, just in case, I reluctantly pull out another ten and put it in his hand. It retreats again inside the hole.

I wait for it to come out again. Sal's voice sails out of the dark, reciting Bundy's address. I repeat it after him in my head to lodge it in my brain.

He says, "Give Blondie my love."

The door slams shut. I shudder.

I'm starting to feel afraid for Anna. Where is she? One day she was there and next there's no trace of her. Now I have to swallow my pride. Now I have to go and see Bundy.

Bundy's not surprised to see me. He's just disappointed I didn't come sooner. So he could tell someone his side of the story.

"I had nothing to do with it. I swear I didn't kill those girls."

That's the first thing he says as he ushers me into his apartment. His voice is cracking as he says it. Bundy's world has collapsed and he's a wreck. The Department of Justice has seized all of his domain names, shut down the sites—every last one of them—and initiated a Federal investigation into suspected pandering and racketeering. His livelihood is gone; his reputation is in tatters.

I'm not interested in his welfare; I only want to know what happened to Anna.

"Bundy," I say, "where's Anna?"

He doesn't answer, so I have no choice but to go in.

Bundy's apartment has to be seen to be believed. He's making money hand over fist but he's too cheap to splash out on anything other than the studio apartment he's always lived in. It's so crammed with stuff that you can barely move; you can barely get through the door.

He ushers me inside and says, "Sit down."

I look around and it's not as if there's nothing to sit on— like the way Anna described Marcus's apartment—it's just that it's all covered in stuff. DVDs, magazines, comic books, toys, dirty underwear. And another thing, Bundy's apartment really stinks. There are trays of half-eaten microwave food, open pizza boxes with rings of crust, completely intact, as if he'd somehow managed to eat the filling from the inside out.

It's not as if I'm intending to stay, as if I even want to be here, so I say, "It's OK, I'll just stand."

I lean against the wall and feel it start to give way behind me, then realize it's not part of the wall at all but a floor-to-ceiling tower of those white paper boxes with the wire handles containing Chinese takeout food.

It's been less than a week since the story broke on Forrester Sachs; Bundy's only been hiding out for three or four days. He couldn't possibly have eaten all this food in that time. Unless the anxiety made him binge-eat. Bundy's a little chubby anyway so it's hard to tell if he's gained weight. I figure Bundy's one of those eternal teenagers who never loses his puppy fat; it just gets less cute with age.

There are stacks of baseball hats that still have the tags attached and boxes of trainers he's never worn, never even opened. Bundy tells me he wears a new pair of trainers every day and dumps the old ones in the trash like they're candy wrappers. He says it's his one indulgence. But I suspect the only reason anyone would wear a new pair of shoes every day is because they've got really bad foot hygiene.

Suddenly it dawns on me why it smells so bad in here. Not from moldy pizza and discarded Chinese food. From Bundy's rotting feet. It's the kind of odor that's really hard to cover up and seems to linger on everything, like the smell of vomit. It smells so bad in Bundy's apartment that I'm trying to breathe through my mouth. I want to get out of here as quickly as I can, but Bundy's decided his woes are so great that he wants to tell me his entire life story, from beginning to now. From before he was even born. From the day his parents decided to name him.

Bundy's sitting cross-legged on the floor like a sulking child playing with his toys. "I'm not a bad person," he says. "I was just made this way." As he says it, he's absent-mindedly stuffing a Chewbacca action figure headfirst into a pussy-in-a-can.

Bundy's apartment is crammed with toys—plush toys and sex toys—and to him they're all the same. A pair of Care Bears are positioned on all fours, facing away from each other, both split at the seams to accommodate a double-ended dildo that's been forced into their stuffing. There's a Teletubby wearing a strap-on as a face mask. It's as if he tried to upgrade his obsessions and got stuck halfway, somewhere in the middle between adolescent and twenty-something jerk-off, but ended up hopelessly infantilized, obsessively compulsively sexualizing everything in his reach that was previously wholesome and pure.

He has a huge life-size poster of Britney Spears on the wall, wearing Daisy Dukes with the buttons undone, and her hands on her hips as if she's about to peel them off, a white cotton crop-top that seems specifically designed to show off the curve of her tits, and a look that says, You know you want to fuck me, but think again, Buster.

It's Britney Spears in her prime, when she was every man's fantasy, the all-American hot-bodied blond cock-tease. And before she broke a million male hearts by reminding them of the psycho girlfriend you wished you'd never met, let alone thought of putting your cock inside.

Bundy clearly prefers the fantasy Britney to the reality Britney, and he's made some further modifications so that she better fits his image of the perfect woman. He's customized the poster with body parts cut out of porno mags. Britney Spears has a pussy for lips and an erect penis sticking out of her shorts. Not just any penis. A big black cock that's almost as big as her head. I look at Bundy's new-improved genitally enhanced Britney and think, He's one sick puppy. And I scan the room to see if he has any tranny porn because I'd bet anything that's his bag, but quickly give up because it would be almost impossible to spot amongst all the other crap.

He also has a large collection of Star Wars figures lined along his mantel, but only Wookiees. He's not interested in anything other than Wookiees. Bundy tells me he's always loved Wookiees. And he thinks it might be the same reason he only likes women with natural pubic hair, women who never shave.

Bundy says that's the reason he's so fixated on blow jobs—"the receiving, not the giving," he takes pains to point out to me—is that it really doesn't matter whether she's shaved or unshaved. Because he never gets that far.

For him, oral pleasure staves off hirsute disappointment. But the upshot is he's continually sexually unfulfilled.

Bundy's pouring out all his woes to me, his sexual history, his personality flaws, and I don't want to listen anymore. I want to tell him how angry I was about receiving money after visiting the Juliette Society.

"You set me up," I say.

I can feel myself getting mad but I don't want to show it. I don't want to give him the pleasure of seeing that he's rattled me.

"Set you up how?" he says. "With Anna?"

"The money, for that party."

"What party?" he says.

"The Juliette Society," I reply, like he doesn't know.

"Who?" Bundy says.

I say it again.

"The Juliette Society, Bundy."

"I don't know what you're talking about," he says. "I never paid the girls. I only took the money."

I'm confused, but I need to get to the real point of my visit. "Bundy, I'm seriously worried. Where's Anna?"

"I don't know," he says. "I swear I don't know."

Just like he swears he didn't kill those girls.

"Did you do the same thing to Anna," I ask angrily, "try to extort money from her?"

"I wouldn't do that to Anna," he says. "I'd never do anything bad to her. I love Anna. I've wanted her so bad," he says, and he's almost close to tears. "I don't even care if she's shaved or not."

Bundy tells me he tried to get with Anna so many times and did everything he could to impress her. She's the only woman he's ever spent more than ten bucks on, other than his mom. He bought her gifts; he bought her jewelry. But Anna always brushed him off.

"She told me she loved me like a brother," he says, "but she prefers men to boys."

Bundy's looking up at me with big sad eyes and he wants me to tell him it's OK. But there's not a whole lot I can say because I know exactly what she means. He's only pining for Anna because she broke his heart. And, as a coda to his tale of woe, he keeps repeating the same two things over and over, like a broken record.

"I didn't kill her," he says, "and I didn't kill those girls."

"I believe you, Bundy," and as I say it, I realize I do believe him. "But do you have any idea, any idea at all about where she might be?"

And, finally, he comes out with it. "There was this party she was going to. You might find her there."

"What party?" I ask suspiciously.

But before he's even replied, I realize that I'm going to have to go there and I don't have a choice.

21

I'm walking after dark through the grounds of a large Italianate villa—the location of the party Bundy arranged for a car service to, the place he said I might, just might, find Anna. It's also the night before Bob's election and there's so much to do that Jack's sleeping over at the campaign office.

I'm following a path that winds through little dips and climbs and curves. Wherever I am, I can see this sprawling villa up on a hill, cast in silhouette by the light of a full moon sitting low in the night sky and half-obscured by a great hulking cumulus cloud that just hangs there because the air is so still.

There is only one path—it doesn't split off or meet with others—but I never see anyone else ahead of me, even when it starts to straighten out, and no one walks back toward me. The path looks exactly the same all the way along: lined with dirt and outlined by boulders, beyond which are dense thickets of bushes and trees peppered with wildflowers and orchids so vivid and luminous in hue that they seem to glow in the dark. The path is lit by this strange ambient light with no apparent source—the kind of half-light that makes everything seem alive—which falls off just a couple of feet on either side of the path.

I'm wearing the same red cape that I wore at the *Eyes Wide Shut* party and a pair of black Mary Jane flats, and I feel like Little Red Riding Hood hurrying home to Grandma's. The silence, the stillness, the solitariness, and the blackness are all creeping me out. I'm walking as briskly as I can, willing my destination to appear around every turn. But it never does.

I'm scurrying along this path, in the dark, heading to who knows where, and two thoughts are spinning through my head over and over, first one and then the other.

What am I doing here?

Fuck Bundy.

And I can't think of enough ways to curse Bundy because I know, I just know, he's set me up again but I have to find Anna and I don't have any choice. I curse Bundy's birth, I curse his parents, I curse his stupid tattoos, his ugly penis, and his stinking feet. I can't still the voice in my head and it becomes so deafening and insistent that I have to check I'm not saying it aloud. Not that there's anyone around to hear me. I'm running in circles through my head and, every so often, I stumble on the answer.

Anna.

I'm here to find Anna.

I have to find Anna.

Just thinking it steels my determination to reach my goal, and I quicken my pace.

I'm so lost in my thoughts that I forget where I am and it takes the edge off the anxiety and the fear of walking alone in the dark, because although there's not a soul in sight, it's teeming with life I can hear. The way the sounds of nature fill the air when you're walking through a forest, even if you can't see the source. I don't hear the sound of a forest; I hear the murmur of sex, the humming of fucking, the sounds of pleasure unbound. Laughter, shrieks, grunts, and moans. The slap of skin on skin. And when I peer into the darkness, off the path, I think I can make out limbs entwined in branches, bodies bent over boughs, buttocks sprouting from bushes, figures rutting in the undergrowth. It feels like Eden before the Fall, when sex and nature were one, primal, carnal, and wild. Temptation surrounds me.

Although it seems like I'm moving toward the house, I can't be certain that's where the path is actually leading because sometimes it doubles back on itself or slips into a series of sharp zigzag turns. It doesn't take long before I start to lose my orientation and I have no idea whether I'm going forward or backward, up or down. Yet I can always see the tall, thin ornamental tower of the villa, like a beacon or a lighthouse, to mark my way.

I feel like I'm walking through the opening montage of *Citizen Kane*, those famous first shots that begin so ominously with a No Trespassing sign hanging off a chain-link fence, then bleed into that long, slow vertical pan up across more fences, railings, gates, and balustrades—each more ornate, more solid, more foreboding than the last—followed by a series of slow fades through the ruins of Xanadu, the monumental folly Kane built to celebrate his wealth, with his forbidding Gothic mansion dominating the background like a tombstone.

I think of those fences and gates as the barriers and constructs of my personality, the ones I erected all through childhood and adolescence to protect me from the world. I'm so wrapped up in my own life that I'd forgotten all those invisible fortifications were even there and, instead of protecting me, all they do is bar my way from looking inside of myself, from seeing who I really am. And now I realize I don't want to walk through my entire life that way. I don't want to end up like Charles Foster Kane: facing death, but still in denial of what drove him. A haunted man locked up in his haunted house, condemned to rot along with his estate.

This estate, the one I'm walking through, is as derelict as Kane's, but the farther I walk, the more whimsical and eccentric it gets. It's a ruin designed to look like an antiquity, but built to bamboozle the archeologist who would one day stumble upon it. I'm walking past buildings just set back from the path that seem to tower above me as I approach, but when I get closer I see they're built to a forced perspective and exist as nothing but skewed facades with flights of stairs that go nowhere. I pass a half-finished amphitheater that has seats and no stage and rows of columns bearing the faces of sprites and devils. Vast crumbling stone statues peek out over the treetops and from behind the undergrowth—of giants, gods, goddesses, nymphs, mythical creatures—all engaged in some form of sexual congress or exhibitionism. A giant turtle carrying a giant phallus on its back. A sphinx cupping its breasts as water spurts from the nipples. A colossus in battle armor holding his monumental engorged penis like a sword, ready to vanquish his foes.

I figure this place must have been built by some cash-rich financier with unlimited resources at his disposal as a monument to his outsized sexual imagination. Then, like Kane, he became impotent through age or dissatisfaction or putrefaction, and bequeathed his creation to Mother Nature, who embraced the stone deities as her own, swaddling the naked figures with mosses, vines, roots, and weeds.

I feel the figures watching me, I hear the sound of sex in the trees and undergrowth, and I hasten along the path, turning a corner, round a copse of trees, and coming upon a small tree-lined avenue with interlocking branches that form a canopy. It leads up to a large rock set into the hillside, carved into the face of an ogre—chubby and round, with a beard, small beady eyes, and a mouth containing just a handful of small uneven teeth. It makes me think of the vagina dentata graffiti splashed on the wall outside the Fuck Factory. This is a vagina with teeth, eyes, and pubic hair.

An inscription is carved around its upper lip, and stained in red like a tattoo:

AUDĀCISSIMĒ PĒDITE

The ogre's mouth is open wide, as if it's laughing or screaming, I can't tell which. Or maybe just screaming with laughter at some private joke. The ogre is looking at me, laughing at me, as if it's recognized someone who doesn't belong. Part of me feels like I just want to run inside its mouth and hide, no matter what I might find in there, in the pitch black, just so I don't have to meet its gaze anymore. Because that's where the path leads, into the mouth of the ogre. That's where it ends. There's nowhere else to go, other than turn back and retrace my steps, but I have no intention of doing that. I have to find Anna.

I can hear music, the sound of drums and flutes. It seems to be coming from the ogre's mouth.

I'm wavering between anxiety and determination, and I wish Anna was here. I think, What would Anna do? But I already know the answer. None of this would faze her. She'd just skip inside gaily because, to her, every experience is a new adventure, a new challenge, a new frontier to cross.

The murmuring sex is speaking to me. It says, "Come inside." So I do.

Inside it's so dark that I stumble on a rock almost immediately and nearly fall face forward. I extend my arms out on either side to touch the walls, the ogre's mouth and throat. They are so close that my arms are still bent at the elbows but I can stand upright without stooping. The walls are cold and damp to my touch.

I feel my way along, stepping gingerly, until gradually my eyes start to adjust to a soft light up ahead. I arrive at a long staircase, cut into the rock with a rusted wrought-iron balustrade, leading down into a natural cave system. The roof of the chamber droops like the ceiling of a canvas tent during heavy rain and its surface is covered with long spindly stalactites, brilliantly colored reds and browns at the base, yellow and white by the tip—like the spines of a giant sea urchin. Water drops from the spines into small pools in the rock surface and, as it does so, it reverberates and echoes around me like a bell. Rivulets of water run underneath my feet and I have to hold on to the iron rail to stop myself from slipping. It too feels wet to my touch, as if it's rotting. The air is stale and sharp.

It feels like I'm descending into the belly of the earth through the gullet of the ogre, like Jonah wandering aimlessly through the whale. There's nowhere to go but onward, wherever that may lead.

I can see the bottom of the staircase now and I look behind me to see how far I've come and figure I'm about halfway down. The farther down I go, the louder and more frantic the music gets. It sounds like a hubbub of voices all yelling to be heard.

At the bottom of the steps is a passage that's barely wide enough for one person and I have to bend down as I walk through. After a few hundred yards it opens out onto a platform that looks out over a large grotto, with stairs cut into the rock leading down to it.

I'm standing halfway up the face of the cavern and opposite, at the other end, there's a natural waterfall that emerges through a deep fissure in the rock face above it that opens onto the night sky, through which the moon shines down, illuminating the grotto with a spectral silvery light. Flaming torches fixed to the walls provide another source of light, just enough to see that the walls of the grotto are painted with a vividly colored fresco of the garden I've just walked through, with the path winding through it and the same stone statues I saw peeking out from behind the foliage. The floor of the grotto is covered in a luminous pink moss that clings to the rock face and glistens and shines in the torchlight like burnished gold.

At the base of the waterfall, the water runs off in two streams that form an island. On the island stands a small round colonnaded stone structure, like a podium or bandstand, that's open on one side and spotlit by the moon. Arrayed around either side of the podium are several figures wearing white robes and oversized cartoonish animal costume heads, each playing an instrument—either a hollow-bodied hand drum or small cymbals. Two of the figures are playing long wooden flutes that flare out at the end. The music is so loud and piercing as it echoes around the grotto that it fills the space with a disorientating clamor of conflicting rhythms and pitches and I can feel it reverberating through my body.

On the podium is a throne with upholstered red velvet seating trimmed in gold and a lion carved into each of the two front legs. And on the throne sits a veiled figure in long flowing white robes that are so loose around the body it's hard to determine its sex. At its feet is a woman, a naked woman with blond hair, just like Anna's, and my heart skips a beat when I see her, but I can't tell if it really is Anna because she's too far away and she's kneeling with her head in the lap of the robed figure, whose gloved hand rests on her head, the way a cleric might do when granting a parishioner absolution from their sins.

This woman has clearly committed great sins because her back is covered in a crisscross of painful-looking red welts and another robed figure is standing behind her with a bull-whip drawn back, ready to administer more. I think back to the time Anna showed me the marks on her wrist and how horrific it looked, and I realize how naive I was, how that was really nothing at all.

Five other naked women, two blondes, two brunettes, and one redhead, are kneeling in a semicircle at the base of the steps leading up to the podium, facing toward the throne, their hands on their knees and their heads bowed. Waiting their turn.

The music is so loud I can't hear myself think, so loud it feels as if it's slowly erasing my identity and filling it with sound. What I can't let it steal is my purpose. I have to find Anna. I repeat it over and over in my head like a mantra.

I start to descend the stairs slowly and as I get closer to the floor of the grotto, I realize it isn't covered in moss; it's covered in bodies, a writhing mass of copulating bodies, of hair and skin and sweat. The carpet of bodies covers every inch of the base of the grotto and creeps up the sides. They're so entwined that it's impossible to discern where one separates from the other. Heads are buried between legs and arms. Torsos seem blessed with multiple pairs of limbs. Legs emerge from shoulders, arms disappear between legs and emerge from behind waists. Hands are fixed to breasts. Penises sprout from bended knees. Mouths are either open in ecstasy or filled with some appendage or other. And it's as if they've all been whipped into a sexual fervor by the music.

And I thought I'd seen it all in Anna's company—on the SODOM website, at the Fuck Factory. I thought I'd seen just about everything. I was almost starting to become jaded, but I've never seen anything like this. Not even in the movies.

I put one foot forward carefully, stepping into this teeming mass of bodies and, as I do, it seems to register my presence and start to separate and open up, forming a path for me to walk along. I'm moving through these bodies and I feel so self-conscious yet, at the same time, completely inconspicuous because no one is paying me the least bit of attention, as if I'm walking through a crowded city street, one person amongst many, amongst hundreds and thousands, lost in the hustle and bustle.

I glance up at the podium, just in time to see the blond girl stand up and fall back into the undulating swarm of human flesh. Her prone lifeless frame is being tossed back and forth across the floor of the grotto like a body surfer being passed over a mosh pit. Arms reach out to grope and grab her and pull her down. Others push her up and onward.

It reminds of the opening scene of *The Wild Bunch*, where the children are sitting at the side of the road watching an army of red ants swarm over and devour two scorpions. And they're watching this terrible spectacle of ritual sacrifice with delight, poking the creatures with sticks to excite them further, encouraging cruelty without conscience.

I watch in horror as the blond girl gets sucked down and swallowed by the pack, her body lost in the spill. And it's not as if I can do anything about it. Just before she does I get a good look at her face, enough of a look that I can see it's not Anna.

Another girl gets up and takes her place at the foot of the veiled figure. The whip is raised, and comes down on her back with a terrifying force and speed. Her body tenses as it hits, her shoulders arch out and her spine in. Her head tilts and her mouth drops open, like a wolf howling at the moon, but her screams cannot be heard, because the music drowns out everything—the sound of the whip, her screams, the mass of bodies around me writhing and fucking—everything but itself.

The bodies continue to peel away in front of me and I'm almost in the center of the cavern now and close enough to the podium to see the faces of the girls, to see that none of them are Anna either. The girl in front of the throne has been lashed into unconsciousness and she's slumped at the foot of the veiled figure.

This is a weird fucking scene. The weirdest. Too damn weird for me. Right now, I just want to run and get the hell out of here, but I can't. I'm at the mercy of this swarm of bodies.

The music is pounding in my ears. My heart is beating so hard that it feels like my chest is going to explode. It's beating so hard that I can feel myself start to panic and hyperventilate. And it takes every ounce of willpower to stop that from happening, to slow my breathing down and regulate, so I can take stock of what to do and where to go. And now it seems to me as if the bodies are not opening to accommodate the path I've chosen but that, instead, they're leading me, and as long as I keep walking, the bodies will let me pass.

Soon enough, I'm almost at the other side of the cavern and I can see an opening in the rock face, a passage out, and I realize that's where they're leading me. Each step is more excruciating than the last. Until, finally, I can't take it anymore and skip over the last few bodies to safety.

I dash through the opening as fast as my legs will carry me and race down a narrow passageway lit by torchlight, and I don't look back until I hear the music decrease in volume, until all I can hear are the echoes of my footsteps as they hit the floor. The passage splits into two, then three. I don't exactly know where I'm going. I just keep on in the same direction—straight—even when the path bends and seems to turn in on itself. It all looks so familiar and not at the same time, and I feel like I'm back in the bowels of the Fuck Factory again.

The passage straightens out. Up ahead, pools of light spill out from a series of arched openings carved into each wall—alternating, so no two are opposite, like the rooms on a hotel corridor.

As I approach the first, I hear the murmur that filled the air around me as I walked through the garden above, but less ethereal this time, more urgent, as primal as the roar of the crowd at a sports event.

I edge up to the opening and peer inside. The chamber is about the size of a large garage. Like the grotto, the walls are painted with a mural, an interior scene—with windows, paneling doors, and even adjoining rooms—making it seem as if the space extends much farther back than it does. It feels like a theater set.

In the middle of the room is a large wooden scaffold. A girl is bound halfway up its central column. She's naked, her arms raised above her head, her wrists bound together, palms out. A belt of rope constricts her waist like a girdle. Another section, knotted in the middle of her chest, runs around her breasts and over her shoulders like a brassiere.

Her body is stained with black drips and splotches as if she's been spattered with ink. Two hooded figures stand on either side holding large black candles as big as Olympic torches, pressing them to her body and bowing their heads, as if administering a sacrament and offering benediction.

Around the scaffold, men and women fuck in an animalistic frenzy, oblivious to my presence. They all wear costume masks of some description—carnival masks, animal masks, rubber masks bearing the visage of presidents, politicians, personalities, and historical figures. The energy in the room is off the hook, combustible like phosphorus. The smell is overwhelming.

I feel like I'm standing on the edge of my dream, looking in, captivated by the girl on the scaffold. A candle is held against her breast. Wax drips onto the nipple, coating it like frosting. As it collects on her body, she gyrates her hips and grinds her pelvis, the way you do when you're desperate for a pee with no toilet in sight. Her legs are bent back at the knee, the calves bound behind thighs with coils of rope, so that when she moves her legs it looks like a butterfly gently airing its wings. Or a beetle that's been flipped onto its back and its legs continue to paw the air aimlessly, going nowhere fast.

Her mouth hangs opens, her eyes are thinned to slits, and I'm drawn to the expression on her face, unable to work out if she's begging for more or pleading for relief. Looking at her there, tied to a stake like Joan of Arc surrounded by a baying crowd, suspended between euphoria and anguish. I don't know if I want to fuck her, save her, or take her place.

I back away and continue down the passage, passing by chamber after chamber and, as I do, I peek inside. Each one looks like a scene from the SODOM website: a girl in some kind of stress situation or scenario—tied up, caged, chained, restrained—an audience, galvanized and aroused by the spectacle that has been presented for them. I stand at the entrance to each chamber just long enough to check that Anna is not inside, then move on. I'm walking through these catacombs and after a while it feels like I'm walking around in circles. Either that or the punishments just all start to look the same.

Then I come across a room that looks empty. Curiosity gets the better of me and I walk inside. Like all the other chambers I saw, all the furnishings are painted on the walls, except a small dais, made up as a bed, and a marble statue standing opposite it.

A man's voice from behind says, "What took you so long?"

He sounds so familiar to me. This voice, I know it.

I turn around to see the man in the harlequin mask, the man from my dream, my sex partner from the Juliette Society party. A sense of relief washes over me at the sight of a familiar figure. He's wearing a knowing smile and a black hooded cape. He was expecting me, but I can't work out how.

"I'm looking for someone," I say.

And I scan the room as I say it, even though there's not a lot to scan.

"Well, here I am," he says, intent on drawing my attention and my eyes back to him.

"Not you," I tell him. "My friend. Anna."

"Do I know her?" he says.

"I don't know . . . ," I reply, looking into his eyes.

"Should I?" he says. That smile flickers across his face again. I don't really know what this is about or where it's leading, but it feels like he knows more than he's letting on and he's teasing me.

"Come," he says, walking toward me and extending his hand. "I want to show you something."

Willingly, I take his hand and it wraps around mine like a glove, so familiar, comforting and warm. He leads me over to a marble statue in the corner of the room.

From the back, the statue looks like a man with really hairy legs. He's kneeling down and bending forward with his arms out in front of him, either in the midst of prayer or masturbating with his back turned so that no one can see. As we get closer, I see that he's doing neither.

It's a statue of a man, and there's no other way to say this other than to be blunt—it's a statue of a man fucking a goat. Well, not exactly a man, but a half-man/half-goat, with horns, like the devil. The top half is human, the bottom, goat. Technically, I guess, it's really a goat fucking a goat and no laws of man, nature, or God are actually being violated or transgressed. But still...it is fucking, there's not really any doubt about that, because the goat-man has his penis inserted into the goat's lower regions. If a goat has a vagina—this is really embarrassing; I don't know if a goat has a vagina—then, yes, it's inserted into the goat's vagina.

The goat, like most goats, even when they're female, has a beard. It's lying on its back, with its hind legs up in the air. The goat-man is fucking it and tugging on its beard at the same time. And the goat, it's not looking terribly happy about this state of affairs, it has to be said. In fact, it looks terrified. Or maybe I'm just projecting. But I'll tell you this, the whole scenario looks pretty creepy, even if the statue itself is beautifully carved and rendered.

"Do you know what this is?" he says.

"Pretty explicit," I say. "Other than that, no idea."

"Take a guess," he says.

"Ancient Etruscan pornography?" I ask.

"Close," he laughs. "A couple of centuries off. It's Roman. Pan. The god of fucking."

I'm listening to his voice and it's really bugging me because he sounds so familiar, but I just can't place it.

"Do you know where this comes from?" he says.

"The Playboy Mansion?" I say.

"Herculaneum," he says, as if I should know. "Italy, near Pompeii. This was found in the private villa of Julius Caesar's father-in-law, who was himself an extremely powerful and influential figure."

And he gives Pan a friendly little pat on the ass.

"Can you imagine what went on there?" he declaims. "What kind of activities this inspired?"

"House parties?" I say.

I'm just joshing him. I want him to think I'm smart and funny. I want him to like me.

"Correct," he says, without a trace of irony.

At least, I finally got something right. I expect him to elaborate, but he doesn't.

"This isn't the real one, unfortunately. The original is in Naples, but it's a very good copy—all the details are present and correct," he says, running his index finger slowly and methodically along Pan's erect penis, as if checking for dust. "And it serves its purpose."

"Which is?" I say.

"Don't be coy," he says.

"I'm not," I say.

"This is what it's all about," he says.

"This? A half-man fucking a goat?"

"Here. Now. This place."

"Now that you mention it," I say, "what is this place?"

"This," he says, "is the garden of earthly delights. The marriage of heaven and hell."

"What the hell are you talking about?"

"The Juliette Society," he says.

As soon as I hear the name, I'm back in the place I first heard it. Back in that bathroom with Anna. And I thought it was just a silly name for an elite swingers club. Apparently not.

"Sounds like some kind of sorority," I say.

"Far from it," he says. "The Juliette Society are a people united by one idea, a shared philosophy, all dedicated to the pursuit of sublime pleasures. We have common interests, shared goals, and unlimited means."

"Sounds like a club for filthy rich people who like to get their rocks off," I tell him.

"It's not a club," he says. "It's a tradition. A bloodline through history. One that can be traced back to the pre-Christian mystery religions, pagan cults that operated openly during Roman times."

Great, I think, now he's decided to give me a history lesson.

"As the cults became more popular, the Roman authorities began to see them as a threat to power and order," he says. "So they stamped down on them, broke them up, and rounded up their devotees."

The mystery religions are sounding a bit like the Fuck Factory of the Ancient World, but I'm not sure he quite means it that way.

"What the authorities didn't know was that a lot of public figures and executives in the Roman Empire were also secretly members of these cults," he says. "They were hunted down, imprisoned, and put to death. They almost wiped us out, but the cult reconstituted itself after the purge and the core executive came to the conclusion that the best way to safeguard its survival was to pursue three key objectives: limit the threat, manage its activities, minimize the risk."

"Wait," I say, "you've completely lost me now. Are we talking about corporate governance or fucking?"

"Fucking?" he says, almost sounding surprised that the word even came out of his mouth. "This is more than just about fucking."

"You keep saying that," I say, "but you're not telling me what."

"Lust," he says, drawing the word out like a hiss. "And power. We couldn't let them take that away from us, so the cult went underground and hid itself in plain view."

"How can you hide in plain view? That doesn't make any sense."

"It makes all sorts of sense," he says. "Let's put it this way, what kind of story can't be verified?"

"Anything that appears in the *National Enquirer* or on TMZ."

"Exactly," he says. "Gossip. Rumor. Myth."

"And?"

"And you can't prosecute a rumor or disprove a myth," he says. "It continues to exist, perpetuate itself and have influence, but it can't be destroyed. It can only evolve and transform. So, since that time, it's been known by many names."

And he reels off a list of names that sound like the titles of cheesy horror B-movies.

The Cult of Isis.

The Secret Order of Libertines.

The Hellfire Club.

"The name it's known by now is the Juliette Society," he says. "But they all derive from the mystery religions."

"What was the mystery?" I ask, intrigued.

"The mystery wasn't a thing to be uncovered," he says. "It

was a place to be invoked, a place like this. A final destination, not a stop on the road."

He's talking in riddles.

"And how do you get to this place?" I say.

"How did you get here?" he says.

"Car service," I say. "Dropped me off at the main gate. Password: Fidelio. Security looked at me strangely. I think they were expecting Tom Cruise. Instead they got me, Tom Cruise with tits."

"Very funny," he says, but he's not laughing. He's not even smiling.

"That's not what I meant," he says. "There are three stages of initiation."

"Which are?"

"Disorientation of the senses."

I've been there.

"Intoxication of the body."

Seen that.

"Orgiastic sex."

Done that. All present and correct. And here I am.

It wasn't a chance happening, or a random series of events that brought me.

I was led here.

"Now you know how you got here," he says, like he knew what I was thinking. And there's that smile again. I just can't read him.

"Whatever the Juliette Society is, I don't want any part of it," I tell him. "I just want to find my friend."

"You're already a part of it," he says.

"I don't belong here!" I tell him wildly.

"If you got here, you belong here," he replies, looking directly into my eyes.

"But why?" I ask.

"Because the others didn't."

"What others?" I say.

"The ones who didn't make it," he says. "You see, the ones who give up halfway, or quit, the ones who balk at the initiation, they were sacrificed."

Sacrificed, I think. Did I hear that right? And I shiver inside, trying not to look as weirded out as I feel.

"Is this one of those situations where after you've told me, you're going to have to kill me?"

And I'm only half-joking.

He laughs, but I don't think it's because he got the joke, and he doesn't say no.

"We are more alike than we are different, you know," he says. "More alike than you'd want to admit. Hard as it is for you to fathom. We are not as others."

"Why me," I say.

"You have a talent."

"And what's that?" I say.

"You're incorruptible, irreducible. You understand."

He's not asking me; he's telling me. But I don't think I do.

"I'm trying to," I plead. "I really want to."

I wish he would stop talking like this. Even so, I'm completely entranced. I feel like Alice, attempting to converse with the Mad Hatter and the March Hare, getting all wrapped up in some inverted logic that's beyond me but seems like it would make perfect sense if I would just accept it.

"But you already get it," he says, smiling. "How lust and power, sex and violence are just two sides of the same coin. And your desire to know more, to experience it for yourself, brought you here. To me."

He's feeding me a line. I know because I've heard it before—from Anna.

And I know who he is now, this mysterious stranger in the mask, my dream man. He's the guy Anna told me about, the one she said was her favorite out of all her boyfriends, the one who understood her best.

"You know Anna," I say.

He doesn't answer.

And I know what this is now. This is that scene in *Last Tango in Paris*, the only one that anyone really knows or cares about.

The one that begins when Maria Schneider walks into Marlon Brando's apartment, calling out to announce her arrival. Not getting any response, she thinks no one's home. But Brando's sitting there on the floor, eating bread and cheese, saying nothing, not letting on, just waiting for her to arrive.

He already knows what's going to happen. He's already decided where this is going. What he's going to do. She's oblivious. And she makes herself oblivious because, in some ways, she wants it to happen too.

He's been waiting here for me too, because he knew that I'd arrive. And I turned up right on cue.

Ready for my butter scene.

"Are you afraid?" he says, moving toward me.

"No," I say, realizing it's true.

And I'm really not. But even if I was, I wouldn't give him the pleasure of knowing.

All I'm thinking is, What's his game? And where is Anna?

"Should I be afraid?" I ask.

He pulls me toward him and I don't resist because I understand that this is where it's all been leading.

I wanted to come here. I made it happen.

I came by necessity. I had no choice.

I had a talent. And I was spotted.

He pushes me down onto the dais on my back. He already knows what he wants and he's going to take it. I look up and see the statue. I see a goat and a horny devil on top of her. Myself and him in unholy union. But he doesn't reach for my beard; he reaches for my throat.

By the time I realize what he's doing his hands are already upon me and everything's moving so fast that it's moving in slow motion.

His hands are clasped around my throat.

I try to scream. It comes out as dead air. I struggle but he knows that he's stronger than me. I'm pinned to the platform with the full weight of his body bearing down.

I'm utterly helpless but completely alert and aware.

It's too late to react, too late to escape.

I can feel his hands slowly tighten around my windpipe.

"Silly girl," he leers. "You didn't have to come."

He leans into me, until his face is right on top of mine and all I can see behind the burnt leather mask are his eyes, glaring and crazed.

I flash on what happened to all those girls. I flash on what could have happened to Anna. And it all seems obvious now. It all seems so clear.

I should have paid closer attention. I should have listened to my head and not my body. I should have seen this coming.

Nobody wants to die. Not here, not like this.

I don't want to die. Not here, not like those girls.

But it's too late for second thoughts.

He's squeezing the life out of me. He wants to see it go out. He wants me to feel what they felt.

And I summon every ounce of strength and every last drop of air in my lungs to rasp:

"Screw you."

It comes out as a gurgle. He leans down until he's in my ear and I hear him whisper, "Can you feel me?"

His hands tighten.

Then everything goes black.

The next thing I know I'm lying on my back, looking up at a vast, uninterrupted expanse of blue sky that stretches from one horizon to the next. No sun, no moon, no clouds. And even though the color is flat and featureless and completely uniform, it seems like it's arched over me, as if I'm looking at the curvature of the earth. I feel a slight breeze brush against my body but, at this point, I can't tell if I'm submerged underwater or floating through the sky.

Ghostly white gulls glide above my head like sentinels.

And if it weren't for the tips of their wings, that look as if they'd been stained with India ink, I'd think they were just floaters drifting in front of my eyes from staring too long into the infinite blue. They soar across my field of vision, some bigger than others on colliding paths at different altitudes, even though it looks as if they're all inhabiting the same plane. I see a flock of starlings dart back and forth across the sky like a shoal of fish, turning on a dime to catch the current.

I raise my head to look around. I'm lying naked in the middle of a large stone platform raised no more than a foot from the ground. There is a ruby red silk robe with elaborate gold embroidery spread out underneath me like a sheet. And my arms are half in and half out of each arm of the robe. Stretching out from the platform in every direction, as far as the eye can see, are rows of empty bleachers.

I start to feel dizzy so I rest my head again and look up at the sky and I feel like I'm flying, like I'm soaring through the atmosphere with the birds. I feel something catch in my throat, something like a feather. It tickles my throat and blocks it at the same time. I can't breathe and I start to panic. I choke myself to try and dislodge it. Nothing comes out of my mouth, but whatever was there has gone now and I gasp for air, as if it's the first breath I've ever taken. As if I've died and been reborn. With that gasp comes a searing pain that shoots across my throat, down into my chest and through my lungs, as if I'm breathing in fire.

And I think I hear Jack whisper, "You've arrived."

I open my eyes to greet him.

*   *   *

I open my eyes, wait for them to focus and realize it's not Jack, not the stranger in the mask, but Bob who's looming over me, his face clouded by shadow. Bob is the man in the mask. And I don't know why but I'm not at all surprised.

I see him draw back his arm. And I feel a sharp sting on my cheek as he slaps me. My head shoots to the side as if it's spring-loaded.

He grabs my chin, turns it toward him, and slaps my face again. Harder this time.

"Wake up," he shouts. "Not time to die."

I look at him and I only see his face for a split second before everything becomes blurry as the tears well up in my eyes.

He reaches for my wrists, not so he can stop me from striking him again, but to pull them down. Toward his neck.

He says, "Let's switch. Choke me."

His hands are on mine. My hands are on his neck.

He says, "Harder."

And I squeeze.

He says it again.

"Harder."

My hard is evidently not hard enough.

He says it again and he's shouting it now, over and over and over. Like a sports coach trying to make his athletes burn. And I'm incensed.

"Harder."

I'm acting without thinking.

"Harder."

I squeeze tighter.

"Harder."

His hands loosen their grip on mine and fall by his side. I keep applying the pressure.

"Harder."

It feels as if I'm turning a screw that's already tight to the wall. But I want to give it one more twist, just to make sure, and it takes all my strength just to turn the screwdriver.

I see his face blush and redden.

I tighten my grip.

His lips are moving and no sound is coming out.

I'm bearing down on him with all my weight now, with strength I never knew I had, and his face is beet red. His eyes wide, the pupils dilated. His body absolutely still and rigid.

Then I catch sight of his mouth and it's curled at the corners into this little smile that's positively evil. Like he knows exactly what he's doing to me. Or maybe it's because he's in excruciating pain. I can't tell, because it's almost impossible to differentiate between a grimace and a smile.

And I really hope it's the former, because I get it now. I understand what this whole thing's about. This sick little gathering. The power to hold life and death in their grasp. And this is how they get their kicks.

This is Bob's kick.

Taking the ultimate risk.

I can feel his pulse weaken under my fingertips. I can see him slipping away. I can end this all now. He wouldn't fight back. I can squeeze the life out of him. Right here, right now. I can take his life, the way he took it from those girls, how he took it from Anna. Because that's what I figure has happened. I can even the score. I can stop this from happening again. No more victims.

And although he might enjoy it, the sick fuck, it wouldn't be for long. By then it would be too late for second thoughts.

This is what he wants. He knows he can't lose.

If I kill him, he dies safe in the knowledge that my life is over too.

If I kill him, it would be far too easy.

I can see the life ebb out of him. So I pull my hands away.

He doesn't move. The color drains from his face.

The bastard's dead. I know it. He's fucking dead.

I scream his name—"Bob!"—over and over. I slap his face. Pound on his chest.

I'm starting to panic. There's no way I'm taking the rap for this.

I do it all again. Harder.

I'm about to give up when I see a flicker behind his eyeballs.

So I slap him. Once on each cheek.

He gasps for life, drawing air into his lungs. It's accompanied by a hideous rasping sound.

I'm staring at him in desperation, dumbfounded. I want him to live. I need him to live. Not for his sake.

For mine.

It takes three or four goes and it looks as if he's going to make it. He's coming back from the brink now. He's going to pull through.

I can see his lips moving but I can't make out what he's saying. His voice is barely a whisper. I move my head down level with his.

I hear him say:

"Gena...which tie...which tie shall I wear."

The twisted fuck. Still obsessed with appearances. If only Gena knew.

And I wonder if she does and just lets it lie. Is she just deluded and blind? Does she close her eyes to the indiscretions? Or doesn't she see the signs? I can't help but think Gena suspects and that's the story of her corkscrew smile.

Bob's coming round now, but I'm not about to sit here, cradle him in my arms, stroke his head, and nurse him back to health. And I'll be damned if I'm going to stick around to watch. I have to leave before he remembers where he is, who I am, and what just happened.

This party's already got way too old for me. I've seen enough and I know exactly when it's time to go. So I walk out while he's still lying there on that slab, still gurgling, half-conscious and incoherent.

I don't turn around.

I don't look back.

I'm blessed to be alive.

22

It's election night. I'm home alone watching the results come in live on TV. And when they cut to Bob DeVille, he's already triumphant. He's ahead by a clear margin, smashing his opponent, and he knows he's going to take this election. He already knows he's going to win and you can see it on his face. Kind of a foregone conclusion, don't you think?

Name me a politician that doesn't get away with murder.

It's almost a perk of the profession. And DeVille's got it down to an art.

To me, he's DeVille now. Not Bob. That just feels too familiar. A little too cozy for comfort. Now that I know what I know. It changes everything. Calling him Bob, that would be a bit like being on first-name terms with the Hillside Strangler.

DeVille is standing at the podium flashing a victory sign and a Colgate grin with his arm around Gena's waist as he prepares to make his victory speech. He looks so suave and so self-satisfied. And he's wearing a fucking cravat. I must be the only person watching this who knows why. He's wearing it to hide his fuck bruises. To protect his dirty little secret.

Gena is pointing at random people in the crowd, doing that same thing with her mouth that Hillary Clinton does at campaign rallies. Gawping in surprise, incredulously, and frantically waving at random people in the crowd as if she's just seen a long-lost family member—pretending that she knows them. Gena's doing it because she's convinced she's one step closer to First Lady and she better start looking the part.

The DeVilles are performing for an exuberant crowd who have been bused in from miles around to fill out the numbers and make it look as if the senator-in-waiting has his finger on the pulse of an electorate giddy for change, when he's probably just polled the lowest numbers in the history of the state.

And they're putting on a good show. You'd never know that they were anything other than what they present themselves as. The all-American couple. Loving, faithful, and shining with good health.

When it cuts to a wide shot that shows the whole stage, I can see Jack standing there off to the side with the rest of DeVille's team. Nothing could spoil this moment for me. Because I'm so proud of Jack, I really am.

Even though pride comes with a caveat because I know the real DeVille now, not the cardboard cut-out politician on TV who says he wants to show people "the real me." I know what he's capable of. I know what he's a part of.

I ask myself the same questions again. What is experience worth? And what does it cost?

This is what my experience is worth. I understand things now about sex and power and how they connect and interact that some people never get to discover during the course of their entire lives. And I'm still so young. But I'm also going to have to live with this my entire life. I can't say that makes me happy. If I'm really honest, it makes me feel uncomfortable. Because I know that I'm only a step away from DeVille.

I could tell Jack what happened. I could blow the whole thing wide open if I wanted to. But we only have one life to live and I dream and fantasize like everybody else about the things that everybody wants: security, family, happiness, love. And I don't know what the future holds, but I do know one thing that's not in the future I see for myself. A whistle-blower.

My instinct for survival is a lot stronger than my desire to save the world. So I could play the hero if I wanted to, but do I want to be known as that person for the rest of my life? Do I want to live with the consequences? Where would that leave Jack? What would it do to us?

By doing that I'd have to tell Jack everything. And I'm not ready to take that step yet. Some things should remain left unsaid. Secrets are best kept, not revealed. This one has to stay with me. At least for now. But I'll reserve the right to change my mind at any time.

What would you do in my position?

Think about it. It's not so easy, is it? There's no simple solution or obvious exit plan.

This isn't like one of those Hollywood movies where everything gets tied up neatly in the final reel. Where the bad guys get their comeuppance, the forces of chaos and evil are defeated, order is restored. And the hero or heroine gets to live another day and return to their regular lives. Their home, their wives, their children, their dog. And I really don't need to tell you this, but real life isn't like that. Hollywood endings only happen in the movies.

The way this story ends is more like that long tracking shot that leads to the end of Godard's *À Bout de Souffle* where Jean-Paul Belmondo's character, a petty criminal called Michel, is resigned to his fate, after his American girlfriend, who's played by Jean Seberg, has just told him that she doesn't love him and she's informed on him to the cops. And she does it just to get his attention. She does it out of spite.

Being a gangster in a gangster movie, and aware of that fact and smarter than most, Michel already knows where all this is going to end up. And we know too.

Remember what I said?

Plot subservient to character.

So Michel, he's been shot in the back and he's stumbling down the street, stumbling toward oblivion. He makes it to the crossroads and then he falls. And this is really it, the end he envisioned for himself. But more banal, because he looks more like the victim of a minor traffic accident than a dangerous criminal shot down in a hail of gunfire by law enforcement.

The last words to come out of his mouth before he succumbs to his fatality: "Makes me want to puke." That's his sardonic parting shot to a world that never loved him and he never loved back. That's his "Rosebud" moment. But rather than leaving some grand revelation as he makes his final exit, his words are misheard, misconstrued, reinterpreted—we never find out which—as "You make me want to puke." A rejoinder, not to the world but to the woman he loved, who betrayed him—his Achilles' heel, the femme fatale standing over him as he's making a travesty of his big death scene.

But when this is relayed to Jean Seberg, her command of French, which, up to this point in the movie, seems to have been estimable for a young American girl, suddenly fails her. She doesn't understand the French word *dégueulasse* and has to ask what it means.

And that's where the movie ends.

She's left not only realizing the enormity of the events she's set into motion through an act of casual self-regard, but also faced with the prospect of laboring under a misapprehension for the rest of her life.

That he died hating her guts.

If only all movies could end that way. If only all movies could end like life.

Unresolved.

Because, beginning from the day we are born...no, before that, beginning from the moment we are conceived, our lives are nothing if not a series of loose ends. Romantic, sexual, professional, familial, and probably a few others besides. And it takes every iota of our being to stop from getting tangled up in them.

Some people spend their lives obsessed by the loose ends, the what-ifs, could-have-beens, and what-will-happens.

But not me.

Technically, at this precise moment, I'm a loose end. And DeVille knows that. He could get rid of me if he so desired. He has the power. He could just click his fingers and make me disappear. Like Anna. He could pay someone to do away with me, and cover it up the way I figure he did with Daisy and those other girls. And he'd never have to suffer the consequences, never have to pay the price. He'd carry on flashing that Colgate grin on TV and no one would be any the wiser.

But he won't lay a finger on me; I'm pretty certain of that. And I'm not about to spend the rest of my days looking over my shoulder, watching and waiting for that person to arrive. I'm not afraid. I'm sure DeVille's assessed the risks and decided that I'm a loose end he can afford to live with.

Why do you think I'm so sure?

Well, you know what they say.

Knowledge is power.

DeVille made a promise to Jack. He said if they won the election, he'd give Jack a role in his administration. Jack has no reason to think that obligation won't be met. I intend to see DeVille follows through. And I'm sure he will, because DeVille needs smart guys like Jack on his team to make him look good.

And who am I to deny Jack that opportunity? Who am I to put the brakes on his ambition?

Anyway, it's not me DeVille has to fear.

It's Jack.

How he'd react if he found out.

This is how these things work. You need to know that. No one has any incentive to go public. It's not in anybody's vested interest.

That's the true nature of power. The occult nature of power.

It's hidden. And it remains hidden.

So the Juliette Society, it just carries on.

Girls like Anna will continue to disappear. Or turn up dead.

And some poor sap like Bundy gets to take the rap. Because he's disposable and doesn't know enough about the bigger picture to take anybody else down with him. Ultimately, Bundy's one link in the chain that can easily be replaced. There will always be girls who are willing to pander and guys who are eager to assist. It's always been that way and it will always be that way.

We're tied together now—Jack, DeVille, and me. Like the Mexican standoff in *The Good, the Bad and the Ugly*. An eternal triangle. We're standing within a stone circle, diametrically opposed. It's a game of looks now, watching and waiting to see who makes the first move. All I know is, I have no intention of ending up in an unmarked grave. And mutually assured destruction benefits nobody.

Or it's like the end of *The Italian Job*, where the gold is at the front of the bus, the people are all in the back, and the vehicle is balanced on a precipice. One wrong move and the whole shebang will tip over the edge.

That's what this is.

Checkmate.

And this is what I'm taking away from this whole little adventure.

Sex is the great equalizer.

Acknowledgments

I can never say thank you enough to Marc Gerald and Peter McGuigan, who believed in me and pushed me to make this a reality, when I doubted myself. Chris and Masumi for their continuous guidance, invaluable research, and input. MV Cobra for your love and light. Anthony D' Juan, my mentor, and one of my dearest friends, who constantly gives me faith in storytelling. Thanks to my friends Saelee Oh, James Jean, Dave Choe, Yoshi Obayashi, Kristin Burns, Candice Birns, AJ, Brian Levy, and New School Media. Catherine Burke, David Shelley, Kirsteen Astor, Stéphanie Abou, Kirsten Neuhaus—you've all put so much time and effort into making TJS everything it could be, thank you!

I've had an incredible amount of support from everyone at Grand Central Publishing, Little Brown Book Group UK, The Agency Group, and Foundry Literary & Media.

Acknowledgments

Noel Clarke and Mat Schulz, thanks for looking out. Last but certainly not least all of the filmmakers and writers who continue to inspire me: Godard, Fellini, Buñuel, Friedkin, Tohjiro, Jean-Baptiste de Boyer, Angela Carter, Voltaire, THE MDS.

About the Author

Sasha Grey was one of the most successful stars of the Hollywood porn industry. Since she left the adult film industry at twenty-one, Sasha has gone on to star in *Entourage* and Stephen Soderbergh's film *The Girlfriend Experience*. *The Juliette Society* is her first novel.